Drama High, Vol. 2

SECOND CHANCE

Drama High, Vol. 2

SECOND CHANCE

L. Divine

Dafina KTeen Books
KENSINGTON PUBLISHING CORP.
http://www.kensingtonbooks.com

*"The only lasting truth is Change/
God is Change."*

—OCTAVIA E. BUTLER

This volume is dedicated to the many Ancestors who, through their sacrifices, opened the roads for new life to come through. Octavia E. Butler's writings, like Alice Walker's, have challenged my thoughts and actions as well as made me realize the true potential of a phenomenal Black female writer.

When I heard she'd made the transition to the Ancestor world, I stood in my kitchen and cried. It was the same pain I felt when Aaliyah, Lisa "Left Eye" Lopez, Professor X, Marvin Gaye, Bob Marley, Gregory Hines, Rosa Parks, Easy E, Tupac, the Notorious B.I.G., Florence "Flo Jo" Griffith Joyner, Joshua Johnson and countless other prolific artists and activists became Ancestors before the world was ready to let them go in the physical.

Thank you, Octavia E. Butler, for not only gracing the world with your presence, but for also leaving behind your inspiring ideas through your timeless words. I pray to channel your ingenuity. Your candle will always be lit upon my shrine.

Prologue

Okay, I still can't believe they suspended all of us, especially when my girls and I didn't want to be fighting in the first place. Ain't that just wrong? You see what I mean about people just straight hatin' on us up in here? I swear. Well, I'm glad we're at South Bay High and not some school in the hood. Those schools would have no problem calling the police or kicking you out on the spot for something like this.

We didn't even get a real suspension; we got in-house suspension where they just make us sit in the conference room all day and do book work from all our classes. It seems like the teachers really enjoy giving us book work too. Like they've just been waiting to give some student a crapload of work to do that the rest of the class never sees.

We all know why they don't actually suspend us. The administration doesn't want students to be absent from school; South Bay High is known for all its fancy accreditations. And, in order to keep them, having the least amount of student and faculty absences is top priority. So, unless you do something drastic, you won't get sent home, not even for a day.

Well, Trecee did get kicked out, but she deserved it. That

heffa came up here with the intent to create drama, and we really don't need any more. Misty got in-house too, but I doubt seriously it'll affect her one way or the other. She'll probably think of it as a damn vacation, knowing her. It's only the first week of school, and already I'm looking forward to June. Enemies can do that to a sistah.

Do you know that broad Misty had the nerve to call me and apologize for almost getting me killed by Trecee's crazy behind? Not to mention the fact she set up the whole thing to bring herself closer to KJ. What the hell kind of apology can take that fact away, I would like to know. She's straight trippin' if she thinks I'm going to give her another chance to make amends. As many times as she's broken her word about starting mess, I couldn't care less. I've had it with her crazy butt.

Then there's KJ. I don't know what to do about him. Ever since all this drama with Trecee started, he's been trying to get back with me, but I don't know if I can trust him. And, I also kinda like this cat Jeremy. Okay, not kinda. I've been jocking Jeremy on the low for a while now, and it's a first. I've never dated a White boy before.

Jeremy and I have grown kinda tight in class this week. The two days I was there—before being banished to the library—he sat next to me and wrote little notes on his notebook making fun of Mrs. Peterson. I've seen him around campus, but we've never had a class together before. When I was sent to the library for the rest of the week he came to visit me every day during class when he was supposed to be going to the rest room. He's just so sweet.

Jeremy and I seem to have a lot in common. He listens to Southern style and East Coast rap as well as West Coast music, like me. He likes to read and just kick it, like me. He works hard, even though he doesn't have to. His parents are loaded. And, he's the finest boy in the entire school.

* * *

Even with all of this week's BS fresh in my mind, I'm still looking forward to the weekend. If for no other reason, so I can put Drama High behind me for a couple of days.

~ 1 ~
Press 'n' Curl

*"She can walk with a switch and talk with street slang/
I love it when a woman ain't scared to do her thang."*

—L.L. COOL J

My weekly hair routine is like a ritual. When Mama gets her hair done, she calls it a *rogacion de cabeza* or a cleansing of the head.

I love the way my hair looks and smells when it's pressed. I like to use Pantene and sometimes Thermasilk. My other tools include a Gold 'n' Hot blow-dryer and flat iron, two hot combs and an oven, five silver clips, a comb, a scrunchie and some Smooth as Silk hair spray. My girl Shawntrese's mom does hair and works for the guy who makes this spray. It's the bomb.

I lightly press my edges before separating and straightening my hair. It's kind of pretty, the way my hair shines and smokes when I press it. It shimmers like ocean water in the afternoon sun. I'm basically frying my hair, but I still love the way it smells. Almost like sweet, burnt cantaloupe.

"Jayd, why do you press your hair when you know you just gone braid it up tomorrow, like some little thugette," my mom says, while retrieving her manicure set from under the bathroom sink. It's her night to do her nails, before her very social weekend officially begins.

My mom hates having a daughter who wears cornrows in her hair. She's ultrafeminine, and I can be too. But, I also like to wear baggy jeans and boxer shorts sometimes. It's just more comfortable to me. Same with my hair. It's cool to wear it out sometimes. But, truth be told, it's just easier to braid it up.

"Mom, now you know I can't be going to work with school hair. I got to be fresh for the weekend, just like you," I say, smiling at her. She's standing in the bathroom door, holding her big Tupperware container full of nail stuff: cotton balls, polishes, polish remover, tissue, cuticle cream and clippers, nail files and buffers of all shapes and sizes, a stick-on design booklet, some lotion with a box of plastic wrap to make her feet extra soft, and baby oil for her pumice stone. Her heels are hella rough, just like mine. She tosses me the evil eye before stepping into the living room to tend to her feet and toes.

"Jayd, me doing my hands and feet is totally different from you doing your hair." She sits on the living room floor and dumps the Tupperware contents onto the carpet. She comes back into the bathroom and fills the container with warm water and soap to soak her hands and feet in.

"You go through this entire three-hour production every Friday night to wear it like some little dude on the street all week. I just don't understand it."

"Mom, lots of sistahs wear their hair in rows."

"Yeah, and they're all gay."

"Mom," I say. She can be so stereotypical sometimes.

"So, you saying me, Alicia Keys, and Queen Latifah are gay," I say while pressing the first layer of my hair. I start at the back of my neck and work my way up to my crown, which takes at least a half hour. I have to be careful not to burn my shoulders and chest. I use a thick washcloth under the hot comb while I pull it through my hair. If I do it right, I can get a little bump at the ends without having to use my hot curlers.

"I don't know about them other girls," my mom says while trying not to spill the water from her Tupperware-container-turned-foot-soaker onto the carpet, "but you better not be.

It's a wonder you got any little boys running around after you at all, especially KJ."

"What is that supposed to mean?" That was more than a little insulting. My mom can stab a sistah when she wants to. I don't know why she gets like that, especially with me.

"Oh, Jayd, you can be so sensitive sometimes. All I'm saying is that dudes usually like sistahs who wear cute, girly stuff all the time. And girls who wear their hair like girls, not like Snoop Dogg."

"But, Mom, women in Africa have been wearing their hair like this since the beginning of time." As my mom rolls her eyes again, quickly losing interest in the conversation like she does any time I disagree with her, the phone rings.

"Hello-o," my mom coos into the phone. "Oh, hey, baby. You know I'm doing my nails tonight. What's up?"

That must be her main dude, Ras Joe. He's a big dude with long dreads hanging down his back. He's hella light-skinned with them funny-colored eyes. And, he's got money. I don't know how he gets it, but he got it. And he loves spending it on my mom.

Maybe there's some truth to what my Mom's saying. I've never had a dude buy me stuff before like she has. Maybe if I showed a little leg on the regular, dudes would treat me more like a lady.

What am I saying? I sound like Misty now. Besides, all that glitters damn sure ain't gold. Ras Joe is cool, but he don't hang around all the time. My mom has to sit by the phone and wait for that fool to call. That ain't treating nobody like a lady, or even a friend for that matter.

I also think Ras Joe got a family at home, but I ain't sure. My mom don't tell me stuff like that. She talks to her girlfriends, my play aunties, about her personal life. But, I do know she ain't never been to his house, and I don't think she ever met any of his kids.

"Baby, now you know Friday night is my night to beautify myself for the weekend. I'm nowhere near ready for you tonight." I don't even know why she play like she ain't going out with him. She's already taking her feet out of the water and picking out polish.

"All right, baby. See you in a little while."

See, what I say? Now I'm gone have to speed up my pressing process to get out of her way. I know she's going to want to shower before polishing her nails. But pressing don't take too long, and that's all I need the bathroom for. I can style my hair in her bedroom mirror.

But I can't decide how to do my hair. I want to put some cornrows in, but I'm too tired, and I have to get up to go to work tomorrow morning. Granted, it ain't as early as my 5:30 A.M. wake-up call on school days, but 7:30 A.M. is still early to me.

Don't slip up and get caught, 'cause I'm coming for that number one spot. There's Ludacris announcing a phone call from somebody right in the middle of my hair session. Everybody that knows me knows Friday night is hair night. And, depending on if it's just a simple press and curl or something a little more sassy, it could take all night long.

"Hello."

"Hey, Jayd," says a male voice I don't immediately recognize, though something about it does sound familiar—and White. Who's this dude? And then I remember.

"It's Jeremy. What's up?"

"Hey, Jeremy," I say, sounding shocked as I don't know what.

"You sound surprised to hear from me. You didn't think I'd call you, huh?" He got that right. With all that went down today with Trecee and KJ, I'd kinda forgot I exchanged numbers with Jeremy in class the other day.

"Nah, actually I didn't. What's goin' on with ya?" I say, trying to sound like I'm happy to hear from him. But honestly, I

don't want my combs to get cold or burn because I'm talking
to him.

"Did I catch you at a bad time? You sound a little busy." He
sounds so cute when he's nervous.

"Well, Friday night is my hair night," I explain.

"You're doing your hair? I thought that's what girls said to get
rid of guys they don't want to talk to," he says, only half joking.

"Not Black girls. Depending on what we're doing to our
hair, it can be an all-night production," I say, taking the two
pressing combs out of the oven. I use a white washcloth to
set them on. If the imprint from the comb is black, it's too
hot. But, if it's light brown, the combs are just right to get my
kinks straight.

"So what you're saying is you really do have to do your
hair and you can't talk to me now." God, he sounds so sexy
over the phone.

"I can call you back a little later." I glance over at the clock
radio to see what time it is. "It's about eight-thirty now. So,
give me until about nine-thirty or ten o'clock and I'll be
done," I say, touching my hot combs to the palm of my hand.
They're cooling off now. I got to go.

"Well, actually, me and my friends are going to hang
tonight. I wanted to know if you wanted to join us."

What! No plans. No warning. Uh-uh. A sistah got to finish
her hair and get some rest. It's been a rough first week of
school, and I need to chill out. But damn, I want to hang
with him and his crew too. I want to get to know this boy. I
got to be smooth, but not rude or desperate. And quick. My
hair gets dirty from all this airplane pollution by my mom's
house. The damn planes going into LAX fly right over her
building, and I know they leave all kinds of crap in the air.
And speak of the devil, here comes a plane now.

"What the hell is that loud-ass noise?" Jeremy asks, sounding almost annoyed.

"I'll tell you when it passes," I shout into the phone. Folks that don't live near the airport just don't understand. My mom's immune to the noise. When she hears one coming she just turns the TV up. I'm kinda used to it too. But it can get annoying, especially on the weekends when it seems like a plane passes every ten seconds.

"That was a Boeing 747."

"Did it land in your backyard?"

"No. I don't have a backyard here."

"Where is here?" Jeremy says, sounding a little confused.

"I'm at my mom's house in Inglewood." Now I really have to go. My hair is cold, so are my combs, and the oven's baking. Electricity ain't free. "Can I call you tomorrow?" I say, trying to sound unhurried.

"Yeah, sure. Well, do you want to hang out tomorrow night, or will you be doing your nails then?" Oh, I see he's going to be a funny one.

"So, you got jokes? Well, let's see how funny you are tomorrow night. Are you going to Byron's party?" I ask, momentarily forgetting all about Mickey and Nellie wanting us to make an entrance together.

"I wasn't planning on it. But, if you want to go, we can cruise by," Jeremy says. Is he always this easygoing?

"I already told my girls I would be there, so I should make an appearance. I'll call you after I get off work."

"Work? What time will that be?"

"About six o'clock."

"All right then, I'll see you tomorrow, Jayd."

"Have fun, Jeremy, and I'll give you a call tomorrow—nails done and all," I say.

"Later, funny girl." I hang up my phone and put it on the counter.

I have a date with Jeremy the White boy tomorrow night. What am I going to wear? How should I do my hair? Well, I could row it. I mean, he must think it looks cool like that, right? Or should I wear it a little different, show him another side of Miss Jayd Jackson? I don't know. My mom got me wanting to change up my stylo now.

Whatcha doin', man? I'm coming for that number one spot. There's Luda again. Who's this now?

"Hello," I say, sounding hella irritated.

It's a private number. What's the point of Caller ID if people can still block their numbers?

"Hey, girl. It's your daddy. Why you sound so snappy?" Why is he calling me this time of night? Usually by now he's asleep on his couch in front of the TV.

"Oh, hey, Daddy. I was just doing my hair and the phone keeps ringing. What's up? Shouldn't you be asleep on the couch by now?" It ain't like me and my daddy chat all that much, so something must be up.

"What are you doing the last weekend of this month?"

"I don't know. Working, I'm sure," I say, a little snidely. He don't break me off no money. He gives my mom the court-mandated child support, which she then splits with Mama and Daddy, leaving nothing left over for me.

"Well, can you get the afternoon off that Sunday? We're having a little barbecue for your uncle Willard. He's moving back to Mississippi with his new wife, and I want you to be there."

He's always trying to make me go to family stuff, and I can't stand it. Them people don't like me or my mom. And they're afraid of Mama. The Jacksons are good, Southern Baptist folks. They have a fish fry every Friday night, play Dominoes, Bid Wiz, and Spades every Saturday night, and go to church all day long on Sunday.

"Daddy, I can't miss work. I need the money, remember? Besides, Sundays are no good for me anyway. You know I got to go back to Mama's and get ready for school." He don't know nothing about my life.

"What if I pick you up from work and give you a ride back to your grandmother's on Sunday?" This must be big. He don't usually make me offers like that.

"Why you want me to go so bad? I barely know Uncle Willard, and I don't know his new wife. I didn't even know he wasn't with the first one anymore, to tell you the truth." My mom's standing in the bathroom door again, looking at me from the corner of her eye as if to say, "Hurry up and finish in the bathroom so I can get ready for my man." I better wrap this up without too much protesting. Family is family, as Mama says.

"Jayd, don't be difficult. Just come. You may have some fun. You could even invite your little girlfriends, what are their names?" he says, acting as if he really ever knew.

"You mean Nellie and Mickey?"

"Yeah, them girls. How's school going anyway? Didn't you start back this week?"

"Yes, Daddy, but I really gotta go finish my hair now. I'll talk to you later."

"So, will I see you in a few weeks," he asks, not letting me off the hook.

"Yes, I guess so. Now, I need to finish my hair."

"Oh, yeah, and wear it pretty, not in them thug braids you always have in your hair. You're such a pretty girl, Jayd, with good hair too. You need to take advantage of that and stop trying to be so hard all the time." He doesn't even realize how badly he just insulted me. My parents are enough to warrant me a couple of episodes on *Dr. Phil*.

"Bye, Daddy."

"Bye, baby."

Now maybe I can finish my hair. I'm too tired to put any braids in it now, that's for sure. I guess I'll just go with a simple press and curl and worry about the finishing touches tomorrow.

~ 2 ~

The Date

*"Never enough, render your heart to me/
All mine you have to be."*

—PORTISHEAD

"Welcome to Simply Wholesome. What can I get for you?" I've been sweating the clock all day. It's almost time for me to get off, and all I can think about is my date tonight with Jeremy.

"May I have the spinach enchiladas, a small green salad hold the sprouts, with a wheat germ and ginger root smoothie?" She's going to be on the toilet all night long.

"That will be thirteen eighty-five." I can't believe how high the prices are here. Man, if I didn't work here, I don't know how I'd be able to eat this food.

I know it's some soldiers in here. Where they at? There's Destiny's Child again announcing yet another text message from KJ.

"Jayd, please call me so we can talk about this whole Trecee thing. I want 2 put it behind us and get back to us. R u coming to Byron's party 2nite? Maybe we can kick it, like old times. Luv, Your Man."

If he only knew that I got a new man to kick it with now. I can't wait to get off work and call Jeremy. I know everyone's gone trip when we show up at the party together. I've been looking forward to it since last night. I couldn't even sleep, I was so excited. And, I can always get my sleep on, even on my mom's little couch.

Should I text message this fool back? Nah. Let him sweat, like he's been doing since yesterday. For real, though. Last weekend I didn't have a man at all. KJ broke up with me and I was dreading going back to school. Now I got two dudes on my jock, and the first week of school is over. Life just keeps on going.

Speaking of which, I look at the clock and see it's finally time for me to roll. I can call Jeremy while I'm waiting at the bus stop. I would ask my mom to pick me up, but I know she's still sleep from her late night. She walked in the door as I was leaving for work this morning.

"Later, y'all. See you in the morning," I say to no one in particular. Everybody around here is real laid back.

"All right, Jayd. You take it easy." Shahid always speaks to me, even if he's in the middle of taking a customer's order. He's the coolest boss ever. He doesn't even look like the owner; he blends in with everyone else wearing dreads, tattoos, and low-key jeans and T-shirt. You'd never know he was a baller unless you saw him roll up in his black Jaguar. It's his only indulgence.

After cashing out my drawer and clocking out, I walk out the side door and down the stairs toward the bus stop across the street. It's another hot, sunny day in L.A., and the people are out. The cars are gleaming, the sun is shining. But the exhaust from the buses and beat-up cars passing by mixed with the L.A. smog is enough to make me drop dead of lung cancer right here on the street.

Most of the bus stops in L.A., just like in Compton, don't have pretty little benches and covered spots like in the South Bay. Instead, they're raggedy, tattered, and uninviting. So, I just need to find a place to lean so I can call this cat and see what's crackin' for tonight. I saved his number in my phone last night and gave him a special ring tone, so I know when it's him calling.

"Hello," says a woman's voice. It must be his mom. This boy gave me his home phone number? That's rare nowadays.

"Hi. Is Jeremy home?" I ask, trying to sound all sweet and innocent, like I ain't jockin' her son.

"Yes. May I tell him who's calling, please?" Wow. So proper and all. If somebody calls for me at my mom's or Mama's, they usually get a rude grunt followed by a loud-ass "Jaaaaaaayd! Pick up the phone." Thus, the evolution of my cell.

"Yes. This is Jayd."

"Hold on while I get him for you, Jayd," she says with a deep, Southern drawl. It almost sounds like Mama's.

"Justin, tell your brother to pick up the line. He has a call from Jayd," I hear her say to one of Jeremy's brothers.

He picks up immediately. "Hey, Jayd. How was work?" He sounds even yummier than he did last night.

"Work was cool, thanks for asking."

"So, your hair and everything's all done? No more excuses for not hangin' out with me?"

"Oh, you've got more jokes, I see. So, what did you have in mind?"

"Well, I was thinking, instead of going to Byron's party, we could go to the movies and just hang out at the pier afterward," he suggests.

"But, my girls are expecting me," I protest.

"I know, and if you want to go to the party, we can. I just thought it would be nice to get to know you outside the South Bay High crowd." He's got a good point. I don't want to run into KJ and Misty tonight, and I know they'll be there with all the other folks. And, I'd much rather hang out with him tonight, if I have to make a choice.

I wonder how late this boy's trying to hang. I forget these White folks I go to school with don't know anything about a curfew. At Mama's I can't even really go out. But if I should, I know to be home before 11 P.M. No question. It's always been like that for the girls. The boys, on the other hand, have no curfew at all. Look at Bryan. He may come home, he may not. Let me try something like that. They'll be talking about my ass whipping from Mama for years to come.

"Well, I'm over my mom's house, so as long as I get home before she does, it's all good. And, she usually hangs out pretty late." That's the understatement of the year.

"Cool. So, what time do you want me to pick you up? The evening flicks start at around 8 P.M."

"It's 6 P.M. now. By the time I get home, shower, dress, and do something to my hair, it'll be at least 8 P.M.," I say. I hope the bus isn't too crowded. My feet are barking after standing up all day. I have to sit down for the twenty-minute ride back to Inglewood. "Let's say 8 P.M., then."

"All right. You want to give me directions now or call me later?" He's so polite. Good home training.

"I'm just chillin', waiting for the bus to come. So I can give them to you now if you're ready. Where are you coming from?"

"I'm in P.V. You said you're in Inglewood, right?" Damn, he lives in Palos Verdes? His parents must be ballers, for real. That's where all the hellafied rich folk live. I heard Johnnie Cochran even had a house up there when he was alive.

"Yeah, Inglewood. You know where the Forum is?" I say, offering up familiar landmarks because I'm sure he doesn't know his way around Inglewood.

"Yeah, where the Lakers used to play. Do I have to dial a code at the gate or anything?" He's so cute. None of these apartments around here have security gates.

"No. Just come on up and knock on the door. See you at eight. By the way, how should I dress?"

"I don't know. However you want to, I guess. I've never had a girl ask me that before. Just be yourself."

Myself. Well, which self should I be? The little rough-neck Jayd, the dashiki-wearing Jayd, or the laid-back, jeans-and-a-cute-top-from-Baby-Phat Jayd. That last Jayd seems most appealing. Yeah, that's the Jayd going out with Jeremy tonight.

"All right, then. I'll see you soon, Jeremy."

"Bye, Jayd."

So, he wants to go to the movies and hang out at the pier. Which pier? I wonder. He must be talking about Redondo. I know it's gonna get cold no matter where we end up, so I better take my jacket too. And, what about my hair? It's so flat now. But after ten minutes by the beach I'll look like a troll doll. I'd better give Nellie a call to let her know there's been a change in plans.

"Hi. You've reached Nellie's voice mail. Please leave a message after the tone and I'll get back to you when I can. Toodles." No answer. She's probably getting ready for tonight. I hate to leave a message, but it's better than not calling at all, I suppose.

"Hey, girl, it's Jayd. Sorry, but I won't be at the party tonight. I made plans with Jeremy. I hope you understand, and tell Mickey to be good and I'll see y'all at school on Monday. Holla back." I know she's going to be pissed, but she'll get over it.

When I get home, I decide to touch up my press and just let it lay back in a tight ponytail on the right side of my neck. I'm wearing my cute capri jeans from Lerner's and my pink and white Baby Phat tank with my Baby Phat flip-flops. I gotta downscale the diva in me a little. I don't want to overdress for the beach crowd.

Usually when I would go out with KJ, he would give me explicit instructions on what to wear and how to wear my hair. I was there to accentuate his outfit, basically an accessory. It's kind of cool just wearing what I feel like and not worrying about anyone saying anything about my toes hanging out at night, although I'm still a little self-conscious. And, I don't want to be cold. If I don't cover up my feet, I should wear something over my shoulders.

As I open the living room closet to get my jacket, I hear a knock at the door.

"Who is it?" I call out.

"It's Jeremy. I'm here to pick up Jayd."

Oh, no, this dude is early. This I'm not used to. I still have to put on my perfume, check my nose one more time, and say a little prayer that I don't embarrass myself in front his fine self.

"Just a minute, Jeremy. I'll be right there." I quickly spray on some Escada Rockin' Rio and dab a little Egyptian Musk Oil behind my ears. My mom swears it drives Ras Joe out of his mind. My mom's still in her room, recouping for tonight's adventures I'm sure. I leave her a note on the fridge telling her where I'll be and with whom. I check everything else and say a quick prayer before opening the door.

When I do, I find Jeremy looking hella good. He's wearing some typical White boy South High gear. Levi's that are hella worn-out, loose fitting, but not too baggy, a T-shirt, a baseball hat with the rim folded real tight, and some brown, suede Birkenstocks on his feet. This cat is straight out of P.V.

"Hey, Jeremy. Sorry to keep you waiting."

"Hey, Jayd." He looks at my ponytail, my big gold hoops hanging from my ears, my jeans, and finally, my feet. I've always been self-conscious about two things: my breasts and my Flintstone feet. I took care of my overly large breasts last year, but I think I'm stuck with my feet for life.

"You look cute in sandals. Ready to go?" I don't know if he's joking or not, but I ain't gonna compromise the one and only compliment I've ever received on my feet.

"Thank you. Yeah, I'm ready. Will I fit in with your friends, or is the jacket too much?"

"Jayd, you never struck me as a fashion queen," he says as I turn around to lock the door behind us. "Damn, how many locks you got?"

My mom has four bolts on her door. She's been robbed a couple of times, so she's not playin' anymore. Now she just gotta worry about getting in the door in time if she's running from somebody.

"I know. My mom's a bit paranoid."

"Is she here? Does she want to meet the White guy taking her daughter out?" he asks, only half joking in that way of his. He has the most beautiful smile. It's like his eyes just light up when he smiles. And his teeth are perfect.

"Did you wear braces?" I ask.

"Where the hell did that come from?" he says, still smiling. "Yes, I did. Now answer my question. Does your mom want to meet me?" How do I tell him my mom's tired out from her date last night, and conserving her energy for her date tonight, without making her look bad?

"She does, but she's got cramps. She said to tell you to be careful with her baby. So, be careful with me."

Jeremy takes my hand and leads me down the narrow stairway to the front where his car's parked. What a sweet ride. His car is infamous around South Bay High. It's a powder blue '65 Mustang convertible with cream-colored leather interior. The original wood paneling is perfect. It's the nicest car I've ever been in.

"What did you do to get this car?" I say, knowing his dad's an engineer with eighteen U.S. patents, so far. That's another detail about Jeremy's life that's pretty widely known.

"Actually, it's kinda the family first car. My two older brothers both drove this car until they went off to college. Now I get to drive it until I go to college." He opens the door for me, and I slide onto the leather seat. It smells like leather polish. Everything's shining like he just got it washed.

"You mind if the top is down? Or is it too much wind on you?"

"Nah, I'm cool." Good thing I wore my hair back.

"I thought maybe we could skip the movie and just kinda hang out. It's a nice night and I want to be outside. And, I want to talk to you, and we can't do that in the movies."

I agree with him. The movies are cool, but it's not conducive for getting to know someone. KJ and I used to go to the movies on the regular, and the only thing he was interested in was making out. This date's already off to the right start, as far as I'm concerned.

We end up in Manhattan Beach by the pier. It's a trendy little spot. There are bookstores, chic clothing stores with shit I could never afford, and coffeehouses. My favorite coffee spot is right on the corner, The Coffee Bean & Tea Leaf.

"You mind if we stop here? I want to get a Café Vanilla."

"Yeah, I like Coffee Bean too. I usually get the Chocolate Ice Blended," Jeremy says.

"Well, aren't we just the exact opposite of each other," I say, eyeing the joint to see if there are any other Black people around. Nope, not a one.

"You wanna sit down in here or on the patio?"

"On the patio's good," I say, claiming a seat with a sidewalk view.

"I'll get our drinks." He's such a gentleman. If I was with KJ, I'd be paying for my own coffee, since he's not into the whole coffee shop thing. And we definitely wouldn't be sitting down and talking up in this place.

When Jeremy comes back outside with our drinks, we talk until the place closes. I find out he's a true surfer dude. He wakes up at 4 A.M. to get out and surf every morning. His mother's from Louisiana and his dad's from Brooklyn. His mom's a Baptist, his dad is Jewish, and he and his two brothers don't know what to believe and don't really care. He's the baby of the family. They have a dog, Ganymede, that doesn't bark.

"I've never heard of a dog that doesn't bark. Are you sure she's not broken or something," I say, sipping the last of my drink.

"No, she's not broken. She's a basenji."

"A what?" I ask. The only dogs in my neighborhood are pit bulls, dobermans and mutts, and they all bark.

"A basenji. Better known as the African barkless dog," he says, sounding very proud.

"Now I know you're lying. Ain't nothing in Africa quiet, especially not a dog. What's the point of having a dog that doesn't bark?" I ask.

"Well, I'm not getting into the history of Ganymede's ancestors, but my mom specifically chose her because she doesn't bark." Now, that's strange. Usually people get dogs to warn them of danger, which they do by barking. So why wouldn't she want a dog that barks?

"Okay, Jeremy, whatever. What about the name Ganymede? Where did that come from?"

"Actually, I named her after one of the moons of Jupiter. It's my favorite planet." He pulls up his right sleeve to reveal a tattoo of Jupiter on his arm.

"I've never known anyone to have a favorite planet," I say, avoiding the secondhand smoke floating our way from the other people sitting outside. We must be the only nonsmokers out here.

"Well, I don't much believe in things I can't see. So, you can kinda say Jupiter's my concrete evidence in something else out there bigger than us."

"So, you don't believe in God at all?" I ask. I've also never known anyone who's an atheist. This date is just full of first-time adventures for me.

"No, I don't. Between my parents' arguments about their beliefs and my own aversion to anything religious, I just don't care too much about God and religion and anything like it," he says, finishing the last of his Ice Blended.

"Really? So, how do you think Jupiter came to be?" I ask, enjoying the conversation's new direction.

"Well, like I said. I believe something made us and the solar system, obviously. But, all the God stuff and spirituality and shit is just made up. I remember talking to Mrs. Bennett about it one day in class, and she almost passed out," he says, referring to my most hated teacher, aside from Mrs. Peterson.

"Please don't mention her name to me. I'm having such a nice night."

"I know. A lot of people can't stand her. But, she's cool to me. Besides, she's the only teacher who challenges my intellect and allows me to challenge hers." Jeremy's hella smart, but doesn't flaunt it. I really like that about him and everything else so far. When the coffee shop's staff tells us they're closing, I fear the date might be over.

"Well, I'm glad I got to know more about you. And thank you for the coffee. I had a really good time."

"Are you trying to get rid of me or something? It's only midnight, and the car doesn't turn back into a pumpkin until 2 A.M. Care to see it happen?" Damn, he's sexy when he's being a smart-ass.

"You know what, you don't have to be funny. I just assumed that since the place is closing down we were going home."

"Why would you assume that? The night is young. I want you to meet some of my friends outside of school, if you're up for it."

Oh, hell, where's he taking me? You know how all them movies end with the little Black girl being sacrificed or something crazy like that. But, I'm going to risk it 'cause I don't want the night to end just yet.

We get back in his car and cruise down Pacific Coast Highway toward Palos Verdes. It's a perfect night to be by the beach. The moon's full, the sky's clear, and the air is chilly, but not too cold. As if he'd read my mind, Jeremy reaches into the backseat and grabs his poncho pullover, a surfer must-have, and hands it to me.

"Here. I know it can get a bit cool, especially for people who aren't used to cold beach nights." He's damn right about that. This little cute jacket I brought ain't doing nothing to keep me warm. This poncho looks like it's just what I need. And, so does he.

"Thank you, 'cause a sistah is getting hella cold," I say, pulling the poncho over my head, careful not to mess up my already poofy hair.

"Why'd you do that?"

"Do what?" I ask, self-conscious.

"Try not to touch your hair. The poncho won't hurt it, you know."

"Oh, no, but it will. You see what the ocean air has already done to it. I don't want your friends to see me looking like a madwoman."

"Your hair is really important to you, isn't it?"

"You just don't get it, do you? My hair is very sensitive to the elements. The slightest change in air temperature, moisture, or something as simple as putting on a poncho can permanently affect the style of my hair for the night."

"Well, I think your hair looks sexy like it is. Besides, you look way better than any of the people you're going to meet tonight." This dude's really diggin' me, ain't he?

* * *

We pull up to what looks to me like the middle of nowhere. Or rather, the deserted beach where they sacrifice people in horror flicks. He parks the car on the sand, grabs my hand, and leads me down a steep sand hill. At the bottom of the hill, right off the beach, I see a bonfire and smell marijuana burning in the wind.

As we get closer, I can hear drumming and a guitar. People are just lying around, kickin' it. Most of them look high off something; the rest look like they're mesmerized by the motion of the waves.

"Jayd, meet my surfing crew. Crew, this is Jayd." They all look at me and nod a cool "What's up?" before returning to their individual trances.

"So what do you think?" Jeremy asks, as we sit down on the cold sand.

"Honestly, this is the most peaceful I've felt in a long time. All night I haven't thought about the drama of this past week at all. Thank you for taking me out. I'm having a good time."

"Well, I hope it won't be the last." Jeremy pulls me in close to him and wraps his arms around me. He smells like vanilla incense and Polo cologne. It's at this moment I realize I could easily fall in love with him.

I purposely turned off my phone when we left the house because KJ has been on my jock all weekend. And, I know my girls must be bugging out over the fact that I'm not at Byron's party. They've probably been trying to reach me all night. I don't want anything ruining our night, especially not any annoying phone calls or text messages. And, it's perfect. I can't wait to go home tomorrow night and tell Mama all about my date with Jeremy.

~ 3 ~
Jaw Jackin'

"You ain't saying nothin' homie/
You ain't fresh azimiz."

—LIL' BOW WOW

On our way back to Compton Sunday evening, my mom and I have a chance to talk about my date with Jeremy. I'm glad too because I've been itching to tell someone about it and Nellie and Mickey aren't answering their phones.

"So, how was the party last night?" my mom asks as we merge from the 105 freeway to the 91. She drives like a race car driver in her little Mazda. I hope she teaches me how to drive before my test at the DMV in a couple of months. If I play it right, I can have my license by Thanksgiving. I'm saving up for a car, even though my dad promised he'd help me to get one when the time comes. But, I don't know about trusting him to get the kind of car I need. That's why I put a small portion of my paycheck away in the bank every month. But I will have to remember to ask my dad about my car situation next weekend when I see him.

"We didn't actually make it to the party. We ended up having coffee and hangin' out by the beach with some of his friends instead," I say.

"Really? And that was okay with you?"

"It was better than okay. I had enough drama at school all week long. I didn't need any more from the same haters while trying to get to know Jeremy. I didn't expect him to be such a gentleman. But last night gave me a good insight into his character. And, so far so good," I say, smiling like the Kool-Aid man. "When he dropped me off last night, he didn't even attempt to kiss me or feel me up."

"Is that right," my mom says, not completely convinced of Jeremy's chivalry.

"Yes, it is. He just walked me up the stairs and gave me a big hug," I say, defending my man.

"A gentleman, huh," my mom says, glancing at me from the corner of her eye and giving a sly smile. "What's your definition of a gentleman?"

"Well, someone who opens the door for me, gives me compliments, and who doesn't pressure me about sex from jump street," I answer, realizing I'm comparing Jeremy to KJ. Not that KJ didn't open a door for me once or twice. But, being complimentary ain't his thang, and neither is waiting for the cookies. KJ tried to jump my bones the first time we kicked it during summer school and would do it now, if he had the chance.

"Well, men who act the gentleman can also be control freaks. Your father was a gentleman, and look at us now," she says as we exit onto Central Boulevard, only a few minutes away from Mama's house.

"Jeremy's nothing like my dad," I say, hurt my mom would even make such a comparison after all the mess my dad put her through.

"All I'm saying is be careful, Jayd. Take your time with this one and make sure he stays a gentleman. Once you give up your opinion, cookies, or whatever else they can take, all the gentleman shit goes out the door."

When I get home, Mama and Daddy's yelling can be heard all the way outside. They have the best fights. Mama gets to talking to Daddy while he gets dressed to go out with the church members, all of whom happen to be women, for Sunday night dinner. Mama knows more than dinner's going on and always tries to get him to tell the truth.

"Look, Lynn Mae, I ain't got to lie to you. I'm a grown man. Good, Christian, and God-fearing, unlike yourself. If you want to come to dinner, come. You're always welcome back in the church," Daddy says, knowing good and well Mama ain't going nowhere near them church folks.

"You're such a lying ass. You don't even know when you're telling a lie anymore. Church dinner my ass. Who is it this time, huh, Ray? One of them little young heffas, or did you have a taste for some old cat tonight?" Mama can get raw when she's pushed.

"If I wanted some old cat, I'd stay home." And that was checkmate. Daddy left, and Mama went outside to work in her spirit room. She said she was working on a potion for one of her clients, but I think she was working on one to use on Daddy.

After the house drama, I don't bother telling Mama about my in-house suspension tomorrow. I'm sure they'll send a letter home tomorrow, on which I'll promptly forge my mom's signature and turn back in Tuesday morning. They never check, and my mom doesn't want to be bothered with menial stuff like that. I'm not looking forward to suspension, but I am looking forward to seeing Jeremy tomorrow. I'm still buzzing from our date last night. I didn't get home until 2 A.M. and barely stayed awake at work. All I want to do now is sleep and hope tomorrow goes by fast.

When I get to campus, I immediately report to the main office to serve my time. Nellie and Mickey are waiting for me by the principal's office, which is next to the conference room. I've never been suspended before, so I don't really know how this works. But, Mickey was suspended last year for fighting Misty, so she knows the ropes.

I'm still pissed KJ didn't get in-house with us. Being an athlete has too many perks. And, not to mention he's still harassing me. He's texted me three times already this morning and left me several messages last night, mostly wanting to know where I was Saturday night and if I was hangin' out alone. He's on my jock hard now, just like he should be. I feel like I'm serving time for my man while he's on vacation with another woman. This ain't my ideal romantic situation, and KJ's got his nerve trying to get back with me now.

"Hey, y'all," I say, trying to sound chipper, even though I'm really not looking forward to this part of my day. "Ready for Alcatraz?"

"Jayd, it's not that bad," Mickey says as she and Nellie take a seat on the benches outside the principal's office. I walk up to Mrs. Cole's desk and lean up against the side, waiting for her to return and lead us to the conference room.

"Speak for yourself, Mickey," Nellie says, flipping her perfectly straightened hair over her shoulders and rolling her eyes in disgust. "I'm way too cute to be on lockdown like some criminal. I have a reputation to uphold."

"You have a reputation of being a tight-ass, and I doubt it'll be tarnished by this little episode," Mickey retorts. "Besides, this might be good for your reputation. Everybody needs a little bad girl in them, right, Jayd?"

"I have enough bad girl in me. I could do without the school's intervention," I say, anxiously eyeing the busy office. The warning bell just rang, and students and teachers alike are buzzing around hurrying off to class.

"We missed you at the party," Nellie says, sounding disappointed. "We dressed alike and everything. All eyes were on the two cute Black girls when there should have been three."

Oh, here we go again. This girl gets salty at the drop of a dime. But, I know it's all in love.

"Nellie, you know I wouldn't have missed the party if it was in my control. Also, I had enough of Misty and KJ during the week. I really didn't want to deal with their energy on the weekend too," I say. I hope she understands my decision. "I would have been cool with you ditching me to get to know a guy who could be your soul mate." I'm still high off Jeremy from Saturday night. I can only imagine how our first kiss is going to feel.

"Energy, soul mate? What the hell happened to you on Saturday, Jayd?" Mickey asks, mocking my vibe.

"So you did get my messages," I say, nudging her in the shoulder with my elbow. "Why you didn't call me back? I'm crushed."

"Oh, shut up, girl. You know you couldn't care less about me returning your call. We had to recuperate from Saturday night," she says, returning my nudge.

"Yeah, girl, it was heavy up in Byron's house. Shrimp, caviar, chocolate soufflé, you name it. I had niggeritis all day Sunday." Mickey is crazy.

"I'm quite sure that's politically incorrect," Nellie says, looking offended.

"Whatever. You know I'm right," Mickey says, rolling her eyes at Nellie. "So, Jayd, how's the White boy?"

"He's real cool," I say, ready to drop the details of our date. But the killjoy arrives right on cue. I bet she was listening to our entire conversation on the low.

"What's up?" Misty says as she enters through the double doors connecting the main hall to the office. No this girl isn't talking to us after all the shit she's put us through in only the first week of school.

"Did you hear something?" Mickey says, looking around the office as if she doesn't know it's Misty talking.

"No, I didn't," Nellie responds, playing along. "I thought I heard a rat, but it couldn't have been. The administration would send an exterminator immediately if there were any pest control problems on campus."

"Not if the pest's mother worked here," Mickey says with a giggle. She and Nellie can be so rude sometimes. But, I do agree. The school would be better off without Misty around.

"Again, I try to be friendly and this is how I'm treated," Misty says, feigning hurt. She could really care less if Mickey or Nellie speak to her; she just gets pleasure out of their reactions. "Cat got your tongue, Jayd," she says, noting my silence.

"I have nothing to say to you, Misty."

She shoots me a look of pure hatred. I wish she would say something slick to me, 'cause this morning I'm not in the mood and I will snap back at her.

"If Mrs. Cole asks, tell her I went to the ladies' room," Misty says, walking back through the doors leading to the main hall.

"That bitch has got some nerve, greeting us like we're homies. She's lucky we ain't in Compton right about now because I'd whip her ass," Mickey says.

"Good morning, ladies," Mrs. Cole says as she walks toward her desk from the principal's office carrying two DVDs and a set of keys. "Nellie and Mickey, you'll be in the small conference room adjacent to the principal's office. Misty and Jayd will be in the large conference room, next to me." How Misty and I got placed in the same room for in-house suspension is beyond me. Doesn't she know she's the reason the fight happened in the first place?

"Can I please be in the same room with Nellie and Mickey?" I ask in my nicest voice possible. I'm liable to smack Misty eventually, and that will only get me into more trouble.

"I'm afraid not, Miss Jackson. Rules are rules. Where is Misty anyway? The bell rang five minutes ago," Mrs. Cole says as she walks toward the small conference room and unlocks the door to let Nellie and Mickey in. Not one of us answers. "That girl's habitually late," Mrs. Cole says in response to our silence. "You girls are on first lunch; Jayd and Misty will be on second." Damn. I don't even get to talk to my girls at lunch? This is punishment for real. "Jayd, why don't you go into the large conference room; the door's already open. I'll be there in a second."

"See you later, Jayd," Nellie says as she follows Mrs. Cole into the small conference room.

"Yeah, you and Misty have fun," Mickey says sarcastically.

The conference room reminds me of the one on *The Apprentice*. There's a large, marble table in the center and ten plush leather chairs around it, which take up the majority of the space. At the head of the room is a large white board, and a television and DVD player stand in the corner. There's a large window on the other side of the room, where there's also a sink and small refrigerator.

I choose a seat at the far end of the table, farthest from the door. I can't believe my girls get to kick it with each other all day while I have to sit in this room with my nemesis. What did I do to deserve this? Speak of the devil, there's Misty's loud voice announcing her return. As she enters the room, the scent of her cheap perfume fills the space, nearly choking me.

"Damn, Misty. What are you trying to cover up with all that perfume?"

"Don't hate. You're just pissed because your precious reputation has been tainted by this little visit," she says as she seats her wide behind into the chair across the table from me.

"Excuse me, ladies. There's no talking. This is suspension, not vacation," Mrs. Cole says as she enters the room to cue the DVD player to our disciplinary video. "This three-hour presentation will show you the consequences of being a problematic student. After the video, you will be excused to lunch. When you return, you must complete your regular class work and a multiple choice quiz about the video before leaving for the day."

"A quiz? I thought this was suspension, not an extra class," Misty says. Mrs. Cole makes an ugly face at Misty. Not even five minutes and already Misty has managed to irritate her.

"Again, this isn't a vacation, Miss Truewell," Mrs. Cole says. "And, being an office aide, you should really know better than to be in this predicament in the first place. I'll have to talk to your mother about your status when she gets here," she says, looking at the clock on the wall. Misty's mom is late, as usual. "Mr. Adelezi will be in to talk to you girls about the incident later. Now, again, there's absolutely no talking. If I hear any voices, we'll have to extend the suspension for another day."

I don't know about Misty, but I'd rather be in class than sitting in the office all day. I want to see Jeremy and talk to my girls. At least they let us out for lunch. I'll just have to catch up with him then.

"So, Jayd, we missed you at the party Saturday night. Your girls were there. Where were you?" Misty asks, ignoring Mrs. Cole's warning. Does she listen to anyone?

"Misty, haven't you caused enough trouble? Do you really want to be in here for another day?" I whisper, trying not to get caught talking. Mrs. Cole left the door cracked, and I don't want her to hear my voice. If anyone gets caught jaw jackin', it should be Misty.

"Mrs. Cole can't hear us. She keeps that stupid radio on all day long, listening to boring classical music. So, we can catch up, like old friends." Misty must be on something if she thinks I'm going to confide in her.

"Misty, I'm not interested in catching up with you about anything," I say, reaching into my backpack to retrieve my notebook and pen.

"Ah, come on, Jayd. You can tell me all about your little date with Jeremy," she says, smiling like she knows something, but she doesn't. This is how she gets her information—by tricking her subjects into divulging their info because they think she already knows, but not me. I know her too well.

"Shut up, Misty, and watch the movie. I've really had it with you. First, you start all this BS with Trecee, and then you have the nerve to call me and apologize like we're in kindergarten. Please know I want to kick your ass, but you're not worth it. So, don't mistake my calm for forgiveness because there's none where you're concerned."

Misty looks genuinely hurt, which makes me feel a little bad, but not much. She deserves all the lip I can give her under the circumstances.

"Well damn, Jayd, a sistah can't make a mistake?" she says as she reaches into her backpack sitting in the seat next to her.

"Yes, a sistah can. But you sure as hell ain't a sistah of mine. And for the record, I've forgiven you several times only for you to repeatedly stab me in the back. No more chances for you to hurt me, Misty. From now on, you don't exist to me."

"Are you sure, Jayd? I'm pretty hard to ignore," she says, smiling. That's probably the truest statement she's ever made. Her presence is so powerful there should be a hurricane named after her.

"Ladies, I said no talking," Mrs. Cole says from her desk. "Not another peep, you two." And, with that last warning, Misty and I watch the DVD in silence.

* * *

When the bell rings for second lunch, Misty rushes out before I even have a chance to get my backpack closed. I guess she can't wait to get to South Central's area in the quad and hear or spread the latest gossip, whatever that may be. I haven't seen Jeremy all day, and I'm jonesing for a hug. I grab my backpack and walk through the main hall doorway to find him waiting by the entrance, ready to satisfy my craving.

"How's my little jailbird?" he says, taking my backpack from my shoulder and slipping it onto his before hugging me. God, his arms feel good around my body, and he smells so sweet.

"That's not funny. It's boring as hell sitting in there with Misty all day. At least I don't have to talk to her. But the movie we're being forced to watch is so slow," I say as we walk arm in arm down the crowded hall toward the quad.

"Yeah, the movie's totally outdated," he says like an expert critic.

"How many times have you seen it?" I ask.

"Oh, enough to know it doesn't work. Hungry?" he asks as we approach the snack stand. I'm really hungry, especially since we weren't allowed outside for break and I never bring a snack to school.

"Starved. What's on the menu today?" Before he can answer, I notice Misty's across the yard pointing and staring at me. She's already made up some story to spread since I wouldn't tell her anything about our date, I'm sure. Being alone in a room with her all day and not being able to punch her is pure torture.

"Well, there's pizza, corn dogs and French fries. The usual. Interested?" Jeremy asks, totally oblivious to the looming drama across the yard. Misty has KJ, Del, C Money, Tony, and Shae looking our way. But I'm not going to let her get to me.

"I'll have a slice of pizza. What are you having?"

"I'm having three of the same," he says. "I'll get our food.

Why don't you grab us a bench before they're all gone."
Jeremy walks over to the long line, leaving me to seethe
alone. I wonder what BS Misty's spreading now. That girl can
talk up a storm. I wish I could vibe with Nellie and Mickey
right about now. I'll have to catch them right after school before I catch the bus home and ask if they know what Misty's
up to now.

Lunch with Jeremy was fun, even though Misty and crew
watched us the whole time, making up the sound track to my
conversation with Jeremy, I'm sure. When I got out of in-
house detention, Nellie and Mickey were still in the conference room as the bell rang. I knew they couldn't keep their
mouths closed the entire day. I would be in there with them
if I had a choice in the matter.

When I get home, Mama and Daddy are both out, although I'm sure not together. My uncles, as usual, are in the
streets somewhere and won't be home until well after dark.
Jay and Bryan are in their room playing chess, which leaves
me to start dinner if I want to eat. I wish Mama was home because I need to talk. I'm so tired all I can think about is finishing my homework and going straight to bed. I guess I'll
just have to wait until tomorrow to get advice from Mama.
She always knows what to do.

~ 4 ~
Pullin'

"Don't you know my hair's so strong/
It could break the teeth out the comb?"

—JIGABOOS & WANNABEES CHORUS/SCHOOL DAZE SOUNDTRACK

When I wake up this morning, Mama is already up which is highly unusual. After my shower and breakfast, I go out back to check on her.

"Good morning, Mama. Are you all right?" I ask. She and the dog, Lexi, both look up at me like I've interrupted their flow.

"Yes, Jayd, I'm fine. Just behind in my work. Come find me at Netta's shop after you get home from school so we can sit down and talk. I want to hear all about your weekend." The only thing about meeting Mama at Netta's shop is I usually run into Felicia, Monica, and the other neighborhood haters on their way home from Compton High. They're also tight with Misty, which makes them even more unpleasant to be around.

"Why don't I meet you here and get some of this done for you while you're at Netta's," I say, trying to get out of going to the shop. I'd much rather work in the spirit room than run into any more broads.

"I'll have this done before I leave. But, thank you for the offer," Mama says, giving me a kiss on the cheek before sending me off to school and what promises to be a drama-filled day.

* * *

Since Misty reported yesterday that I missed the party and went out with Jeremy instead, there was nothing but BS at school today. People in our government class were making kissing sounds at Jeremy and me when we walked in with each other and took our customary seats. Everybody now knows that Jeremy and I are dating. And, Misty's having a field day spreading her version of the news. I tried to lay low all day, which wasn't hard to do because Jeremy took me off campus for lunch today. Now he's giving me a ride to the bus stop near my house. I don't want him taking me all the way home just yet; I'm not ready for everyone on my block to be up in my business. After Jeremy drops me off, I head up Alondra toward Greenleaf and Netta's shop, ready for some sound advice.

I like to watch Mama get her hair done. Netta, Mama's long-time hairdresser and gossip buddy, always gives Mama a hot hairstyle that will last through the upcoming week, as long as she wraps it up in a scarf every night. Today, after her usual press and curl, Mama is getting a French twist with a little extra hair to give it some booty. Some of the best advice comes from Mama when she's sitting in that chair. Just like when she's cooking, Mama's on a different level when Netta gets in her head.

"Netta, don't be taking all afternoon. I got beans cooking on the stove," Mama says, while Netta pushes the lever at the bottom of the salon chair to make Mama sit up a little higher. Netta shifts her weight from one side to the other on her cushioned stool behind the chair. Netta's a big sistah, with pretty brown skin and platinum blond hair cropped real low to her scalp.

"I thought you said you wasn't doing no cooking for them

fools this week. That's what you said last week." Netta re-
members everything like a tape recorder.

"Look, Ms. Nosey, I ain't cooking for none of them fool
men in that house, ain't that right, Jayd?" Mama says, looking
to me for validation. I just shake my head and say "whatever"
because Mama knows she ain't telling the whole truth. She
doesn't cook for Daddy anymore, but the rest of them fools
still look to her for some table droppings every now and
then.

"Jayd, I tell you what you should do," Netta says, referring
to the latest episode of *Misty the Meddler*. I already filled
them both in on today's drama. "You need to get your Mama
to put a root on that girl, show her who's boss," Netta says,
careful not to burn Mama's ear. "It seems like every time you
have a problem, that girl's behind it."

"Don't tell that girl that, Netta. She already got them kids
thinking we're a voodoo house," Mama says.

"But, Lynn Mae, you do have a voodoo house, or is this
the wrong queen sitting up in my chair? Now, you want some
hold spray with sheen or shea butter?" Netta asks Mama, already knowing what she's going to do, no matter what
Mama's answer is.

"Hold spray," Mama says.

"Okay. Shea butter it is. That'll give it a little sheen plus
protection from the elements," she says, spritzing Mama's
hair lightly before pressing it, without waiting for Mama's ap-
proval. "Your mama can get rid of any enemies, ailments, issues, you name it. Why you don't give her a root bag or
something, get that little hussy away from her, Lynn."

"Netta, keep your voice down. Walls have ears," Mama
says. She don't like airing her laundry all willy-nilly.

"Well, I'm sorry. But from where we're from, Jayd, your
mama's a modern-day Marie Le Veaux."

"Yes, and they persecuted me like her too," Mama says, looking into the mirror while Netta parts another section of her hair. "I used to love working in the shop with Netta, Jayd. Thought I was gonna do hair for the rest of my life, until I met your granddaddy and moved to Texas and then, eventually, here."

"Yeah, your mama sho' could do some hair, girl," Netta says, taking over Mama's story. "She has a special touch, like every time she washes your head your whole body gets clean. Can't nobody do a head like your mama." Netta's got that right. During certain cleansings, Mama washes my head, and it feels like every problem I've ever had instantly disappears. I know Netta misses working with Mama. Mama said they used to try out new styles on each other. Not anymore, though.

"It broke my heart when them people on Bourbon Street boycotted my chair. Granted, it was the sixties, but they picked the wrong cause to protest," Mama says, looking close to tears. "I never did a thing to them people. See what rumors can do, Jayd? Those people heard I made a doll for the senator's wife, and they got scared to let me in their heads."

"But what does doing hair have to do with a doll?" I ask, a little confused. I've heard this story time and again, but each time I get a little more out of it.

Netta eagerly answers for Mama. "Some people say that if you want to put a curse on someone, you get a strand of their hair and pin it to the doll's head. This will make the person lose their mind." Netta continues, almost in a whisper, "That's why your mama couldn't get no more clients. Everybody in New Orleans knows your mama's a very powerful queen." As Netta says this, I picture Mama with her scarf wrapped tight around her head, like a crown. "Nobody would take the chance on becoming her next victim. They didn't want to end up like the senator's mistress, who wound up with a mysterious brain tumor that made her speak in tongues for the rest of her life."

"Netta, how you gone remember all that but can't remember what kinda spray to use in my hair?" Mama says, trying to change the subject. "Stop all that nonsense before you scare the poor child."

Netta ignores Mama and continues with her story. "Jayd, your mama put all them Louisiana Catholic Creoles in their places when she left with your granddaddy. She didn't look back not once," she says, spraying Mama's hair without missing a beat.

"They thought they would ruin her. No, not your mama. She stopped right in front of the shop we worked in on her way to meet your daddy, put her bags down in the doorway, untied her scarf, and let her long hair hang down, representing the Williams' royal legacy proudly."

Mama pretends to be bothered by the story, but she looks like she's smiling behind the frown.

"It's still considered ill luck to utter the name Queen Jayd, aka Lynn Mae Williams-James, in New Orleans to this day."

"Queen Jayd? I ain't never heard this part of the story before," I say, hoping to get another good story out of Netta. The last time she told this story I found out more about Netta's past too—that she and her husband, Lester, came to Compton in the late 1970s, same time as everyone else from Mama's generation. Netta and Lester started their businesses—he's a mechanic—and wanted to get pregnant, but couldn't. That's when Netta went to Mama for help, and she made it happen.

"People back home never thought it was a coincidence that like Marie the First, your mama named her first-born daughter after her."

"That's common in the South, Netta. You making something out of nothing, as usual."

"And then," continues Netta like Mama never spoke, "your mama names you, her first-born granddaughter, after her spiritual name, Jayd, the green-eyed voodoo priestess and conjure woman."

"Netta, shut the hell up with all that talk and concentrate on my hair." Netta has wrapped Mama's hair in an immaculate French twist while telling the story.

"You need to go back under the dryer and let the spray stiffen," Netta says, leading Mama to the hair dryer. While Mama's under the dryer, Netta continues to tell me about the rumors that were spread about Mama in New Orleans, or as they say it, "Nawlins."

"Your mama's mama was said to be this French woman from Paris herself. She fell in love with this dark Haitian fella named Jon Paul Williams. His mama was a voodoo priestess in Haiti, and he a priest.

"Your mama was pulled toward the priesthood, but wanted your grandfather more. Besides, she was getting tired of people's envy. She left her legacy in Louisiana to become the first lady of First AME of Central Compton. Your mama never did like that title, though."

"All right, Jayd, that's enough for today. See you next time, Netta," Mama says, surprising us both as she takes off her hair cap, pulls the cotton from behind her ears, and grabs her purse from the lounge area.

"All right, Queen Jayd, and little Jayd too. See y'all next week."

While Mama and I walk the six blocks across Wilmington back to Gunlock, I tell her all about my date with Jeremy and the week's drama so far.

"Jayd, if you really like the boy, then date him. Misty will always be around. You just have to learn to ignore her."

"Ignoring Misty is like trying to ignore a bee stinging me. It can't be done," I say.

"Yes, it can, Jayd. You're stronger than your enemies. Always remember that."

As we turn the corner onto our street, I see Bryan talking to someone on the porch, but I can't make out who it is.

"I see your uncle made it home today. Who's that he's talking to?" As we get a little closer to the house, I clearly see it's KJ.

"Jayd, what kinda mess you starting now, girl? Does that boy know you dating Jeremy?" Mama asks.

"I didn't tell him, but I'm sure Misty gave him the four-one-one. KJ and his boys were staring at me and Jeremy at lunch yesterday."

"Oh, that girl is something else," Mama says, shaking her head from side to side. "Just be cool, Jayd. Just keep a cool head and everything will work out. You'll see." As we walk up the driveway, KJ comes to meet us halfway. Bryan stays on the porch looking like he's got a ringside seat and the main event is about to start.

"Good afternoon, Mrs. James," he says to Mama.

"Good afternoon, KJ. What brings you by, unannounced, I assume?" Mama looks at me out the corner of her eye and smiles. Mama's so bad sometimes.

"Well, I was hoping me and Jayd could go out and talk for a while. I haven't been able to track her down since last week," he says, looking in my direction.

"And yet, you still came by," I say. Mama frowns at my rudeness.

"Well, I just wanted to make sure you were all right. It's not like you to ignore a brotha."

Mama feels the heat rising and proceeds into the house. Bryan, smirking, reluctantly follows Mama inside.

"I'll talk to you later, man. And don't forget to listen to my show," he says to KJ.

"All right, Bryan, I'll check it out. Bye, Mrs. James."

"I'm sure I'll see you soon, KJ," Mama says, leaving us alone in the driveway. Once they're completely inside, I let KJ have it.

"Look, KJ, you can't just be poppin' up at my house like you're still my man."

"Why not? Is the White boy hangin' out in Compton now?" he says, oozing with jealousy. I actually like seeing him this way; he deserves it.

"You're not funny. And, so what if he is? It ain't none of your business no more who hangs out with me. Now, if you'll excuse me, I've got homework to do," I say as I push past him toward the house.

"Jayd, what happened to you?" KJ asks, looking a little hurt. "You don't have feelings for me no more?" he says, grabbing my arm and turning me around to face him. His touch sends shivers down my spine.

"KJ, you must have convenient amnesia or something, because I could have sworn you broke up with me last weekend, almost got me beat down last week, and now you want to be all up on me again. You must be out of your ever-loving mind if you think I'm gone let you back in that easy."

"Well, tell me what I can do to win you back."

I look at this boy, shocked. "Nothing, KJ. That's the point. I've moved on, just like you." I snatch my arm from his grip, turn around, and walk up to the porch. A part of me wishes neither of us moved on and could forget everything that happened last week. But, the larger part of me knows better than to let him near my heart again.

"Jayd, wait. Let me at least take you out one more time. Besides, everybody's rooting for us to get back together." No doubt this little bit of drama makes a tasty episode in the days of the lives of the jealous and bored.

"I don't know, KJ. I'll think about it. Now, like I said, I got stuff to do. Good night."

"All right, Jayd. I'll see you at school tomorrow. And don't be acting like you don't know me anymore. It's bad for our reputation."

"Whatever," I say, walking in the house and closing the door. Dudes can be so full of themselves sometimes.

Let's take a long walk, around the park, after the dark. There's Jeremy's special ring tone. Who else better than Jill Scott to sing about my new baby?

I'm cool on KJ for right now. He's trying to make me conform to his and everybody else's expectations of a happy ending. But, just like black hair, you can try to pull it straight all you want, but it always wants to be kinky. And, I want to get to know my new man, not deal with more bull from the old one.

~ 5 ~
Jungle Fever

"I might date another race or color/
It doesn't mean I don't like my strong Black brothers."

—EN VOGUE

Now that KJ's gone, maybe I can get down to business. I've got mad homework now that school's in full motion. It's always been difficult balancing my school, home, and family life, but not impossible. But first, let me call my new baby back. I wanted to get settled before talking to him, so I let his call go to voice mail.

"Hello."

"Hey, Jeremy, it's Jayd. You rang," I say, making myself comfy at the dining room table, books in tow.

"I know your voice, Jayd," he says, sounding all sexy. His voice is heavy and sweet, like molasses. I can hear the smile on his face. "So, what are you up to tonight?" he asks as if it's the weekend.

"My homework and then to bed. What else is there to be up to?" I ask, opening my English textbook. Mama's already wrapped her hair up in a scarf and is headed to the bathroom for a bath before everyone gets home, particularly Daddy. There's an unofficial bathroom schedule in the house: Mama first and everybody else when they can. The only person bold enough to challenge this rule is Daddy.

"Well, I was going to invite you over for dinner. We don't eat until seven-thirty around here."

"Here, as in your family?" I ask. That's a big step, and I want to make it clear that I think so. When I first had dinner with KJ's family, it officially sealed us as a couple.

"Yes. My mom cooks every night. You like Southern food?" Jeremy asks, not knowing my family's also from the South. I learned all about Jeremy's family on our first date. But really, I thought my family history would be a little too much for him, so I kept my answers to his questions light.

"Hell, yes," I exclaim. "My mama's from Louisiana, so we're always eating good over here."

"Really? I didn't know you were a Southern girl," he says with the cutest imitation of a Southern drawl, as if I'm not already finding him irresistible.

"Oh, yeah, my mama can cook her ass off." Speaking of which, Mama asked me to look after the beans a minute ago, and I completely forgot. I hope they're not sticking to the pot.

"So can mine. She's got four men to feed, so she's got mad skills in the kitchen."

"Now, hold on there, White boy," I tease, "don't start using my language. Your mom may be able to throw down and all, but don't forget your place," I say, getting up from my seat to tend to the beans on the stove.

"Say it to my face, shorty," he says.

"Oh, no you didn't go there," I say, pretending to be offended. We're having a good time now.

"Oh, yes I did. You're cute, but still a shorty."

"You know what, Jeremy, I'm going to let you slide on that one for now because I have to save these beans and start the corn bread before my grandmother gets out of the tub," I say as I reach for the cornmeal and flour in the crowded cupboard.

"So, can you come and play or not?" Jeremy persists.

"No, I can't. Too late and too short notice. Besides, my

grandmother doesn't like me going out on school nights, and she doesn't let me stay out late like my mother does."

"But I thought you were at your mama's house?" Jeremy asks, sounding confused.

"No. I call my grandmother Mama, get it?" I ask, still not sure he does.

"Okay, whatever. Can you clear it with one of them to come to dinner one night, after school? I'll take you home, to whomever's house you're at that day," he says very sarcastically.

"You can be a little smart-ass when you want to, huh, Jeremy?" I ask, again teasing.

"Awwwe, baby, I thought you knew," he says. I'm laughing at him now.

"Jayd, are you watching those beans?" Mama yells from the bathroom. That's my official warning to get off the phone.

"I'll clear it with my grandmother and get back to you. Now, I have to go before I get yelled at."

"Can you call me later? I'll be up until about midnight." He's just not knowing my life at all, is he?

"Sweety, after I finish cooking dinner I have homework, as you know, and then I will try to be in bed by eleven, and that depends on if I can get in the bathroom by ten or before."

"Why can't you call me after your bath?" he asks. I like that he wants to talk to me before he goes to bed.

"Because I wake up at 5:30 A.M., and I need my beauty sleep," I say, more serious than he knows. The Williams women are notorious for being ugly and cranky if we don't get enough sleep.

"Damn, why so early? You surf or something?"

"No, silly. It takes a while to get to school on the bus. Compton ain't around the corner from Redondo Beach, ya know," I say, trying to mix batter and stir the beans at the same time. Mama would kill me if she could see me now.

"Yeah, I know. But we'll have to work on your morning transportation soon. Good night." Well damn, I like his directness. This dude's gone get me so sprung on his ass I ain't gone never want to let go.

"I'll hold you to that, Sir Jeremy."

"Please do, Lady J." And, with that last tingle down my spine, we hung up. Lady J. I like the sound of that. I've got to call Nellie and tell her about this. She's still a bit irritated that I blew off her, Mickey, and the party at Byron's on Saturday night, but she's slowly getting over it.

After dinner, I finish my homework, take my bath, and lay out my clothes for tomorrow. Now that Jeremy and I are officially dating, I want to look as cute as possible every day. I better call Nellie before it gets too late. As I grab my phone out of my purse, I notice there's a text message from KJ.

"Hey, Jayd. Just wanted to say good night and I can't wait 2 start over 2morrow. Nite, KJ."

This boy's too much. First he's playing pop-up this afternoon. Now he's sending me good night messages. I've never been so flattered and irritated at the same time. I wonder how long this new KJ will last. I scroll down my contact list and locate Nellie's number. Cell phones are so convenient. I don't have anyone's number on deck anymore—not even my girls'. They're all in the phone.

"Hello," Nellie says, sounding interrupted.

"Hey, girl, it's Jayd. Whatcha doin'?" I ask, trying to break the ice.

"Why you acting like you didn't ditch your girls for the cute White boy and then not even spend break or lunch with us today because you're hangin' with him and his crew?" she says, trying to make me feel guilty, but in a tone that lets me know she's cool and would have done the same thing.

"Girl, it's only Tuesday. You make it sound like I've been gone for weeks."

"Well, it sure does seem that way, especially since we didn't get to kick it yesterday due to our unfortunate incarceration. And, girl, everybody in South Central is talking about y'all, especially since neither of you showed up to the party on Saturday. But, I covered for you."

"Covered for me how?" I ask, wondering what kind of damage Nellie has done.

"I just said you came down with a little fever. Jungle fever, that is," Nellie says, getting a real kick out of her little joke.

"I'm not laughing with you, girl, just at you," I say, hanging my clothes on the back of the door and walking out the bedroom and toward the kitchen for more privacy. "But seriously, though. What am I gone do about KJ? He keeps calling me and texting me. Do you know that fool even came by here this afternoon trying to get me to talk to him?" I say.

"I don't know, Jayd. If it were me, I'd at least give the brotha another chance. But then again, you don't want to miss out on going with Jeremy. He's so cute, popular, and did I mention the boy's got bank?" she says. Nellie can teach a college course on gold digging.

"Speaking of which, Jeremy just invited me to dinner with his family. He wanted me to go tonight, but I had too much work to do, and Mama probably wouldn't let me go anyway."

"Jayd, you need to get some more freedom up in that house. You're the only girl in high school I know who has to cook dinner when she gets home and has a curfew. That's just slavery. I'm going to start calling you Cinderella if you don't speak up for yourself," Nellie says, making me laugh. If she only knew the half of it. I don't talk about my spiritual work with any of my friends, especially not Nellie. Her mom's very Episcopalian, and Nellie's not too far behind.

"And, this too shall pass," I say, quoting one of Mama's favorite Bible verses.

"It'll pass faster if you say something." This is an ongoing argument between Nellie and me. It usually starts because I can't accompany her to the mall and nail shop on a regular basis.

"Look, I want to hang out late on school nights, but I just can't. And, I like cooking. Jeremy says his mom can throw down too."

"What are you going to tell KJ? You know if you meet his parents, it's a big deal," she says, reminding me of the first time I met KJ's parents. They were so nice, and the food was so good. I instantly fell in love with his vibe at home. KJ's a sweet guy at his core. It's just the exterior attitude that needs help. I wonder if I'll fall in love with Jeremy's home too?

"So, are you gone become a surfer chick now? You know you'll have to turn in your Black card if you do that," Nellie says.

"No, Nellie, ain't nobody turning in no cards around here. But, I'm having fun. He's so funny and sweet and fine. I just love his smile and his whole outlook on life. He's so different," I say, wishing I had time to call Jeremy. Mama already gave me the look when I walked out just now. It's way past my bedtime. I'll just have to send him a good night text on the low instead.

"Well, girl, I say ride the wave and screw the consequences," Nellie says, sounding like an old lady. "You only live once. Have fun, girl. And, get him to take you shopping. He's balling."

"Nellie, I am not using Jeremy for his money."

"Well then, can you ask him to take me instead?"

"Good night, Nellie. I'll see you tomorrow," I say, laughing.

"Good night, girl." When Nellie hangs up, I send Jeremy a

quick message saying good night again before turning in for the night. I can't wait to see him tomorrow.

By the time I get settled in my bed, it's eleven-thirty. I've got to be up in a few hours to face the day at South Bay High. Every day seems to be filled with the same drama. But, at least now I have a new face to look forward to seeing on a regular basis.

"Jayd. Wake up, girl. Your man's in trouble. And, it's all your fault!" a familiar voice screams at me from the dark. I feel like I'm outside and the wind is blowing so much I can hardly keep my eyes open long enough to see anything.

"Jeremy," a woman's voice screams from the distance. And then I see Jeremy walk up the steps to the main hall. And in slow motion a huge wave hits him from behind. When the water recedes, Jeremy is nowhere to be found.

"Jeremy," I scream, but it's too late. Why didn't I warn him about the wave? Would it have made a difference, or would he still have been engulfed by the powerful water?

Even with all the gossip about us spreading around school like a forest fire, Jeremy and I are still going strong. So far, so good. Our friends are still getting used to the idea that we're dating, but that's for them to deal with, not us. Every new couple needs to spend time alone to get to know each other and chill before actually solidifying the relationship. And, we're doing just that.

"I really like eating off campus. It's so relaxing to leave school behind, even if for only a little while," I say, sipping my chocolate milk shake from Jack-in-the-Box. KJ and I would go off campus occasionally, but not every day, like Jeremy and his crew. Even if they all don't go, someone at least makes a food run. They hardly ever eat campus food.

"Yeah, it's a relief, isn't it? Makes you remember the world is bigger than high school," Jeremy says.

"You can say that again. I like hangin' with you," I say, grabbing hold of his hand as we walk back to campus from the main parking lot.

"Hey, man. Can I holla at you for a minute?" one of Jeremy's friends says as we start to walk up the stairs leading to the main hall. A strong sea breeze kicks up dust into the air, and something feels like déja vù.

"Sure thing, man. Jayd, give me a second, would you?"

"Yeah, go ahead. I'll wait here," I say, totally missing the signs of the impending drama. As Jeremy talks with his friend, the breeze knocks some napkins left over from lunch out of my hand. They fly everywhere. I chase after them in the wind, which causes me to break out in a light sweat.

As I run around like a dog chasing its tail, I notice Stan and Dan, campus security, watching Jeremy. I look over toward Jeremy and see what they see: Jeremy gives what looks like a cigarette to the dude. I want to warn Jeremy, but it's too late. Stan and Dan close in on them, and all I can do is watch.

~ 6 ~
I'm Your Pusher

*"In this life one thing counts/
In the bank large amounts"*

—LUDACRIS

After Jeremy and his friend were handcuffed and led to the office, I went to class as if nothing happened. I didn't tell anyone in class, not even my home girl, Alia. She's the coolest White girl I've ever met, and she's on the same track as me, so we have most of our classes together.

"Hey, Jayd. Is everything all right? You look a little pale," she says, turning around in her seat to look at me. She's a pretty girl with long, blond hair, usually streaked with multiple fluorescent colors, and dark blue eyes. She's on the girl's volleyball team, although I think she should play basketball. What's the point of being six feet tall and not ballin'?

"I'm fine, girl. Just tired of the drama," I respond, telling the truth without giving up too much info.

"Well, you're not only in the wrong school; you're in the wrong class," she says, referring to our fifth period drama class, which is actually my favorite class of the day despite how I feel at the moment. Our teacher, Mrs. Sinclair, is pretty cool. She's so wound up in her personal life she doesn't bother us too much about assignments. As long as we look busy, she leaves us alone. The only time she gets serious is when we have a show to put on. Other than that, drama class is like a free period. Chance and I usually kick it, but he's not here today. I wonder if he's with Jeremy.

"Alia, have you seen Chance today?" I ask, knowing she'd know. She's secretly had a crush on him since last year. But, she's definitely not his type. He's not into punk girls, although I think they'd make an adorable couple.

"I saw him earlier, but he hasn't made an appearance in class yet. Want to check the theater?" she asks.

"No, that's okay." The one thing about South Bay is it's got hella money. Not only does this school have a full drama program, including a stage crew class and five drama classes, it also has a state-of-the-art theater, boys' and girls' dressing rooms, and the rehearsal room, which we use as a classroom. Most of the students kick it in the theater, but even the drama clique has subdivisions.

The drama stars, who think they're the only talented ones, hang out on stage, practicing monologues for auditions or just playing around. The wannabes hang out in the audience, watching the stars to learn a thing or two, I suppose. And then there are the talented ones, who hang in the classroom and just chill until we have to work. This last subdivision includes Matt, Chance, Alia, Leslie, Seth, and myself. We're usually chosen to perform in short skits and plays. The stars are always the leads in the musical productions, mostly because their parents are the financial sponsors for the drama program.

"Hey, Miss Jayd," Matt says, strolling into the room accompanied by Leslie and Seth, all tardy as usual.

"It's a good thing Mrs. Sinclair doesn't take roll," Alia says as she gets up to give them each a hug.

"Now, you know she's way too busy deciding between her old husband and the new one to be bothered with us," Leslie responds. Mrs. Sinclair and her husband, Mr. Sinclair, the se-

nior economics teacher, have been the most popular teachers' couple for years, or so I've heard. But lately Mrs. Sinclair
has been coming to school driving a fancy little Porsche,
which doesn't belong to her or her husband. She's also
showing a little baby bump, and we all know Mr. Sinclair
ain't the baby daddy: she slipped and told the entire class he
had a vasectomy last year and she was upset about it. I guess
she found a way to get over it.

"Hey, have y'all seen Chance?" I ask as Matt and Seth each
take a seat in the empty row of desks in front of mine.

"Actually, Chance called me a few minutes ago and told
me he wouldn't be here; he had something to handle," Matt
says, reclining back in his seat for his afternoon nap.

"Why are you so worried about Chance? I thought you and
Jeremy were kicking it pretty hot and heavy these days," Seth
says, looking at me with a silly grin. He can be so annoying
sometimes, like the White little brother I never wanted.

"Shut up, Seth. I haven't seen him all day and needed to
talk to him about something." I would try him on his cell, but
our cells rarely get a signal down here in the dungeon. This
is the last classroom on the west side of the campus and is
right off Pacific Coast Highway. We call it the dungeon not
only because of its location, but also because it's the only
classroom that has no intercom speakers, which connect all
the classrooms through announcements from the main office. I don't know if it's because of all the stage equipment or
what, but our cells rarely work in here.

"We're going to sit outside and soak up some sun," Leslie
says as she and Alia head to the outside benches. These White
girls are serious about their tans. "Want to come, Jayd?"

"Uhmm, no. I'm cool," I say. What the hell do I need with
a tan? Sometimes folks don't think before they speak. But,
she's being nice, so there's no need to clown.

"What do you need to talk to Chance about? I'm here if you need to vent, baby," Matt says, sitting up in his seat. But something about his look tells me he already knows why I'm concerned.

"You know, don't you?" I ask.

"Of course I do. You think my boy's going to get busted and I'm not going to find out about it immediately?" Matt says with a big grin across his face. Damn, news travels fast around this campus. I wonder if word's got back to South Central yet. If so, I know Misty and KJ are ecstatic.

"Yeah, we're tighter than the gay mafia," Seth says, and he should know. Anybody can look at Seth and know he's swinging on both sides of the fence.

"Well, how come y'all so cool? I'm freaking out about what just happened, and y'all act like it's nothing," I say, socking Matt in the arm for being so coy about what he knows.

"I didn't want to let on in front of the girls. You know how y'all like to talk. Besides, there's no need to worry about Jeremy; he can take care of himself. And, if he can't, his dad can." Matt has a good point. These rich boys have a whole different set of laws. I wish I could holla at my girls before school's out about what happened with Jeremy, but right after drama class I have to head clear across campus to dance class, and then to the bus stop. I don't think Jeremy will be able to take me to Compton today after all. I'll just have to wait until I get home to get this off my chest.

"Girl, you just lucky they didn't put your ass on lockdown with him," Nellie says, putting her two cents in the three-way conversation between her, me, and Mickey. I barely walked in the door before my cell began to ring.

"For real, Nellie. You just know they would have loved to pin it on you, Jayd," Mickey says.

"I'm still in shock he's a dealer. Jayd, did you know Jeremy and his crew were our local drug cartel?" Nellie asks, sounding as judgmental as ever.

"No, Nellie. I didn't know that Jeremy and his friends were involved in any kind of illegal activity," I say sarcastically, while putting my backpack down on the hallway floor. That damn thing's too heavy.

"Look, y'all, don't overreact. I want to call Jeremy and make sure he's all right before I start judging the boy," I say, rushing them off the phone.

"Judge the boy about what?" Mama asks, coming in from the backyard.

"Oh, nothing, Mama. Nellie and Mickey are just hating on Jeremy as usual," I say, trying to redirect Mama's BS detector. I'm not telling anybody around here about this.

"No, we're not. You better tell Mama the truth, Jayd," Nellie tries to shout through the phone loud enough so Mama can hear her.

"Your girls have your best interests at heart. Listen to them sometimes," Mama says, passing me in the hallway to go to her room. Sometimes she likes to play devil's advocate.

"I'll talk to y'all later," I say, finally hanging up the phone.

"Jayd, what was that all about?" Mama asks while hanging her outdoors work dress on the closet door. I guess she wasn't satisfied with the answer she got. Ready to settle in for the evening, she changes into her multicolored housedress. Mama looks tired and worn down, like she's had one hell of a day filling client prescriptions.

"Nellie and Mickey were just teasing me about Jeremy, that's all. Mama, you feeling all right?" I ask her as I walk into the room. I place my backpack by my bed and sit down on the foot of her bed. "You don't look so good. Have you been taking your herbs," I ask, getting up to get a closer look at her. I worry about Mama sometimes. She works too hard and frets too much, not a good combination.

"Jayd, get away from me. I'm fine, just a little tired, that's all. Have you seen Bryan today?" Come to think of it, I haven't seen him since Monday afternoon, and he's usually my morning companion. He must have a new woman. When any of my uncles—or my grandfather, for that matter—have a new girlfriend, we don't see them for a couple of days straight. Maybe even a week or two, if it's serious.

"No, Mama. I don't know where he is. Knowing him, he's fine, though. He's bound to check in sooner or later."

"Why do boys have to trouble you so? You never know what they're doing or the company they keep," Mama says, picking up her Bible and opening it to the Twenty-third Psalm.

"The Lord is my Shepherd, I shall not want . . . ," she reads aloud, holding her brass Rosary in her right hand and the Bible in her left.

"He leads me beside the still waters . . . ," Mama continues in a trancelike state. Maybe I should be praying with Mama for Jeremy. He's in some serious shit. And I don't think his charming smile or irresistible wit is going to be enough to get him out of this mess. South Bay High has a "zero toler-ance" policy about weapons, drugs, sexual harassment. You name it. I don't think Jeremy's White skin or money will be enough to get him out of this.

"Yea, though I walk through the valley of the shadow of death, I will fear no evil. For you are with me; your rod and your staff, they comfort me . . ." I join Mama, praying for both Jeremy and Bryan. I wonder if I could make a charm bag for Jeremy that would help with his situation, but first I need to talk to him and see what's really going on.

"Surely goodness and mercy shall follow me all the days of my life . . . ," Mama says.

I rejoin her with an "Amen."

"I've been out back all day doing work for other people and haven't done any work for myself. I hate when Bryan stays gone like this. All the boy has to do is call and let me know he's okay," Mama says, taking a bag of loose herbs from the nightstand and putting them in her empty water glass.

"Jayd, could you please get Mama some water?" she says, handing me the glass.

"Sure, Mama. I'll be right back." On the way out the room, I grab my cell from my backpack so I can call Jeremy while I have a free moment.

"Hello," Jeremy says.

"Hey, it's Jayd. Are you okay?"

"Hey, Jayd. Yeah, I'm cool. Are you good? Hope you didn't get too scared. I was just about to call you," Jeremy says, sounding genuinely concerned about me.

"Yes, I'm fine. How are you? What did they do to you?" I ask.

"They just said I have to appear at some stupid hearing on Friday with the principal and the Special Circumstances counselor to see if they want to file charges against me."

"You mean to tell me they didn't arrest you?" I ask, filling up Mama's water glass as slowly as possible. Unbelievable. If he'd been KJ or Del or some other Black boy, his ass would've been in jail already. I place the glass full of the thick herbal concoction on the kitchen counter while I catch up with Jeremy. By now Mama's probably watching the news or something.

"Naw, Jayd. I only had a joint on me, and they can't prove I put the rest of it in my locker, since it's technically public property. And, because my attorneys weren't present when they searched it, we have a pretty good defense. Don't forget, my dad's rich and has powerful lawyers. This is a walk in the park for them."

"But, I thought you said your dad was an honest man," I say.

"So, are you saying I deserve jail time?" he asks, sounding a little hurt.

"No, of course not. I'm just teasing, silly. You know I got your back, baby."

"Yeah, I know. But why would you think they'd arrest me? It was just a joint," Jeremy says, sounding like it's no big deal.

"Well, it's my understanding that South Bay doesn't play, no matter who your daddy is. But, I guess I didn't know who you were, until now," I say.

"And, who am I?" Jeremy asks, goading me.

"You're the man lucky enough to be in Queen Jayd's favor," I say, feeling the power of my words.

"It's going to take more than good favor for me to get out of this one, though. My lawyers need to be on top of it. South Bay High would love to make an example out of one of the Weiner boys."

"The Weiner boys? There must be more to this story than you're telling me," I say, wanting to hear about his own legacy.

"Jayd, where the hell is my water?" Mama yells from her room. Damn, I forgot all about her herbs.

"Who was that?" Jeremy asks, responding to Mama's call.

"My mama. I'm sorry, baby, but I've got to go. I was in the middle of doing something for her when I called to check on you. I'll have to talk to you at school tomorrow."

"I won't be at school tomorrow. I've been suspended for two days. And, they're only allowing me to come to school on Friday because of the hearing," he says, sounding a little more concerned than a moment ago.

"I'll keep you in my prayers, Jeremy."

"I don't believe in all that stuff, remember?" Jeremy asks.

"Yes, baby. But, lucky for you, I do. So, I'll put in a good word for you that all goes well on Friday. It'll take a miracle to explain why your ass had weed on you at school."

"Well then, I'm ordering a miracle, Queen Jayd. Pray for that," he says, teasing me in that sexy little way of his.

"One miracle, coming right up," I say. What he doesn't know is that I'm serious. I passed a pop quiz on my spiritual work this morning, and Mama was so proud of me she's letting me look through her big book of secret recipes as a reward. It's got all of her good stuff in there: him-never-leave-me potion, good-luck serum, enemy-beware spray. You name it, she's got it. It's like looking at a big cookbook for manipulating the real world with some spiritual help. And, I intend to cook up a batch of get-out-of-jail-free cakes for Jeremy tonight. I walk back into Mama's room and finally deliver her herbs.

"Jayd, what took you so long?" she asks, after swallowing the cold concoction down in three swift gulps.

"Slow down. You gone choke if you don't watch out," I say, taking the glass from her and setting it on the nightstand.

"Whatever you're planning to do," Mama says, pulling back the covers on her bed and slipping her feet in between the sheets, "keep track of what you do, who you do it for, and of the outcome," she says as she wipes her mouth with the back of her hand before lying down for a well-deserved rest. "That's the first rule of prescribing."

"What are you talking about?" I say, trying to throw her off my trail. She always knows when I'm up to something.

"I know that look, child. You're up to something, and I know it's got something to do with that boy," she says, obviously referring to Jeremy. If it were KJ, she would have called him by his name.

"Don't worry, Mama. I've got it all under control." I pick up the empty glass and my backpack and head to the kitchen. I've got a lot of work to do before tomorrow comes.

I've never made anything out of her secret recipe book. But, I'm sure I'll have to go to her spirit room to do it right.

"Jayd, where you going?" Jay asks, coming into the kitchen from the living room. He sees me walking outside with my bag and assumes I'm sneaking out.

"I'm going out back. I've got some work to do," I answer as I step over Lexi, asleep on the porch.

"Does Mama know what you're up to?" Jay asks, looking for an opportunity to get me in trouble. Sometimes he acts like he's ten years old.

"Yes, she does," I say, slamming the back door in his nosey face. I'm so sick of people all up in my business. I'm glad for the opportunity to escape the real world for a little while. Maybe this is one of the main reasons Mama enjoys her spirit work so much—it's a sort of retreat from the daily hustle. As I walk past the garage, I look up and notice the sun has just set and the sky is red-orange. I can also smell the night-blooming jasmines permeating the evening air.

When I reach the backhouse, I see Mama has left the door open from earlier. There are all kinds of herbs hanging from the ceiling to dry. The smell of fresh lavender and orange peels overwhelms me as I place my backpack and the recipe book on the oversized wooden table in the center of the room. I turn on the lamp sitting on the opposite end of the table. A mixture of dust and powdered sugar flies off the stool as I sit down and get to work.

"Hey, girl," I say as Lexi enters the room to witness my first attempt at being a true Williams woman. My mom used to tell me stories of how she and her best friend, my aunt Vivica, would come back here and make a mess. But, she also said most of the time her messes worked, as long as she followed the instructions verbatim. So, I'm willing to give it a try, for Jeremy's sake. It would just suck if he went to jail or got expelled right as we're starting to get to know each other. No, I'm not having that.

As I flip through the cookbook, which has all kinds of stories about our lineage as well as prescriptions for spiritual, mental, physical, and social ailments, I turn to the page entitled *Sweet Treats*.

"Get-out-of-jail-free cupcakes. This is exactly what I'm looking for. How hard can it be to make cupcakes, right, Lexi?" I say as Lexi finds a comfy spot on the floor and plops down, ready for whatever I conjure up.

I love being in here. It's like a cozy little kitchen for one. There's barely enough room in here for the antique, wood-burning stove, sink, and ice box, let alone the table, stool, and small bookcase in the corner. The last of the evening sun reflects red and orange hues through the stained-glass window over the sink.

I wash my hands and grab the flour, sugar, blueberries, lemons, and other ingredients from the cupboards over the stove. Gently moving everything off the table but the recipe book, I start looking for the necessary tools for my work: three bowls, two spoons, a knife, a sifter, a whisk to cream the eggs and sugar, five yellow candles, Puerto Rican rum, and some Red Hots candies, for the finishing touches.

"Mama needs more space in here, huh, girl," I say as Lexi watches me from her post. I place the ingredients on the table and start measuring and pouring them into the large wooden bowl. "I don't know how good these are going to taste, but we're going to work it out, girl, and quickly. I got a ton of homework to do," I say as I mix all the ingredients, except for the Red Hots, with the wooden spoon.

As I reach into the ice box to get the butter, I notice a little pouch with the words "him-never-leave-me potion" on it. I open the pouch and pour some of the fine gold powder into the palm of my hand. Oh, I'm going to put a little of this in the batter too, just in case Jeremy gets to thinking he's gone leave me after I help his ass get out of this mess. Also, it can't hurt to have some backup, right? Him never leaving me is the same as him not leaving South Bay High, as far as I'm concerned. A girl needs some insurance, especially after the KJ mess.

It doesn't smell so bad. So far, the batter looks and tastes like regular lemon blueberry cupcakes. But, once I put this gold powder in there, I don't know what's going to happen. I take a little powder with my finger and dab it onto my tongue.

"Tastes like honey and something else I can't quite make out. It shouldn't be so bad, should it, girl?" If Lexi could talk, I think she'd be in total disagreement, because her face is scrunched up and I swear she rolled her eyes at me. "Oh, what do you know? You're just a dog," I say, knowing she's more than a dog; Lexi's Mama's personal gatekeeper.

I take the thick, golden powder and sprinkle a little into the batter. "There, it's done. Now, let's bake these babies and see what we've got to work with," I say, pouring the batter into the cupcake pan.

"Perfect. A dozen him-never-leave-'cause-he-gone-get-out-of-jail-for-free cupcakes, coming right up," I exclaim, proud of my creation.

Becoming completely engrossed in the stories in Mama's cookbook, I don't realize twenty minutes have passed. I open the oven to place three Red Hots on top of each cupcake before they finish baking. The cupcakes appear to be rising to perfection and smell even better. But, as soon as I place the first candy on one of my creations, it falls flat.

"Damn it," I shout, waking Lexi from her comfortable slumber. I knew something was gone happen. I shouldn't have tampered with the recipe.

I put the rest of the candy on the cupcakes and watch all twelve of them fall, one by one. "Well, I'm sure they're still edible, just not pretty," I say, convincing myself I did the right thing. I close the oven and clean up my mess, all the while looking through the recipe book to see if there's anything else that needs to be done.

"Make sure you witness the object of your intentions enjoy these treats." Now, how the hell am I going to do that when I won't see Jeremy until he comes to school on Friday for his hearing? I was going to ask him to meet me at the bus stop after school so I can give these to him. But, I don't want him to look at me crazy if I ask him to eat them right there on the spot.

The timer goes off, and I reach for the oven door. Because they're for a specific purpose, I can't taste them to see how they came out.

"I'll just have to trust that Jeremy likes them, no matter how they look," I say to Lexi, who's completely disinterested by now. I set the dilapidated cupcakes on the table to cool and grab my backpack to take out my homework. I figure I can get in a couple of hours of homework and still make it to bed by eleven. It's been a long day and I'm tired. Mama didn't cook this evening, and I'm too tired to even cut up potatoes to make myself some fries. A bowl of Cornflakes will have to do for dinner tonight. I hope these cupcakes do the trick. I'll just have to wait until tomorrow to find out.

~ 7 ~

From Broad to Snitch

"A bitch is a bitch."

—N.W.A.

Riding the bus this morning will be especially eventful with my little basket full of cupcakes. It's never easy carrying anything extra on the bus. The drivers can be cool when they want to be and allow passengers to carry food, even though it's against the rules.

When I get to the bus stop, Pam, the neighborhood crack head, is sitting at the bus stop talking to herself. Mama feeds her sometimes. But, normally, Pam's too out of it to care if she eats or not. It's not cold, but the morning chill is still in the air, and she's wearing nothing but a tank top, some biker shorts, and flip-flops. Whenever I see Pam, chills come over me like I'm in the presence of a ghost. I wonder where her family is and how anyone ever gets this far out there.

"Good morning, Pam," I say as I sit down next to her on the tattered bench. We're the only two people out this early in the morning, but she's heavily engaged in conversation with herself. She's mumbling and doesn't respond to my greeting, yet I feel obliged to at least get her to make eye contact. "Pam, how are you this morning?" I ask, only to be ignored again. Mama says I should always speak to Pam just to let her know I see her, unlike the other folks around our neighborhood who pretend she doesn't exist.

As the bus pulls up to the curb, Pam finally speaks. "Jayd, tell your mama I said hi," she says as I rise from the bench and head toward the opened double doors of the MTA bus.

"I will, Pam. I'll see you later." Before I finish my statement, Pam's again engrossed in her side conversation with people only she can see.

"Are you coming or not?" the rude bus driver says, rushing me up the steps and onto the nearly empty bus. "And there had better not be any crumbs on my bus when you leave, either," she says, referring to my basket of goodies and the sign on the bus indicating no food allowed.

"I'm not gone eat on your bus," I say, walking to the back of the bus to stretch out before my first transfer in Gardena. Sometimes the three bus rides are a bit much for me. I get tired of the long commute from Compton to the South Bay every morning. I wish I could sleep on at least one of the buses. But, I don't want to risk missing any of my stops.

When my final bus pulls up to the stop near South Bay High, my phone rings, displaying Nellie's name on the Caller ID. What could she possibly want this early in the morning?

"Hello," I answer as I exit the Torrance bus and head up the steep hill toward campus, trying to balance my backpack, Jeremy's basket, and my cell phone all at once.

"Hey, girl. Are you here yet?" she asks. It must be nice to have a mom and dad to take her to school every morning and who'll pick her up if need be.

"Almost. I'm actually walking up the hill as we speak." As usual, the local residents are outside walking their dogs, watering their lawns, and sending their children off to school, all the while watching me from the corner of their eyes, making sure I don't steal their lawn ornaments or whatever other possession they may think invaluable.

"Well, hurry up and get here. We've got news, girl." What

now? I can't even have a nice walk in the morning without some drama jumping off.

"Why you can't just tell me over the phone? I need to return a book to the library before I go to my locker this morning, so I'm not going to have time to talk before first period." I couldn't help checking out one of my favorite books, *Mama Day*, for what must be the fifteenth time while in the library last week. I love Gloria Naylor's writing.

"Because, I want to see your face when you hear what I have to say." This can't be good if Nellie can't tell me over the phone.

"Just spill it, Nellie," I say, halfway up the hill. By the time I get to campus and go to the library, I'll have just enough time to get to Spanish class before the bell rings.

"Girl, rumor has it Misty's the one who ratted out Jeremy's little side occupation. Ain't that some shit," she says as I stop in the middle of my stride to catch my breath. What the hell?

"Are you serious, Nellie? Where'd you hear that from?" I ask, resuming my hike at a much quicker pace than before. Why does that broad always have to be in the middle of some shit?

"Well, apparently Shae overheard Misty telling her mom all about it in the office yesterday. You know Misty's friends with Stan and Dan," Nellie responds. How can a student be friends with campus security?

"So, what are you gone do," Mickey says, shouting through the phone. Nellie must have her cell on speaker because I can hear other students all around them. "See, you should've whipped her ass when you had the chance," she says, reminding me of last week's fight. "Trecee didn't finish the job, and I think you should."

"Fighting is definitely not the answer. But, I agree with

Mickey," Nellie says, reclaiming control of the conversation. "Something needs to be done about that girl."

"I agree with both of you," I say, feeling my heart beat faster as I step onto campus, heading straight for the library. This broad's gone too far now. Snitches are not respected in our hood, at all. And, there's usually only one way to deal with a snitch. But, I don't want to get too ghetto out here with these White folks. Misty isn't worth my education or my freedom. If I fight Misty now, it'll be a straight beat down from the girl formerly known on the street as Lyttle, and that's dangerous territory.

"Excuse me, there's no cell phones in the library," says one of the librarians from behind the counter. She's so old she looks like she's been here since the library was first built.

"I'll have to talk to y'all later. Meet me at my locker at break. Maybe by then I'll have something figured out," I say, not really wanting to hang up in the middle of the conversation. What the hell am I going to do about Misty? Her being a broad I can handle. But, a snitch? Never.

"Hey, Jayd. What's in the basket?" Nellie asks as she and Mickey walk up to my locker. I was unable to concentrate in my first two periods, thinking about how I should respond to this new drama with Misty.

"It's a gift for Jeremy," I say, making sure the basket is completely covered. I don't want them to see what's inside. I know they would make fun of my messed-up cupcakes. But, as long as they work, I don't care what they look like.

"I thought he was suspended," Mickey says, trying to snatch the basket.

"He is. But I was hoping to catch up with him after school," I say, carefully placing the cupcakes back into my locker before walking to class. I also have to figure out a way to get him to eat them in front of me. If I've learned one thing about Mama's recipes, it's to follow them to the letter. "Have y'all seen Misty this morning? I want to have a word with her before I go around accusing her of a crime she may not have committed."

Nellie and Mickey look at each other in total disbelief.

"Are you kidding, Jayd? After everything this girl's done you're still willing to talk to her?" Mickey asks, looking like she wants to slap some sense into me.

"I just want to hear it from her mouth before I jump to conclusions," I say, taking my backpack off to get my English and Spanish books out and place them in my locker before retrieving my government and math books and placing them in my backpack.

"You need a talk show with all the discussing you try and do with this girl," Nellie says, leaning up against the lockers next to mine, getting a bird's-eye view of the busy hall. "Speaking of which, have you told your man about this new discovery?"

"No, I haven't talked to him yet. But, I'm sure he'll call before lunch."

Or maybe we can just chill or maybe . . . And there's Jeremy, right on cue. I retrieve my cell from my purse, eager to hear his voice while my girls wait patiently to continue our conversation.

"Hey, baby. How's lockdown?" I ask, knowing he's probably having the time of his life.

"Very funny, Lady J. I'm chilling, catching up on repeat episodes of *College Hill.* How's school?" he asks, in the sexiest damn voice to ever come through my cell. And, I love it when he calls me Lady J. It sounds so OG.

"It's school. You ain't missing nothing, except for all the gossip about you being the next Scarface," I say, only half joking. I don't want to tell him about Misty quite yet, not until I know the truth. The rumors are growing more ridiculous as the day goes by, and it's still early.

"So, what are you doing for lunch? I wish you could come over, but my mom's here and she's pissed at me. Are you going to miss me?" he asks, sounding a little nostalgic.

"Oh, my God, Jeremy. Do you miss me already? It's only been a day," I say, flattered. Speaking of which, I better go. There's the warning bell. All the other students are already wrapping up their conversations, including my girls.

"Hey, baby, I hate to go, but I'm gone be late if I don't," I say, not really wanting to end our conversation, but I still need to talk to my girls and get to class on time.

"Cool. Don't say anything witty until I get back," he says. I laugh, missing him even more.

"I'll try not to." Before I could recommend meeting up at the bus stop after school, Jeremy suggests another idea.

"Can you meet me at Mrs. Bennett's class after school? She's going to let me pick up my work so I don't fall behind, and I thought I could still give you a ride home, if that's okay with you." He's so sweet, thinking of me in his time of need. I'm so glad I made these cupcakes for him. I just pray they keep my man out of jail and at South Bay High. And, that he trusts me enough to eat them, no matter how jacked-up they look.

"Only for you," I say, and I mean it. I hate Mrs. Bennett. She's notorious for being a supporter of anything anti-Black. Because of her reputation, the school made her host the Black History Month celebration last year. It was a success only because she had movies in her room every day during lunch for the entire month. That was her way of celebrating: showing old Black movies, like *Pinky*, all month long.

I had the twisted pleasure of having Mrs. Bennett last semester for English. She teaches tenth and twelfth grade A.P. English, which means I have to have her one more time if she stays here. She was as much a bitch then as she is now, and I don't normally call broads bitches. But, she and Misty are exceptions to the rule.

"Why do we have to meet in her class? I hate that woman. You know that," I say.

"She says she wants to talk to me about something. I'm sure she just wants me to know she has my back at the hearing," he says, reminding me of his impending appointment with fate tomorrow.

"What does she have to do with it?"

"She's one of my character witnesses. We'll talk about it later. You'd better go before you're late," Jeremy says, and he's right. I only have a few minutes left before the final bell rings.

"Jayd," Mickey says, interrupting my conversation. "We've got to go. See you at lunch?"

"Yeah, I'll see y'all later. We need to finish our conversation. And, Nellie, tell everybody in your class to mind their own damn business," I say as they walk away. I know all of them South Central folk have class together and they're having a field day with this new bit of drama.

"Jeremy, I'll call you at lunch," I say as I start speed walking down the main hall.

"All right, I'll talk to you then. Bye, baby." Ooh, I love it when he calls me baby. I feel like we've been together forever. As I walk down the main hall toward Mrs. Peterson's room, I notice Ms. Toni coming from the main office.

"Hey, Ms. Toni. How are you this morning?" I ask, stopping to give her a big hug. It's always nice to see her.

"Hello, Miss Jayd. You're on your way to government, right?"

"Yes, Ms. Toni. And I know you heard about Jeremy and the whole bust thing, but it's not as bad as it sounds," I say, trying to diffuse this argument before it begins.

"Oh, no? Is that why you haven't been by my office this week?" She's right. I have been avoiding her. But only because I know she won't approve of my seeing Jeremy, especially not now.

"Jayd, what are you thinking? That boy is trouble waiting to happen. Now, usually I don't speak ill of students. But, Jayd, I've seen this happen to young, Black girls time and time again. These rich White boys are all alike."

"All alike how?" I ask, waiting to hear her answer.

"They're spoiled, bored risk takers, Jayd. I've seen too many decent girls ruin their reputations over the wrong boys. You're too smart for him, Jayd. And I don't want you to be pulled down with him. And he is going down for this one."

"He's not going anywhere, Ms. Toni. And besides, I think you're overreacting."

"Am I? Does your grandmother know about his little drug problem?" she asks, knowing I ain't told Mama nothing. As I try to think of a savvy comeback, I notice students rushing up and down the halls, slamming lockers, and sneaking last urgent conversations and kisses before the final bell for fourth period rings.

"Ms. Toni, that was a low blow. Everyone deserves a second chance. Besides, I have to go before I'm late for class."

"Fine, Jayd. But we're not done. Come see me by tomorrow or I'll have you summoned out of government in front of your new man, do you hear me?" Ms. Toni yells after me as I rush down the hall. I really don't want to be late. That'll just make Mrs. Peterson's day, and I ain't about to give her the satisfaction. It's going to be weird not seeing my baby in class, especially since he's my buffer as far as Mrs. Peterson's concerned. I can't wait till after school when I finally get to hug my man.

Thank God the rest of morning is uneventful. Instead of kickin' it with Mickey and Nellie at lunch, I choose to chill alone. I just don't feel like dealing with everybody talking about Jeremy right now, especially not when I'm trying to help him. I decide to calm down before confronting Misty. Instead, I spend my time talking to Jeremy on the cell and filling him in on the day's drama, which has only just begun for me.

When I get to Mrs. Bennett's classroom, hoping Jeremy's already outside, she notices me standing by her door and signals me to come in. I'm almost nauseated by the pungent mixture of gardenia perfume and the strong coffee percolating in the corner. Her room looks like a country inn in a French magazine, with two dozen student desks in the center of her perfect picture.

"Jayd, what are you doing here?" she asks, obviously annoyed by my presence.

"I'm here to meet Jeremy. He told me to meet him after school," I say, pissed that I'm here before him. My plan was to meet him outside and keep stepping. Not to actually engage in a conversation with this evil woman. She's hella snide and creepy, like the witch in the "Hansel and Gretel" story, ya know? Just weird. And she's real tiny and old like all the witches in the fairy tales too. Why Jeremy would ever choose to be friendly with this woman is beyond me.

I wouldn't put it past Mrs. Bennett to give private lessons to some of her male students on things other than the English language, like that other teacher who made her student her baby daddy. I bet she's got a crush on Jeremy and some of his cute surfer friends. She strikes me as the conniving, jealous type. I don't know what it is about her, but this woman gives me the creeps.

"Jayd, what exactly is your relationship with Jeremy, hmm?" she asks, while putting on her thin-framed glasses. She slips into the chair behind her desk and looks up at me over a stack of papers.

"I don't have to answer that. I'll wait outside for Jeremy," I say, turning around to walk out the room. I'm going to kill Jeremy for being late. What could be keeping him?

"Look, Jayd, I don't mean to pry," she says, holding a red ink pen in her left hand and tapping the papers with her right, "but, it's come to my attention that you may be involved in a relationship with Jeremy. Is this true?" she asks.

I turn to face her again. "None of your business," I say, trying to restrain myself from cussing her out.

"Look, Jayd. You and I both live in the real world, right?" she asks, trying to get me to agree with her, but I know it's a trap. This is how she lures in her victims during class. Then, she goes for the kill. "Jeremy is a great guy. Have you ever wondered why he would want to be with someone like you when he could have any girl in the entire school?" she asks, cool as a cucumber.

"What the hell did you just say to me?" I snap, ready to drop these cupcakes and slap the mess out of her. I can't wait to tell Ms. Toni what this broad just said to me.

"Oh, Jayd, please calm down the ghetto attitude. It's so unbecoming of a young lady," she says, picking up one of the papers and reading the title page.

"Seriously, Jayd," she says, looking over her glass rims at me. I want to walk out the door, but I'm glued to my spot. "What does he see in you? Your friend Mickey's the cutest of all of you here." She turns around and reaches behind her, seizing the coffee-stained mug sitting on top of the bookshelf behind her desk. She then reaches over to the coffeepot and pours herself a cup. I hope she drops it and burns herself. I'm seething now.

"Who is the you?" I ask, already knowing she means out of all the Black girls.

"You know who I mean." She takes a sip of her black coffee and continues, "All I'm saying is don't be stupid. He's just dating you because he's curious, Jayd, that's all. I wish our boys weren't so tempted by your kind. But, it seems to happen every year with him."

"Are you on crack or something? How dare you talk to me like this? You're lucky I've got good home training; otherwise I would've told your ass off a long time ago," I say, getting hotter and hotter as the minutes pass. Where is Jeremy? And, what does she mean by this happens to him every year? "You don't know anything about me or my girls or my friendship with Jeremy," I say, not wanting to defend my relationship to this broad, but I can't let her get away with talking to me like this.

"Jayd, don't you think you're in a little over your head?" she asks.

"Things are not always as they appear," I say, wishing I had something to throw at her.

"And, sometimes they are just that and nothing more," she says, looking me up and down like she's reading my life story. I hate the way people like Mrs. Bennett look at me, especially people who think badly of me and my folk: poor, colored people from the hood. It can be any hood anywhere in the world. It's just something about being broke that makes us different in the eyes of the other people. This bitch is definitely one of them with a special twist; she's as racist as they come. And, like all racists, she thinks she's absolutely right with her ignorant ass.

"Tell Jeremy I'll meet him in the quad." I can't take any

more of her bullshit today, not even for Jeremy. How do such evil people become teachers? He'll just have to go out of his way to find me. I've had enough for one day.

Just as I think she's finally finished, she persists in a low, harsh voice barely audible as I walk away, "You're not the right type for him, Jayd. He's way out of your league."

I would turn around and snap back at her, but I don't want to give her the satisfaction. I just want Jeremy to hurry the hell up and come on. As I approach the quad, maneuvering my way through couples making out and other students hangin' out after school, I see KJ and Misty in our old hangout spot. What are they doing here? And, why do I care?

I've been wondering what to say to Misty all day about the snitch rumor. Now's the perfect time to confront her and force the truth out of her. I need to release my anger, and she's the perfect outlet.

"Jayd," KJ says, sounding surprised to see me. "What are you doing over here? Shouldn't you be on the bus by now?" he asks, readjusting himself on the cozy bench made for two.

"And shouldn't you be at practice? Or are you playing a different sport these days?" I say, referring to Misty's everlasting games.

"Whatever, Jayd. Don't be mad because you gave up this man for your new man who's now on lockdown," Misty retorts, smacking her gum loudly, which has always annoyed the hell out of me.

"Speaking of which, Misty, did you have anything to do with Jeremy's bust?" I ask, getting straight to the point. Jeremy should be here any minute, and I don't want him to witness this little episode. This is between me and Misty. No one else. But, I do want KJ to be a witness to this girl's true character, as if he doesn't already know who Misty truly is. He may be ready to move on, but I'll be damned if it's with this girl.

"Don't blame me if your man's a drug dealer. That's on him," she says, expertly evading the question. "Besides, he would've been caught eventually. Criminals always are," she replies with a wicked grin. It's taking all of my restraint not to throw these cupcakes at her. KJ's lying back, enjoying his ringside seat at yet another chick fight.

"Ladies, please, not again. Y'all just got off suspension a few days ago. Do you really want to do this now?" KJ mock intervenes. "Besides, Jeremy's not worth it."

"What?" I exclaim. "Are you kidding me, KJ? Misty basically admitted to snitching, and regardless of the circumstances, you know that shit is foul and deserves an ass whipping," I say, ready to throw blows.

"Misty's a lot of things," he says, checking her ego a little. "But a snitch ain't one of them, right, Misty?" he asks, looking Misty in the eye, awaiting her reply. Instead of denying it, which is exactly what I thought she'd do, she surprises me by telling the truth.

"I didn't mean to tell on him; it just sort of slipped out when I was talking to my mother. And, Stan and Dan happened to be standing right there," she says, batting her long, curly eyelashes at KJ, feigning the innocent victim. I want to slap the shit out of her right now, but I want to get to the heart of the matter first.

"Misty, what did you tell your mother about Jeremy?" I ask, wanting the full confession.

"I just told her I heard he meets his clients after lunch by the parking lot to exchange goods. That's all. Stan and Dan busted him on their own," she responds, conveniently making herself look like a helpless victim, and KJ's falling for her act. I hope that's all he's falling for.

"Your mouth's writing checks your body can't cash, Misty. You need to watch your back," I say, not believing her act for a minute. "If Jeremy goes down for this, you're going with him."

"Jayd, regardless of how he got busted, Jeremy's no good," KJ says as he grabs his backpack from the ground next to his feet and rises from the bench. "When you're ready to come back to me, let me know. You've got the number." And, with Misty hot on his trail, he walks away, leaving me fuming. First Mrs. Bennett, now Misty. Broads come in all shapes and sizes, I suppose.

School let out almost twenty minutes ago, and I'm still waiting for Jeremy. I wonder what's keeping him. I should probably text him and let him know where I am, just in case Mrs. Bennett doesn't deliver the message. I'll tell him about this little episode, but not yet. I'll wait until after his hearing tomorrow. Today I want to concentrate on keeping him at South Bay High and with me for as long as I can, no matter what obstacles our enemies place in our path. Speaking of foes, Ms. Toni walks up to me, catching me off guard as I sit down on an empty bench and send Jeremy a text message.

"Hello, Miss Jackson. What are you doing here after school?" she says, looking over my shoulder at my phone. She's a good foot taller than me and makes me feel like a midget from where I'm sitting. "I hope you're not waiting for that boy," she says, walking from behind the bench to sit down next to me. Placing the envelopes in her hand on her lap, she looks at me and can read the frustration on my face. "Jayd, what's wrong with you, girl?"

"Nothing," I say, pressing send on my cell and flipping it closed. "I'm just tired of people running their mouths up at this stupid school," I say, raising my voice slightly and forgetting who I'm talking to. "Sorry," I say.

"It's okay to be upset Jayd," Ms. Toni says, smiling at me. "Just tell me what happened," she says. "Does it have something to do with Misty and KJ? I saw them walking toward the main parking lot a moment ago."

"Yeah, most of it. Can you believe Misty snitched on Jeremy and no one cares? Had I done something like that, the entire Black student population would be out for me," I say. "And, I know you don't approve of what Jeremy did, but he doesn't deserve to be targeted because Misty hates me."

"Oh, Jayd. You can't control what Misty does. Don't you know that by now?" she says, pulling a tissue out of her sweater pocket and handing it to me. "Crying over that girl is a waste of tears. She'll always start mess because she has nothing else better to do, just like her mama."

"Ms. Toni, that's not nice," I say, laughing a little. I'm glad I ran into her. Talking to her always makes me feel better. Or, at the very least, she makes me laugh.

"Well, it's the truth and you know it. All Misty and her mother do is talk mess, and that's not to be envied or feared. All Misty can do is talk because she can't walk like you do, Jayd. Just know she'll always be around to cause mischief and she won't catch you off guard so often."

"I know you're right," I agree. "But, I just feel like I can stop her with one good beat down," I say, again forgetting my place. Ms. Toni's cool, but she's still an adult and doesn't like to hear me talk about fighting.

"Jayd, the best way to get back at her is by ignoring her. Don't let her get to you, and certainly don't be confrontational. She lives for getting a rise out of you," Ms. Toni says, lifting my chin with the tip of her finger and forcing me to look at her. "Jayd, your future's too bright to let your enemies get the best of you." She sounds so much like Mama sometimes. What would I do without either one of them? I'm lucky to have more than one mother figure in my life, especially at school. If Ms. Toni had been at my junior high school, maybe I wouldn't have gotten into so much trouble back then.

"What if one of my enemies is a teacher?" I ask, not wanting to bring up Mrs. Bennett, but I can't get her off my mind. Ms. Toni has a problem with most of the teachers up here because most of them have a problem with her simply because she's Black. But Mrs. Bennett, in particular, irritates the hell out of Ms. Toni.

"Okay, what else happened?" Ms. Toni asks. "I guess these tears aren't just for Misty, are they?"

"No," I say as I blow my nose into the tissue. "I went to Mrs. Bennett's room looking for Jeremy, and she was just as rude as ever."

"What did she say to you?" Ms. Toni asks in a serious voice. She sits up straight and looks at me hard, waiting for my reply.

"It wasn't so much what she said as the way she said it. She always speaks to me with the most racist tone I've ever heard. And, she called me one of those girls, like all Black girls are different from other girls." And Mrs. Bennett's right. We are different. But not in the way she meant it. Her "different" was inherently negative and unequal.

"I know what you mean. When we have staff meetings it's as if I'm the only other person in the room who hears her racist jargon. She's a crafty one," Ms. Toni says, looking past me and off into the distance. "You know, Jayd. You shouldn't take this lying down. Whatever she said to you should be documented. And, the best way to do that is to request a hearing with the principal, Mrs. Bennett, and your counselor. Your mother or grandmother should also be present, for support," she says, patting me on the leg.

"I don't want to get them involved in something like this. They don't have time to fight my battles," I say. Mama and my mom don't like coming up to school for anything that doesn't involve me graduating. Everything else they feel I should be able to take care of on my own.

"Okay, Jayd. But you need an adult to stand by you. The administration won't take your claim seriously if you don't. So, I'll be there to act as your self-appointed ombudsman. You have a right to one, according to the student bylaws," she says, referring to the bylaws and constitution booklet every student receives in their annual registration packet.

"I don't know, Ms. Toni. It's her word against mine. And, if I don't win, she'll hold it over my head next year in A.P. English."

"Don't worry about next year. Right now you need to let her know she can't get away with treating you as less than equal. Think of how many other students she's done this to," Ms. Toni says. "Think about what I said seriously, Jayd. Unlike Misty, Mrs. Bennett is a person in a position of influence and power. Focus your energy in the right direction and really make a difference," she says, reclaiming the envelopes in her lap and rising from her seat. I get up to give her a hug.

"I will, Ms. Toni." As we embrace, I can't help but wonder what's holding Jeremy up. I also wonder if Mrs. Bennett's going to tell him her version of our little conversation.

"Come and talk to me tomorrow, Jayd. Right now I'm running late for a meeting." As she walks off toward the staff lounge, I continue to wait for Jeremy. If he's not here in the next fifteen minutes, I'll have no choice but to leave in order to catch the next bus and still make it home at a decent time. I hope he gets here soon. The late bus is usually crowded, and I don't want to stand all the way to my Gardena transfer.

~ 8 ~

A Different World

"Hey, being with you is a top priority/
Ain't no need to question the authority."

—A TRIBE CALLED QUEST

When Jeremy finally arrives, I'm calm, cool, and collected. I don't want him to worry about my drama with all of his own on the horizon. Instead, I want him to be in full acceptance mode so he can enjoy a cupcake or two in my presence, as the recipe prescribed.

"Hey, Jayd. Sorry I'm late. Are you all right?" Jeremy asks, gently caressing my face with the back of his right hand. "Mrs. Bennett said you were upset when you left her room. Why didn't you stay and wait for me?" he asks, looking truly concerned. I doubt the broad told him about our conversation. Just thinking about it makes me hot again. But, I don't want to spoil the few moments we have together.

"Oh, I had to catch up with an old friend," I say as I regain my composure and force a smile, even though all I can think about is Mrs. Bennett and Misty. "I'm fine, and you?" I ask as he takes my hand and leads me toward the front of the school where he's parked his car.

"I'm cool. It's only been one day and I'm already bored out of my mind. My mom's got me on total lockdown. I can't even surf. All I do is sit up in the house and watch television or sleep, which is why I'm in no rush to get home," he says as we approach his car. He's not even supposed to be on campus, yet he parks where everyone can see him. The boy's got balls.

"What about your schoolwork?" He's on the A.P. track like me, so I know he's got tons of work.

"Well, Mrs. Bennett's the only teacher who allowed me to come and get my assignments ahead of time. All the other teachers are assholes. They think I won't be back, so what's the point of giving me work," he says, opening the passenger door. Although I detest the broad, at least she has faith in Jeremy. That's probably the only thing we have in common. "May I give you a ride home, Lady J?" he asks as chivalrous as ever.

"Hell, yes," I say. I reach over and unlock the car door for him before putting my basket and backpack in the backseat; there aren't any power locks in his vintage ride.

"So, what do you want to do now?" Jeremy asks as we head off campus toward Compton. I love the smell of his leather interior and coconut air freshener. He keeps this car immaculate.

"Now, you should know there's no spontaneity allowed in my schedule," I say, reminding him of how different our worlds are. "I would love to go to the beach, though. It's a beautiful afternoon," I wish aloud while placing my left hand on his knee. Just as I make myself a comfortable copilot, Jeremy busts a U-turn right in the middle of the road and heads toward the beach. Luckily, there isn't any oncoming traffic or cars behind us.

"Whatever you want, my lady," he says, grasping my left hand from his knee and bringing it up to his lips to kiss it. His lips are so soft, making me wonder what it would be like to kiss him. First kisses always make me nervous. But, I'll get over it if he wants to make today the day for ours.

"Jeremy, I can't get home too late. Unlike y'all out here, I got a curfew at all times," I say, wishing it weren't true.

"I've thought about it, and the way I see it is if I take you home every day, it saves you over an hour on the bus, right?"

"Yes, it would. But, you don't take me home every day," I say, kissing his hand back. So far, this is as affectionate as we've been.

"But, I can. Then we should have a good hour of chill time every day during the week, that is, if you can handle it." Chill time. What the hell is that? Is he kidding me? Mama doesn't even know this boy's dropping me off at the bus stop because I make sure to get home at roughly the same time every day, regardless of how I get there. Now he wants me to willingly kick it with him after school? Well, I can't say no. He's just too irresistible.

I just know Mama wouldn't approve. She doesn't like me socializing too much during the week. She thinks it'll distract me from my schoolwork, not to mention my spirit work. I know she's right, because Lord knows I'm certainly distracted now, but I still want to hang with Jeremy and see where he takes us.

"Yeah, but don't forget I still have to walk home from the bus stop," I say, reiterating how crucial time is in my world. It takes a good fifteen minutes for me to walk home from the bus stop on Alondra to Gunlock.

"Man, Jayd, you got to learn how to relax, baby. Besides, why can't I drop you off at home?" he asks.

"Oh, there are several reasons, the main one being I don't want no more people in my business. Not yet, anyway." I can already hear my uncles talking shit about me dating a White boy, not to mention all the nosey-ass neighbors. They already tease me enough as it is for going to a White school. Now all I need to do is show up with a White boy to seal my fate as the biggest sell-out in Compton's history.

"Now, this is new. You, Jayd Jackson, caring about what people think of you. You never cease to amaze me," Jeremy says, affectionately touching my chin with the tip of his index finger. When we approach the beach I see people are out everywhere. Do these folks have jobs or what? They're walking their dogs, rollerblading, surfing, you name it, everything but working.

"That's a good thing. At least I'll always keep you on your toes," I say as he parallel parks his fly ride in a metered space right off the sand. As Jeremy walks around to open my door, my cell vibrates, indicating there's a text message waiting. I didn't even hear my phone ring. I keep it on low while I'm at school.

"Where were u at lunch? Me and Mickey R going 2 the mall. Call u later. I know you're with ur man now. Everyone's talking about it already. Misty saw y'all leave. Later, girl."

How could Misty have seen us? We were nowhere near the front gate where Mickey, KJ, and most of the other students park. And, why is it news that me and my new man are leaving campus together? Misty's life is way too mundane if this is hot news to her.

"Anything important?" Jeremy asks.

"Not at all," I say as he opens my door and takes my hand. On the sidewalk, I smooth my clothes out and step onto the sand, letting my toes sift through the warm grains. The sun lifts my spirit, and I know this is where I'm supposed to be.

"You look like me when the first wave hits me in the morning," he says. "There's nothing like the smell of the ocean to make you feel alive. Am I right?" he asks, taking a deep breath. He puts his arm around my shoulder and leads me to the shoreline. The bright afternoon sun shimmers against the dark blue water. I feel sorry for people who never experience the beach.

"I've got the blanket, the water, and you. What more do I need?" Jeremy asks.

I experience a brief moment of panic. Running back to the car, I say, "I forgot something."

"I was wondering what was in that basket, Little Red Riding Hood," he says, trailing behind me.

"I shouldn't even give it to you now, making fun of my little basket," I say, pushing him away from me, pretending to be hurt.

"Is that what they're calling the cookies nowadays," he asks, tackling me like he's Chance. I never feel like this when Chance touches me, though.

"Get off me, punk, and open the door," I say, pushing him toward the car. I climb in and grab the basket out of the backseat.

"Nice," he says as I climb back out of the car.

"You better be referring to my basket of treats." As I fix my clothes, Jeremy grabs me from behind while closing the door.

"So, what you got for me?" he asks, nudging his chin into the groove in between my right shoulder and neck. Oh, God, I'm so nervous. I just know he's going to kiss me today. I purposely didn't eat anything but Starbursts all afternoon so my mouth would be sweet whenever he did try. I hope we get it right the first time. I remember my first kiss with KJ was cool, but sloppy. I had to teach him to tone it down a bit.

"I made these for you last night. Now, please forgive their decrepit appearance. But, they should be quite tasty; it's my mama's recipe." I fold back the yellow and orange cloths covering the cupcakes.

"Well, if they taste as good as they smell, I'm a very lucky man. I got a fine girl and she can cook, a double treat," he says, taking a cupcake from the basket and shoving the entire thing into his mouth.

"Careful. You don't want to choke," I say, looking at him devour the cupcake whole.

"These are awesome," he exclaims, grabbing another cupcake from the basket and greedily consuming it. "What are they? Like blueberry and lemon with cinnamon or something," he says, carefully inspecting the next one before indulging.

"Exactly," I agree, not wanting to give up all of Mama's ingredients. I'm just glad he likes them. Now I have to wait to see if they work. By the time we reach the water, half the cupcakes are gone. This boy can eat.

"Hey, you want to walk or sit?" he asks, taking a break from his munchies.

"Sitting is good," I say, leading him to an empty spot in the sand. There are people everywhere, and finding a good spot is hard. He takes the blanket and smoothes it out before sitting down, pulling me with him. I land perfectly in his lap and stay there, for fear of moving the wrong way.

"Make yourself and the cupcakes comfortable," he says, lying back on the blanket and waiting for me to claim my space. I lie next to him so we can spoon and place the cupcakes in front of me. Mickey calls this little move blocking. I call it the ultimate protection. I always had my purse or sweater or something on my lap when I was out with KJ. Ain't no slipping of the hand on my watch.

"Where are the cupcakes?" Jeremy asks.

"They're right here," I answer, guiding his hand to the basket. He takes another and devours it before putting his arm back around my waist, pulling me in close to him. Now, how's he going to initiate our first kiss like this? I guess I'll just have to wait and see. After we lie for a while, I stop tripping about the cupcakes and the kiss and just let the sound of the waves crashing against the shore chill me out. I've never done this before, especially not on a school day. This is what it must be like to live here. It's a completely different world from the one I'm used to.

"Are you sleep?" Jeremy asks, reaching over my waist for the basket.

"No. Are you full?" I ask, flattered that he likes my baking so much.

"Never," he says, moving the basket to the corner of the blanket above my head while carefully repositioning his body over mine, pinning me down on the blanket. Okay, I know he's going to kiss me now. He looks into my eyes and puts his forehead on mine. "I think you're beautiful," he says, kissing the tip of my nose, then my lips ever so lightly. Finally. I return the kiss, matching his lips move for move. I'm so glad we came to the beach today. We kiss for what seems like hours before his cell phone vibrates in his pants.

"You'd better get that," I utter, breaking our embrace. "Besides, I think we'd better go before we lose track of time," I say, catching my breath. Damn, he's a good kisser. I almost forgot where I was. As if I said nothing and his phone never went off, Jeremy kisses me again, this time more intense than the first. And I welcome round two. There's no need to teach this boy a thing; he's got it down. Right on cue, his phone vibrates again, once more interrupting our flow.

"What," he says into the phone without looking to see who it is. "Oh, sorry, Mom," he apologizes, smiling at me while rolling onto his back. He reaches above his head and grabs the water bottle sitting in the sand and hands it to me. I take a sip, 'cause Lord knows I'm thirsty, and pass it back to him. He takes a swig while listening to his mother through the phone and grabs another cupcake from the basket.

"Mom, I'm still at the school. Can we talk about this when I get home?" he says, putting the cupcake up to my lips for a bite. I shake my head indicating it's all his, and he places it into his mouth. I guess even rich White boys have to lie to their parents when they're on lockdown.

"Mom, I'll be home in a little while, all right? Don't worry. I have a feeling everything's going to work out just fine," he says, hanging up the phone and guiding me up by my chin to his lips for round three.

"I think that was fate telling us it's time to go," I say in between kisses. His mom calling didn't even faze him. Now, if my mama called, I would've already been halfway to the car. But Jeremy's just got it like that, I guess.

"Yeah, my mom's worried about tomorrow," he says. "She thinks I'm going to have to go to North P.V. if I get kicked out of South Bay." North P.V. is a continuation school in Palos Verdes where all the bad-ass rich kids end up after every other high school gives up on them. They basically play football and chill all day, waiting for graduation and trust funds to kick in.

"You're not that bad off, are you?" I ask, realizing I don't know much about Jeremy's past at all. Maybe he's been in this kind of trouble before and this is the last straw. What then? Damn, I hope those cupcakes kick in soon.

"Nah, not at all. My mom just thinks the sins of the older brothers shall fall upon the younger one," he says. "Besides, I'm not scared. This is just what I need," he says, pulling me up into his arms. We lie there, holding each other while looking at the day begin to fade. Unfortunately, it's time for both of us to go home.

When Jeremy drops me off at the bus stop in front of Miracle Market, Bryan's just getting off work. As usual, he's got his backpack on his shoulder and a spliff behind his ear.

"What's up, little J," he says, putting his arms around my shoulders, slightly knocking me off balance.

"What's up is you smell like pickles and pig's feet. What the hell," I exclaim, pushing him off me and into the street. His stench is messing up my Jeremy high.

"Damn, girl. I see why you can't keep no man; you're too mean," he says, falling back into step with me on the sidewalk.

"Well, you can ask Jeremy about that one," I say, claiming my new love. Nothing's going to keep us from making this new relationship as solid as gold. Nothing.

"Ooh, Jeremy. Did the White boy win?" Bryan says. KJ and Bryan play ball at Compton High together sometimes, and I know brothas can get to talking.

"Yes, if there was ever any real competition," I say.

"Are you sure you're over the brotha?" Bryan asks. "KJ's cool. Don't be so quick to cut him loose, Jayd."

"So quick? He cheated on me, Bryan. I didn't cut anybody loose. He let himself go." Why do dogs always stick together?

"Why you getting so snappy? I'm just saying niggas make mistakes, that's all. Besides, what do you really know about this Jeremy dude, other than he's White and a drug dealer?" he asks, waiting for my response.

"KJ told you about that?" I ask, not knowing why I'm so surprised. "It's not as bad as it sounds," I say.

"Damn, Jayd, you can't be that naïve. Everybody at South Bay knew but you, apparently," he says, making me feel like a little kid. He's right. I can be very naïve sometimes. But, not about Jeremy or KJ, at least not anymore.

"You know what, Bryan? You're right. I can be naïve sometimes. Like when I first went out with KJ and everybody told me he was a dog. A fine dog, but a dog nonetheless. And, I was naïve for thinking that he really loved me when he was doing nothing more than trying to get the cookies. And, I was also naïve when he tried to get me to forgive him for getting me into that mess with Trecee. But, no more. I'm done listening to everybody tell me what to do and with whom," I say, silencing Bryan. "Besides, you're supposed to be my uncle. What happened to whipping a dude's ass if he hurts me?" I ask, half-serious. My uncles, dad, or any other man I can think of has never gone to head for me, over nothing.

"Whatever, Jayd. You act like you don't know how niggas are, and I'm not buying that. You live in a house full of them. So, you ain't got nobody to blame but yourself."

"Are you serious? How do you ever get girls to go out with you?" He's getting on my nerves and ruining my whole vibe, making the walk home seem longer than usual.

"Girls appreciate my honesty," he says, patting himself on the chest and smiling big, like he deserves a medal or something. When we get home, the rest of my uncles are hangin' out on the front porch, drinking forties, smoking blunts, and talking loud to the neighbors hangin' with them. Mama must be gone. Bryan sits down and joins the session while I go around the back and into the house to call Nellie. I can't wait to tell her about my first kiss with Jeremy.

"Hello," Nellie says. "Who is this?"

"What's up, girl. It's Jayd," I say, like she didn't check her Caller ID.

"What's up, Miss Jackson? Or, should I say, Mrs. Weiner?" she says, being cute.

"Not yet, not yet. What's up?"

"Nothing. Me and Mickey are still here getting our nails done." Only ballers can afford to get their nails done at the mall. I'm glad I got a new man to distract me from how broke I am when I'm around my girls. "What's up with you? Where did you and Jeremy end up going?"

"Ask her how was it," Mickey yells from the background.

"Shut up, Mickey, and stop being ghetto before they kick our little chocolate asses out of here," Nellie says, sounding embarrassed. How the two of them became friends, I'll never know.

"Tell that nosey heffa that all we did was kiss, and it was the bomb," I say, barely able to contain my excitement. I don't want my uncles to hear me, especially not Bryan.

"Oh, Jayd. I'm so happy for you," Nellie says, sounding genuine yet a little apprehensive.

"What, Nellie?" I say, bracing myself for her criticism. "What do you have to say?"

"Nothing, except that maybe you want to move slowly with this one, Jayd. I mean, damn. It's only the beginning of school, and already you've almost been in a fight, got two dudes jocking, and one of them is going to jail," Nellie says, sounding way too dramatic for me.

"Nellie, get over it," I say, feeling tired. "You always act like somebody's mama." I have to admit I'm a little hurt my girl isn't completely excited about me and Jeremy getting closer.

"Just be careful, Jayd. That's all I'm saying. But, I am happy that everything seems to be working out for the two of you," Nellie says, trying to save face.

"Whatever, girl. I'll talk to you later," I say, hanging up the phone. People can piss me off sometimes, ya know. I should've just kept my happiness to myself since I seem to be the only one genuinely happy about me and my new man. Speaking of which, I need to look real cute for him tomorrow. Hopefully, I'll be able to see him before his hearing. I think I'll wear my pretty, bright yellow sundress and white sandals. He needs as much joy in his life as he can get, and so do I.

~ 9 ~

Habeas Corpus

*"Nowadays everybody wanna talk like they got somethin' to say/
but nothin' comes out when they move their lips;
just a bunch of gibberish."*

—EMINEM

As I walk up the hill from my last bus stop for the morning, it's oddly quiet. Twenty minutes earlier than my normal arrival time, my usual spectators aren't out yet. The fresh salt air is rejuvenating and helps cool the sweat generating on my forehead from my uphill hike to school. Finally, a peaceful morning's walk in the South Bay. Good, because I need to focus on the day's looming drama. I already sent a text message to Nellie, asking her to meet me in the quad when she and Mickey arrive. I hope I can catch a few minutes alone to talk to Jeremy before they get there.

I couldn't stop thinking about Jeremy all night. I wonder what happened when he got home. Does his mother yell at him like Mama and my mom do when I've disappointed them? What kind of punishment does he get? I'm sure it's not a skillet upside the head or a shoe thrown from across the room, like the boys at Mama's house get when they're severely out of line.

I thought a lot about what Bryan said too. I should know better than to trust dudes with my feelings. These Negroes around here don't respect me or Mama as women or cherish us the way a woman should be. So, why should I expect any different from KJ or any other dude, for that matter? Well, I like to believe everyone's not raised the same and also that dudes can learn, change, and grow the hell up.

I got up a half hour earlier this morning to say a prayer for Jeremy. I can't believe Misty snitched on him. If he doesn't get out of this, I'll have to say a special prayer of a different kind for her. When I get to the quad, Nellie and Mickey are already there waiting on me. I guess they decided to get here early too.

"Jayd, did you talk to your man last night?" Nellie asks, reminding me that I need to call him again. I've been trying to get through to his cell all morning, but to no avail. I'm sure his folks have got him on lockdown with their attorneys before the big hearing.

"No, I didn't get a chance to last night. And his phone's been off all morning," I say as I push send again on my cell, readjusting my position on the cold quad bench.

"Leave a message, or not." Jeremy's message is so boring. I'm going to have to spice it up when we're officially a couple. No need to leave another message. I've already left five.

"He's still not answering." I feel totally helpless.

"Maybe you should skip first period and hang around the office to see what's going on for yourself," Mickey suggests.

"Jayd, the boy isn't worth you having an unexcused absence on your record, and you know that. This is what I'm saying, Mickey. Sometimes you're a bad influence on Jayd's impressionable, young mind," Nellie says to Mickey, patting me on the head like a puppy.

"What the hell has gotten into everybody lately?" I say, slapping Nellie's hand away from my head. "You seem to think you know more than me about life all of a sudden, Miss Nellie. And, the last I recall, you haven't had a man in a long, long time."

"Well, well, well. I see someone had her Red Bull this

morning," Mickey says, trying to add some comic relief to the situation. But, neither I nor Nellie is laughing.

"Damn, Jayd. I'm just watching your back, like a good friend is supposed to do. And, like a good friend, I'm going to walk away now and let you cool off," she says, picking up her bag from the ground and leaving the quad area, going into the main hall.

"Look, Jayd," Mickey begins, grabbing her bag and standing up, ready to follow Nellie. "Bottom line is, if Jeremy's your man and you want to support him, do it. That's the most important thing. Because, when the shit gets rough, all y'all really got is each other." Spoken like a true ride-or-die chick. That's what I like about Mickey; she's loyal to the ones she loves. "I'll check you later, and good luck to your man," she says as she walks toward the main hall. She's right. I do have to find a way to support Jeremy.

As the bell rings for first period and people start running to their lockers and exchanging vital beginning-of-the-day information, I remember my Spanish book is in my locker. But, instead of going to go get it now, I think I'll wait until first period starts. I bet I can get a hall pass from Mr. Donald, avoiding an unexcused absence while still supporting my man.

Since I changed my outfit at the last minute this morning, I forgot to bring a jacket, and it's still chilly from the morning mist. But I know it's going to be at least ninety degrees by lunch. Even though my pink shirt is off the shoulders, it has long sleeves, so at least my arms will be warm because this miniskirt sure isn't providing me with any coverage. As I walk away from the quad and toward class, I notice Chance coming my way.

"Hey, girl, you look a little cold," Chance says, taking off his jacket and covering my body with it. "Worried about your boy, huh?" he asks.

"Yeah. I must be in another world if I forgot to wear sweats under my skirt and a sweater this morning," I say, putting my arms through his oversized jacket. It smells so good, like leather and Polo for men. "Thank you."

"No problem. Besides, now that you're my boy's girl, I got to protect his assets when he's not around," he says, pulling me close to him and hugging me tight like a brother protecting his little sis.

"Is that what he told you?" I ask, looking up at him for the truth. We're in front of my classroom, and I know the bell's going to ring any second.

"How was the beach yesterday?" he counters with a sly smile.

"What do you know?" I ask, pulling away to look him dead in the eye, but I'm smiling a little too.

"Let's just say you've left a lasting impression on the boy. See you later, Jayd, and don't worry about Jeremy. He always lands on his feet," Chance says as he runs down the hallway to his own class. I wonder what he meant by that. I'll just have to ask Jeremy myself when I do finally see him. Now, about that hall pass . . .

It's eerie being the only person in the main hall right after the bell rings. I left Chance's coat in the room because the entire point of me wearing this little outfit was to give Jeremy some inspiration, if you know what I mean. And, if I do catch him, I want him to see me in all my glory.

As I approach the office, I see the clock says eight on the dot. It took Mr. Donald too long to call roll this morning. Knowing the administrators at this school, they probably started Jeremy's hearing right on time, which means I've more than likely missed my opportunity to catch him and wish him good luck before it begins, but I hope not. Sometimes during hearings the students are left outside while the administrators and parents talk. I hope this is one of those times.

Approaching the end of the main hall, I straighten out my skirt, take a quick glance at my reflection in the window above the double doors, and head toward the back entrance of the main office. "What are you doing, Misty?" I whisper as I open the door to the office to see her standing by the principal's door, snooping as usual. Where's Mrs. Cole? She rarely ever leaves her desk.

"SHHH! Do you want to get us both busted?" she whispers loudly, shooing me away from the office and back into the main hall. "What are you doing out of class?" she asks, closing the office door like she's got some authority because she's an aide.

"Look, Misty, I don't have time for this right now. I want to see if I can catch Jeremy before the hearing begins," I say, pushing past her to step back into the office, but she blocks me again.

"Uhmm, hate to burst your bubble, but the hearings have already started, Foxy Brown," she says. "And, your little White boy's in for it too. I don't care what kind of curse you put on that boy. You're not gone be able to get him out of this one," she says, twirling her extra-curly hair with her index finger and snapping her gum, like a true ghetto girl. "You better get out of here before Mrs. Cole gets back from the attendance office."

"Misty, as usual, you don't know shit. And, what the hell are you doing out of class anyway?" I ask, realizing she's as much in the wrong right now as I am. That's why she's trying to get rid of me; she's on an information mission. Well, she's not gonna know anything about Jeremy before I do. Just as I prepare to force my way past this girl, Jeremy comes out of the principal's office with a short White woman who's wearing a business suit and glasses. She must be his attorney.

"Jeremy," I shout, making sure he hears me. Misty turns around to shoot me a look of hatred and jealousy.

"Jayd. Hey, girl. How'd you get out of class?" he asks, walking toward me with his arms opened wide.

"I have my ways. Besides, you know I had to come and wish you good luck," I say, giving him a big hug and kiss on the cheek. I'd love a repeat of yesterday, but there will be plenty of time for celebrating later, I pray. "What are you doing out here?"

"The principal and Special Needs counselor wanted a moment alone with my parents. Sorry I couldn't call you back. My mom took my phone until after the hearing. She wanted me to be in the zone," he says, holding me by the waist and looking down at me, totally relaxed. I wish I had his confidence.

"Jeremy, I'm going back into the office but don't go anywhere," his attorney says.

"Hate to break up your little love fest," Misty says from her perch on top of Mrs. Cole's desk where she can inspect the entire office. "But, Mrs. Cole's coming, and you really shouldn't be here."

"We wouldn't be here at all if it weren't for your big mouth," I say, tired of Misty's meddling. But from the look on her face, I can tell she doesn't want me to call her out in front of Jeremy, which makes me want to even more. "Baby, do you know how Stan and Dan knew to find you after lunch?" I ask, looking up at Jeremy.

Jeremy looks from Misty to me, putting two and two together, and slowly answers, "No, actually I don't. But, from past personal experience, it was probably another student. People are always jealous and ratting people out up here," he says, taking the words right out of my mouth. All this time I thought Misty hated on me because of KJ. Now I realize she's just one of those people who will always and forever be a hater, no matter who I'm dating.

"Whatever," she says, ignoring Jeremy and returning to her original statement. "All I know is Mrs. Cole is coming, and you should be grateful I warned you," Misty says.

"I have a hall pass, Misty, which means, as usual, your help is unwanted." Feeling my heat, Misty goes back into the main hall. Why isn't she in class?

"How do you do that?" I ask, looking up at Jeremy. He's so cute.

"What?" he says, looking back toward his attorney, who's now waiting for him at the door to the principal's office, and then back down at me.

"Be chill at all times."

"It's a gift. Speaking of which, thank you for being here. It means a lot to me," he says, kissing me on the nose, like the prelude to yesterday's shower of kisses.

"Where else would I be?" I say, knowing my ass should be in class.

"Well, let me get back to my lawyer before she has a fit. She's a real control freak," he says, nodding his head toward her. "By the way, you look good, girl. Damn, you got body," he says, eyeing me up and down with the sexiest smirk on his face. "What are you doing after school?" he asks in a tone suggesting he already knows the answer.

"Well, I was going to get my nails done, and then maybe go to the mall with my girls . . ." I say, purposely giving him a hard time. He knows it's Friday and I'm going to Inglewood. Unlike my girls, I don't get my nails done. Like my mom, I do them myself. Speaking of which, she's coming to get me after school today because she's getting off work a little early, so I won't have much time to kick it, but I'm sure we will make it work.

"Yeah, right. I'll see you after school, all right? I'll call you as soon as I get out of here and let you know the verdict," he says. How can the same arrogance KJ exudes come across as sexy, cool confidence on this dude? I must be sprung. "And, what happened to the coat Chance gave you? He sent me a text warning me about your gear already," he says, sounding a little possessive. I hate when guys do that crap. "You should put it back on. I'm sure it looks good on you."

"Yes sir, Jeremy sir," I say, saluting him like I'm in boot camp.

"I didn't mean it like that," he says, looking hurt and a little embarrassed. He can be so sensitive sometimes.

"Jeremy, let's go. We don't have all day," his attorney says. "Your parents have other things to do, and so do I."

Misty has snaked her way back to the chairs outside the principal's office, like she's been sitting there all along—she's good at what she does—watching us. Mrs. Cole returns to her desk, scoping the scene. I better wrap this up quick before I find myself on lockdown with Misty again.

"I'll see you after school," I say, stretching my lips up toward him as he meets my kiss halfway. "And good luck," I say, walking back into the main hall and toward my locker to get my Spanish book before returning to class. No doubt this little rendezvous will be all over school by break, if Misty has anything to say about it.

As I walk back to class I notice Mrs. Bennett walking toward the office. She notices me too and gives me a sly smile. I can't wait until this hearing is over so I can concentrate on fixing her ass next.

English class may as well have been German today, for all I know. It's impossible to concentrate on Emily Dickinson when my man's future hangs in the balance. I hope he didn't crack under the pressure. These administrators up here could easily double for ATF interrogators. As I walk toward the quad to meet up with my girls they rush toward me, almost running.

"Girl, have you heard the news?" Nellie says, almost out of breath. Mickey, two steps behind Nellie and also out of breath, spills the beans.

"Misty just told everybody in South Central Jeremy's been cleared." I can't believe it. My baby's free. Now, that's some serious work those cupcakes did. I can't wait to tell Mama my first prescription worked. But first, I have to write it down or she won't hear me at all, which means I won't be telling her for a while. I have too much going on to think about bringing my journal up to date.

Let's take a long walk . . . And there's my man now, calling to share the good news.

"Girl, let's sit down. I'm tired," Mickey says to Nellie as they claim an empty bench and leave me to talk to Jeremy in peace.

"Hey, baby. I heard. Congratulations," I say loud into my cell like he just won the lotto.

"Thanks, baby. It was tough. They grilled me like I damn near committed a murder or something, but my lawyer was intense," he says, sounding relieved, but not surprised.

"I'm so happy for you. I can't wait to hug you after school," I say, feeling tingly just thinking about his touch.

"Ah, baby. My family's taking the law firm out to dinner tonight, and I have to go and tie up some last minute legal shit with my dad. So, I'm sorry but I won't be able to make it back by the time school's out," he says, sounding regretful. I admit, I'm disappointed, but it's cool. I want to be ready when my mom gets here. It's rare for her to pick me up after school, and I don't want to keep her waiting.

"It's okay, Jeremy. I understand," I say, trying not to sound too upset.

"But," he says sweetly, sensing my hurt, "what are you doing tomorrow night? My parents are having a family dinner to celebrate, and I would love it if you could be there." Oh, snap. It's time to meet the parents already? I don't know if I'm ready for all that yet.

"I'm sure your family just wants to celebrate with the actual family, Jeremy. It's kind of a personal victory, you know," I say, trying to get out of it. I don't really want to meet his parents, not yet, anyway. It's just too soon. I get attached to families and hate when it doesn't work out. Like KJ's parents. I love them and wish we could keep in touch, but I'll probably never talk to them again.

"Look, if you don't want to meet my folks, just say so," he says, sounding as hurt as I did a moment ago.

"No, baby, it's not that. It's just that we're not officially a couple yet, and I don't want to give your family the wrong impression."

"What impression is that?" Jeremy says, sounding defensive. My girls are looking at me, waiting for me to get off the phone so we can talk about the news.

"The impression that we are something that we're not yet," I say, restating the obvious. Why can't he understand my apprehension? I'm sure he's not ready to meet Mama yet, no matter what he says.

"Look, Jayd. It's just dinner. Please come. Besides, I have you to thank for my victory too. The cupcakes and the kiss gave me all the good luck I needed to win." If he only knew how true that statement really is.

"Well, it's just dinner. And, I am a little curious to see if your mom can cook as well as my mama," I say, surrendering. Mama's always telling me to be sweeter, so here goes one of those times when I try with compromise.

"Thank you, Miss Difficult," he says, laughing. "I thought I was going to have to kidnap you from your mom's house," he says, remembering it's Friday and therefore my night to go to Inglewood. "Speaking of which, do you have a ride? I can ask Chance to give you one," he offers, forgetting Chance is my friend too.

"I can ask Chance myself, but no thank you. My mom's coming to get me after she gets off work."

"All right, Ms. J. Call me tonight after you're done with your hair," he says.

"Sure thing, baby. And I'm looking forward to tomorrow, no matter how hard of a time I just gave you."

"So am I. And don't worry. It'll be fun. My family will love you," he says, and I'm reassured. Truth be told, I'm really looking forward to seeing where this dude lives. I know it's a fly-ass crib if it's in the Palos Verdes Estates. It's basically Bel Air by the beach. What am I going to wear?

"I'll talk to you later and see you tomorrow, Mr. Weiner," I say, now a little nervous about my gear. I'm sure I'll find something to wear by tomorrow evening.

Before I can fully squeeze in next to Nellie on the bench, she's already on my case. "Hey, was that your lucky man?" she says sarcastically. She's been throwing salt since yesterday, and it's getting on my nerves.

"What's your problem, Nellie? You were all for me and Jeremy getting together before. What's all this hatin' I'm feeling?" I say, dusting the dirt off my shoulders like I'm Jay Z.

"That was before I knew the fool was Scarface," Nellie retorts, as melodramatically as ever.

"Nellie, you need to calm your ass down," Mickey says. "Her man ain't done nothing that my man don't do on a daily basis. Do you all of a sudden have a problem with my man too?" she asks.

"You both need to readjust the company you keep, with men, that is," she says, turning her head away from us, like she's our moral superior.

"Screw that, Nellie," I say, feeling myself get hot. I didn't mean to start no shit, but enough's enough. "You can't stand up here and judge us because of what our men do. And, it's not your place to tell us about the company we keep, either."

"Hell, yeah, Nellie. You're tripping, girl, and it ain't even cool. You sound like you need to be in the office, sulking with the principal," Mickey says, getting up from her seat on the quad bench to go to the vending machines. I need a snack too.

"Mickey, I'll come with you. I need something to shake off this negativity," I say, rolling my eyes at Nellie. "You want something?" I ask Nellie because I just can't help it. Even when she pisses me off, she's still my girl. I know she means well, but sometimes you'd think she doesn't live in the same city we all do. Compton ain't that big, but man, is she sheltered.

"Nah, I'm cool. And I'm not trying to discourage your relationships. I'm just saying, be careful," Nellie says, sounding a bit remorseful, but still judgmental.

"Nellie, everybody's got skeletons," I say, trying to cool the vibe. I don't want to fight with my girl, especially not now. I want to celebrate Jeremy's victory, not feel bad about it. But speaking of skeletons, KJ and his crew walk up right on cue.

"Well, well, well, the White boy wins again," KJ says, drawing laughter from his crew and mine too. Misty, Tony, and Shae have come along to taunt me as well. I turn and give KJ the evil eye.

"I didn't know it was a competition," I say, stepping toward the vending machines.

"It's always a competition, baby. Or didn't you know?" KJ says, stroking the tip of my chin just like a pimp.

"Whatever, KJ. I've got to get something to eat before the

bell rings," I say, realizing I've wasted the entire break dealing with bull.

"You know, Jayd, you don't have to do this. You've made your point. You can get another man. But, a drug dealer? Really, Jayd? You'd rather be with him than me?" KJ asks, rubbing his chest like he's the man, with his crew smiling and nodding their heads, cheering on his supersized ego.

"KJ, I'd rather him over you any day. And, in case you missed Misty's announcement," I say, glaring at Misty, who's also rolling her eyes at me, "he was found not guilty. So, stop hatin'," I say, pushing him aside as I head for the vending machines, then on to third period. "I'll see y'all later," I call to Nellie and Mickey as they make themselves comfortable to flirt with KJ, Del, and C Money before the bell rings. I guess Mickey forgot about her munchies. As I walk away, KJ continues his tirade.

"Whenever you're ready to come back to Black, baby, I'm right here for you," KJ shouts. What is it with him? Has he completely lost his humility? "And, you're working that skirt, girl. But the jacket's covering up the most important assets," KJ adds as I finally leave the quad area. I look back to make an ugly face at KJ, and Misty again rolls her eyes at me, obviously irritated by KJ's last comment and my man's freedom. Oh, well. Like Mama says, it never pays to be evil, especially not to a Williams woman.

I hope I run into Chance before the bell for third period rings. It's starting to heat up, so this jacket is becoming a bit annoying. And, I just need a hug from someone who's happy about Jeremy too. I can't wait until tomorrow night, now that I'm all excited. I was going to ask Nellie if I could borrow something of hers to wear, but never mind now. She'll probably sabotage the outfit on purpose. And Mickey would be no help, since she wears a size one. So, me as myself with my own clothes will have to do for the Weiner family dinner.

* * *

When my mom and I arrive at her apartment, it's still early evening, which leaves me plenty of time to do both my hair and nails tonight. I wish I didn't have to work tomorrow. I hardly ever wear any polish other than clear on my fingernails because my hands are in water or food all day at work and during the week at Mama's house. So, there's no point in painting my nails when they'll be chipped by the end of the first day. But I try to keep my toes polished at all times. Noticing my preoccupation with my hands and feet, my mom walks over from where she's seated in the dining room to where I'm sitting on the couch.

"Jayd, you want me to do your nails tonight after I finish with mine? Boys like pretty hands and feet," she says, taking my hands into hers and examining my long fingers and nails, which are identical to hers and Mama's. She's never offered to do my nails before.

"Honey," she says, making herself comfortable on the couch next to me. "Something tells me Jeremy's special to you. Am I right?" Feeling like I've just been read, I nod my head in agreement. "Well, if that's the case, I want to help you be at your best. From what you told me about your last date he seems like a keeper, especially if he treats you like a queen. So, I'll help you pamper yourself tonight, and I'll pick you up and help you get ready tomorrow after work." She's never offered to do that either.

~ 10 ~

All in the Business

"Why you all in my business?"

—WHITNEY HOUSTON

I could barely concentrate on work today, I'm so excited about tonight's dinner. Since my Mom gave me a ride home after work, I have more time to look my most fly for Jeremy.

"You're not nervous about tonight, are you?" my mom asks while inspecting the outfits she laid out on the couch when I was at work. She picked out outfits that make me look respectable and cute at the same time. It's nice when we bond, although it's not often enough. She can be hella cool sometimes, like a big sister. And, she knows all about looking fly for her man. "Believe me, Jayd, they'll like you. And wearing one of these ensembles, they'll love you." I didn't tell her about his little run-in with the law, or that this dinner is in celebration of his stroke of good fortune, courtesy of my special touch.

"I'm a little nervous. But, I think I'll look good enough to hide any issues I may have." I approve of her choice in outfits. She's narrowed it down to two favorites: a cognac, shoulder V-neck tee and some flood-length jeans from Baby Phat with some gold heels, or my black, high-heeled boots, with her yellow Akademiks silk tee and some low-rise jeans. "Both

outfits are just right, Mom. How do you do it?" I say, giving
her mad props.

"It's a gift. Now, just pick an outfit and you're good to go.
I've got to go meet Ras Joe at the Bar and Grill for the game.
So, have fun and tell Jeremy dinner's here next time. It's time
I meet this new man in your life. Tell him we like White boys
too," she says, switching her thin frame through the hallway
to her bedroom to dress. I look over at the clothing options
and decide the boots and tank might be a little too much for
these conservative White folks. So, I'll go with the cognac tee
and heels. Sexy yet sophisticated—just what I'm going for.

Jeremy already called and told me he's on his way, so I
better get in the shower now. Luckily, my mom's just changing clothes and heading out the door, leaving me time to get
myself together in peace. I'm lucky I have my mom's apartment to escape to on the weekends. Here I almost feel like a
normal girl.

"Jayd, I'm out. You know how to reach me if you need me.
And don't be out all night, either. I know them White folks
let their kids stay out until sunrise, but not here," she shouts
from the front door. My mom probably won't be home before sunrise herself, so she's really got her nerve. But it's not
her I have to worry about. If I should ever come home after
my mom, all she'd have to do is tell Mama, who would have
me on lockdown for years to come.

"Have fun, Mom, and I'll be home before you," I yell to
the closing door.

"Okay, baby, and have fun. I want to hear all about it in the
morning." And she's out.

When Jeremy arrives, I barely have time to get my mascara
and lip gloss on before he kisses me like he hasn't seen me in
years.

"Slow down, baby. We've got all night," I say, pushing him

off me and into the living room to wait while I make the finishing touches.

"I'm glad because I want to look at you all night. Damn, girl, you're fine," he says. I blush. "I feel underdressed, and it's my damn dinner party," he says, looking over his tie-dyed Rip Curl T-shirt and some blue boardshorts with the brown suede Birkenstocks to match.

"So, this is your mom's house? Very nice," he says. He looks like a giant sitting on my mom's couch.

"Yeah, it's all her. Let's go before we get caught in traffic on Crenshaw. You know the lowriders will be out tonight," I say, realizing maybe he doesn't know. When my mom was growing up, Sundays were the night to cruise down the Shaw. But the police put a stop to that. And now, everybody just rolls out on Saturday after the sun sets.

"That's cool. I've always wanted to see what Tupac was talking about." This boy is too much. He has no problem with his naiveté in my world, and that's what I like about him the most.

"I'm going to let that one slide because I'm feeling too good, but remind me to bring it back up at a later time," I say, grabbing my beige corduroy jacket from its hook and heading for the door. "I'm ready. Let's go," I command, like I'm his boss.

"Yes, ma'am," he says, rising from the sofa to follow me out the front door. "I like it when you're bossy," he says, kissing me on the lips.

"Good, because you need some direction, Eminem," I tease, pushing him out the door and down the stairs.

"I'll just take my time getting to the car while you lock the fifty bolts," he teases back.

"How many locks do you have on your front door?" I ask, genuinely curious.

"You'll soon find out," he says as we walk hand in hand

down the long walkway to his Mustang. It's a peaceful evening, and no one's outside. We should have a good view of the setting sun if we go down PCH to Palos Verdes Boulevard. I've never been, but from what I've heard, that's the only way to get in and out of the estates.

As we approach PCH from Aviation Boulevard, the scenery quickly changes from airport cargo and industrial businesses to beach condos and strip malls. Jeremy speeds down PCH, passing South Bay High on the left.

"Do you want to stop at the school?" he asks sarcastically. I've heard of students hanging out on campus during the weekend, but never witnessed it. And I know Jeremy isn't part of that clique.

"No, that's okay. I get more than my share of this place during the week," I say, enjoying the cool, salty air blowing against my face. The sun's quickly setting, and the beach folks are ready for the night life to begin. It's pretty live around here. There are plenty of coffee shops and clubs to keep it crackin' all night. As we approach the estates, I lose track of the unfamiliar street names because of all the twists and turns to get up the hill. The view is breathtaking. All I can see for miles is water and mountains.

"Is that Santa Monica?" I ask, pointing to bright lights far in the distance.

"Yeah. And that's Malibu further to the left," he says, releasing my left hand and pointing out of my window.

"Watch the road, man. Watch the road," I say, only half joking. These curvy roads up here scare me a little. Bike riders and rollerbladers fly by, also making me nervous.

"Don't worry. You're safe with me," he says, taking my hand again, making me feel instantly protected.

After another mile or so, we arrive at a two-story brick home with an enormous front lawn. There are four cars parked in the crescent driveway: a black CL 55 Benz, a silver

Range Rover, a red convertible BMW Z 4 Roadster, and a classic red Corvette.

"My grandfather would go absolutely crazy if he saw this car," I say, referring to the Corvette as we walk up the driveway toward the massive front porch. "Well damn, you only need one lock for this huge door," I say, a bit taken aback by the solid oak and stained-glass door with a brass hook and one lock above the antique door handle.

"Yeah, it would be kind of hard to break through this thing," he says, opening the door and leading me into his home. As we walk into the foyer, his mother comes in from the living room to greet us.

"Come on in, darling. You must be the Jayd we've all been hearing so much about. I'm Julie, the mom of the household," Jeremy's mother says, looping her right arm through my left and leading me into the dining room, where everyone's already seated and waiting to devour the ten-course meal filling the table. It's a Martha Stewart kind of moment. Jeremy's right behind us, getting a kick out of this, I'm sure.

"Hey, what took you two so long?" Jeremy's father asks. "We almost started without the man of the hour," he says, picking up a bottle of Moet and pouring himself another glass before pouring one for Jeremy, and then one for me. Julie seats us next to each other, with Jeremy at the opposite head from his father. I wonder if they eat like this all the time.

"Inglewood isn't down the street, Dad," Jeremy says, placing his right hand on my left thigh under the table.

"Let me introduce you to everyone, Jayd," Julie says, ever the Southern belle. "This is Michael, our eldest son, and his wife, Christi, Justin, our middle son, and his girlfriend, Tammy, and this handsome man is my husband, Gary." Jeremy seems to be the most relaxed person in his family. Michael looks like he's suffocating, and Justin looks ready to go. "Everybody, this is Jeremy's Jayd," she says, obviously amused at my embarrassment. As if sensing my need to be rescued, Christi jumps in.

"Inglewood? That's where my dad is from, originally, that is. Now if you say he's from anywhere but Palos Verdes, he's liable to put a hit out on you." I can see why. He must be passing for pure-bred rich Negro, because her mom's obviously White. And, she looks like one of those sorority kind of girls. Real prissy and well-mannered. Nellie would love to be friends with this broad.

"Yeah, your dad is pretty high strung about being from here," Michael says, agreeing with his wife. I hate to admit it, but maybe Mrs. Bennett was on to something here. Tammy's a cool-looking surfer chick, and she looks like she's mixed too.

"So, are all the stories we hear about Inglewood true?" Justin asks, passing the first dish around the table. There are three empty bottles of Moet on the table, so everybody has obviously started drinking.

"Hey, back off, everyone. There'll be time for twenty questions later. Pace yourselves. She'll be here all night," Jeremy says, trying to protect me. I'm sure I'm an interesting anthropological study to these folks. But I'll play the game to eat this food right about now. I haven't eaten anything all day because work was so busy, and I didn't really get a break today. And besides, I think Jeremy was telling the truth about his mom's cooking. This spread looks like it could go toe-to-toe with Mama's Christmas dinner.

"I hope you like Cajun cooking, Jayd. I hear your family's originally from Louisiana," Julie says, sounding a lot like Mama, but her accent's a little more proper.

"Yes, ma'am, that's right. My mom's family," I say, remembering Mama's warning about talking too much and telling all our business. She always has to remind me about running my mouth.

"Well, I'm sure you can appreciate all this food, then. We have crawfish étouffée, black-eyed peas, glazed sweet potatoes, sweet potato rolls, green bean casserole, barbecued shrimp, crab salad, and for dessert we have chocolate fondue, caramel pralines, pineapple cake, and peach cobbler. My boys can eat." I'm impressed. If this dinner tastes as good as it looks, I might have to get some private lessons for myself.

"So, can you cook, Jayd?" Christi asks, again drawing attention away from Julie, who seems annoyed. I sense some drama between these two women.

"Hell, yeah, she can," Jeremy answers in between bites. "She made me the best cupcakes before the hearing. I think they had something to do with my good luck," he says, winking at me.

"Is that right?" Julie asks suspiciously. "So, you're the one who made those cute little cupcakes Jeremy brought home on Thursday," she says while ever so carefully picking up the tail of the jumbo shrimp from her pristine china plate. Before placing it in her mouth, she pauses and asks, "What part of Louisiana did you say your family's from, Jayd?" I know better than to answer this woman truthfully. She gives me the chills, like our neighbor, Esmeralda.

"I didn't," I say, realizing how defensive I must sound, quickly rethinking my answer. "I mean, I don't know exactly. My mom never talks about her life down South. And my grandmother didn't really know her family. So, she actually ended up in Texas with my grandfather's family. And that's where our history begins, as I know it," I say, carefully leaving out all of the vital information about Mama's legacy, but giving enough of an answer to satisfy her, I hope.

"Oh, that's a shame. There's so much power in knowing one's family heritage," Gary says while pouring more étouf-fée into his bowl. "I can trace my ancestors all through the Diaspora back to Poland, before the Holocaust," he says proudly.

"When's the last time you went to temple, Gary?" Julie says, touching on a seemingly ongoing argument.

"As I've been telling you for the last thirty years, my love, I'm not Jewish by religion, but by heritage," he says, making a good point. If they weren't drunk, I think this could quite possibly be an interesting debate. Is it possible to get a con-tact high from alcohol? I haven't had a sip of my champagne at all, although I will partake in a toast if there is one. But everyone here seems to be high off something. Maybe it's the food. I haven't touched my plate because I've been too busy answering autobiographical questions, but I'm eager to taste everything.

"I love your outfit," a soft-spoken Tammy says to me from the other end of the table. She has a perfect beach tan, which the white and pink puka shells hanging around her bare neck set off well. She looks like a pretty troll doll. She could be Pacific Islander, or maybe Latina. I'm sure she's sick of people asking her about her race, so I'm not going to let my curiosity get the best of me.

"Thanks. And I like your necklace. I've always wanted one of those," I say. I just don't think I could rock puka shells with my gold hoops and bangles.

"You should get one. I think it would look very nice with your complexion," Justin says, eyeing me like I'm prey. I heard about him being the playboy of the three brothers. Justin is a slightly taller and tanner Jeremy, with long, golden brown dreadlocks hanging down his back in one thick pony-tail. Goddamn, he's beautiful.

"I'll think about it," I say, mesmerized by his intense smile.

"I'll show you where to get them. I bought hers from this cool spot in Venice," he says, lightly flicking the shells around Tammy's neck, making her blush. She's obviously sprung on this boy, and he probably cheats on her every chance he gets.

"If anyone's going to show her where to get anything, it'll be me," Jeremy says, sounding slightly possessive, and it makes me smile. I'm glad to know he cares that his brother's shamelessly hitting on me in front of him.

"Down, you two," Michael says. It's clear he's the family's unofficial referee. "Excuse my family, Jayd. Moet tends to make us all act on impulse," he says, pouring himself another glass.

"I'll take one of those, please," I say, referring to the rolls in front of Michael.

"I was starting to wonder if you didn't like my cooking," Julie says, referring to my untouched plate.

"Oh, no. I'm just pacing myself. I'm actually starving," I say before finally digging in. "Oh, this is good," I mutter through a full mouth of shrimp. I should have worn stretch pants because I feel like throwing down.

"I'm glad you like it," Julie says in a tone that again gives me the chills. "My boys have to have women in their lives who can cook as well as their mother can, isn't that right, Christi?" Julie says. Christi makes an unpleasant face.

"Hey, Ganymede," Jeremy says as the cutest light brown dog hops onto his lap, settling in for the rest of the evening's festivities.

"That's our barkless dog," Gary announces, sounding a little annoyed.

"Yes. We're very proud. She's a pure-bred basenji," Julie says, like she gave birth to her. "She's won several awards and has been in every dog show on the West Coast for the past seven years."

"Yeah, but can she warn us when someone's breaking into

the house?" Gary retorts. "We spend more money on that damn dog than we do on our groceries every month."

"Gary, not in front of company," Julie says, immediately silencing her husband. "Besides, you're hurting Ganymede's feelings."

"Jayd, you want to see the rest of the house? We can take our plates upstairs." Jeremy is already setting the dog on the floor and picking up his plate and napkin. He reaches for my hand, and I can see he obviously needs a break from his family.

"Sure," I say, picking up my own plate and napkin. I grab his hand and follow him out the dining room and up the stairs.

"Oh, son, don't let us run you and Jayd away," Gary calls after us.

"I just want some peace. It's my celebration, right?" he says. We're already at the top of the stairs, and I don't know if Jeremy's dad even heard him.

"Sorry about my parents. They can be a bit intense sometimes," Jeremy says, leading me into the first of five rooms. "This is my room," he says, flicking the black lights on, revealing a wall covered in glow-in-the-dark stickers of planets and stars. The furniture and bedding's all black, really setting off the iridescent walls.

"Wow," I say in surprise. "I like your room. It's bigger than my mom's entire apartment." There's a walk-in closet to the left of the door, revealing a bathroom on the other side. In front of us is his king-sized waterbed and a computer desk with the bookshelf attached. There are four surf boards and two boogie boards leaning up against the wall, next to the desk. To the right of the door is a sitting area with a large black leather couch with a matching recliner, a black marble table, and a huge flat-screen television. He takes our full plates and sets them down on the table.

"Do you like video games?" he asks, walking over to the couch and picking up the controller to his Xbox.

"Not really. What's out here?" I ask, walking toward a set of French double doors, not yet done with my inspection.

"Oh, that's just the balcony," he responds modestly. I open the doors and see the most stunning bonsai trees.

"Is clipping bonsai a hobby of yours?" I ask, really impressed by his many hidden talents.

"No. All Mom. She has them all over the house," he says. "I help her maintain them, but that's it. I just like sitting out there for the view," he says, meaning the ocean and all the other houses on this side of the hill.

"It's beautiful. You're really lucky," I say, more than a little envious.

"Not as beautiful as you are to me. I mean that, Jayd," he says putting his arms around my waste. He leans down and kisses me softly at first, then very passionately, much more intense than our first encounter. I respond, matching his every move, not letting him get away from me. Unlike KJ, I don't feel like he's attacking me with his tongue. This kind of intensity I can deal with. After what feels like an eternity of making out, we decide to come up for air to finish our dinner, which is cold by now, but we still devour it quickly. Kissing can work up an appetite.

"So, Jeremy, how long do you usually wait before having sex with a girl," I say in between bites.

"Where did that come from?" he asks, almost spitting out his food. I grab his napkin from the table and wipe his chin.

"All the kissing got me to thinking, that's all."

"Well, it depends on the girl. The ball's always in her court as far as I'm concerned," he says. "Women are in control of sex, and it's better that way."

"Okay, you know you're unusual, right? Most dudes want

the cookies when, how, and where they want it," I say, wishing I'd brought my drink upstairs.

"It's been my experience that sex is more enjoyable when women are in control," he says with a sly smile I've never seen before. I may be in for more than I know with him. "But, we have plenty of time to talk about sex," Jeremy says, setting his empty plate back on the table and reclining back into the couch, watching me finish my food. After we finish eating, we decide to see what the folks downstairs are doing.

"Where'd you guys disappear to?" Michael asks from his comfy spot on the living room sofa.

"I was just showing Jayd around upstairs," he says, wiping the rest of my MAC Lipglass from his bottom lip while I place the empty plates on the dining room table.

"Yeah, whatever," he says to Jeremy. "Mom was asking for you, Jayd. She wants to show you the photo albums."

"Oh, she's in a good mood if she's breaking those out. You usually don't get to see her boys in diapers until the third or fourth date," Christi says, almost nostalgically and a little bitterly too. "You're as good as in now," she adds, taking another sip of champagne. She looks different now, somehow more unhappy or pissed or something.

"Why don't we skip the torture and take a drive. I want to show you more of P.V. before you turn back into a pumpkin," he says. I'm with him. The less time spent with his mom, the better. Something about her—I can't put my finger on it—creeps me out.

"You can't just leave. Mom will have a fit, and we'll have to take the brunt of it," Justin says, coming in from the game room. He and Tammy are shooting pool while his dad watches television on the couch next to the pool table. I would love to see the rest of the house, but maybe when no one's home.

"You barely ate," Gary calls out.

"Tell Mom I had to get Jayd home before it gets too late."

"Yeah, I have to get up early and go to work," I offer, hoping to ease the tension in the room.

"You should really say bye before you go," Christi says. Now she's smiling like she's enjoying something.

"Who knows where Mom went off to. She could be in the cellar looking for another case of champagne, and that could take all night," Jeremy says, already heading for the door. "We're out."

"I'm following you," I say, taking his hand as he leads me out the front door and back down the driveway, toward the car. "Why were you in such a rush to get out of there," I ask as we hurry down the hill.

"I'm just trying to save you, shorty," he says in the worst Southern accent I've ever heard.

"Save me from what," I ask as he opens the passenger door for me. When he walks around to the driver's side, I reach over to unlock his door.

"Thanks, Lady J," he says, starting the engine.

"You didn't answer my question," I insist. It's one thing for his mom to creep me out. But for him to bolt like that when they said she was looking for me is another thing entirely.

"Look, my mom can be pretty protective when it comes to us. She likes to intimidate the women in our lives, and it usually starts with the after dinner baby pics," he says, backing out of the driveway. As we pull away from the house, I see a silhouette of a woman seated on the back porch, just off the driveway. It's Julie, and she's been sitting there the whole time, watching us as we left her house. What a strange woman. "You're not mad, are you?" Jeremy asks. I don't think he noticed his mother at all.

"No. I just didn't want to be rude."

"We weren't the rude ones. Besides, it's supposed to be a

celebration. And, I would much rather celebrate alone with you than in there with them," he says, putting his hand in its customary place on my thigh as we drive back down the hill. "Now we can take our time driving and just chill and enjoy the view." And the view, unlike life, is serene and drama free. It's back to work in the morning and then to my Dad's in the afternoon. So, he's right. We should just enjoy each other for as long as we can.

~ 11 ~
Smokin'

"He's like the lighter to my cigarette (watch me smoke)."

—ASHANTI

Even though the view is perfect, I can't help thinking about what just went down. I met Jeremy's family for the first time, and he wanted to run. What the hell was that? And why is each of his brothers with a Black girl? I want to take this time alone to talk to him about what Mrs. Bennett said, but I don't want to ruin our vibe. Well, there's really no other way to bring it up. Honest and direct usually works for me.

"Jeremy, do you like me because I'm me or because I'm Black?" I ask.

"What?" Jeremy asks as he makes a left onto Pacific Coast Highway instead of the right I was anticipating, which would have led us back toward Inglewood.

"Where are we going?" I ask.

"First tell me why you asked me that," he says, turning down the radio to hear my answer completely.

"It's come to my attention that you have a habit of dating girls with brown complexions," I say, trying to keep it light, yet still get my point across. I don't want to tell him Mrs. Bennett's the one who told me. But I need to know the truth.

"Well, if I do have a thing for Black girls, is that a problem?" It's also come to my attention that Jeremy has a habit of not answering my questions directly. His evasive behavior annoys me a little. But, it's also part of what attracts me to him.

"Yes, it is, because that means you don't really like me for just being me. What if I looked at you and first liked you because you're White, then because you're fine. Wouldn't that bother you too?"

"So you think I'm fine," he says as he turns down a small street with dilapidated houses and overgrown lawns. This must be the White ghetto. I had no idea it existed so close to the beach.

"Just answer the damn question," I say, playfully smacking him on the arm. "And, where are we going?"

"We're going to meet up with Chance at Leslie's house. I told him I'd stop by and meet his new girl if I could. I hope you don't mind. They'll help us celebrate my victory better than my family did." I've heard Alia talk about Leslie's family, and I must say I've never actually wanted to go to her house. Chance and Leslie's older sister, Carly, used to date. But when Carly got with this pipsqueak dude, Alec, Chance decided to put aside his hurt ego and maintain their friendship. That's just the kind of guy he is. Leslie's house has become the other Drama Club hangout, but for the talented ones, not the stars who hang at Matt's crib; they wouldn't be caught dead on this side of town.

"Yes, Jayd, I think Black women are beautiful. I also think a lot of other women are beautiful too. But it's more than outside appearances with me. I like girls who are confident and sure of themselves. And, if they happen to be gorgeous, well, that's just an added incentive for me to go for it," he says, parking in front of what must be Leslie's house. It's completely quiet, and there are no porch lights, making me feel even more apprehensive about going inside. "Now answer my question. Why did you ask?"

"Like I said, it has come to my attention that you may have jungle fever, and I just want to be clear that I don't." Before we can finish our conversation, the front door to Leslie's house opens, letting out a low light. I can see people inside lying on the floor and Chance coming out with some girl I don't recognize. "Who's that with Chance?" I ask as Jeremy gets out the car and walks around to open my door.

"Oh, who knows? He's always picking up strays," Jeremy says. I hate to admit it, but Chance does have a thing for strung-out White girls. I don't know what it is, but the more stupid, addicted, or ugly they are, the more he loves them. "Is she who I should be dating instead of you?" he asks as we walk up the driveway toward the porch.

"No, and that wasn't my point. I don't want to be your flavor for the month," I say, instantly feeling vulnerable. Jeremy stops walking to look down at me.

"Jayd, seriously. Where is this coming from? Did my mom say something to you?"

"No, she didn't. Actually, when I went to meet you at Mrs. Bennett's class on Thursday she and I had a little confrontation."

"So that's why you were upset. Why didn't you tell me then?" he asks, looking sincere.

"I didn't want you to worry about her bullshit with all of yours so fresh. Besides, I'm a big girl."

"I know you're a big girl, but Mrs. Bennett's even bigger and anything that hurts you hurts me, too," he says, looking wounded.

"So, now you're my bodyguard?" I ask, grinning at his cute self.

"Of course I am," he says, smiling back at me. I hope he keeps that smile when I tell him my decision.

"Well, I'm glad you feel that way, because I've decided to file a grievance against her."

"Why? You'll get nothing out of it except more grief from her. I see the way she treats students in her class who've gone up against her, and it ain't pretty."

"But that's exactly why I want to do it. She can't keep getting away with it."

"Whatever you want to do is up to you. I just think you're wasting your time and energy." Why is he so mellow about everything? Does he ever get pissed off? If he's like this all the time, I don't know how we'll ever survive. I need a little spark in my man.

"Hey, dude. I thought you told me you couldn't make it because you had a big family dinner or some shit to attend," Chance says, barely able to hold up his date, who must be drunk because she looks like she's about to pass out. "Hey, Jayd."

"Hey, Chance," I respond, leading the way up the porch with Jeremy right behind me. "Who's your date?" I ask, knowing she doesn't go to South Bay. In fact, she looks too old to be in high school.

"Oh, this is Jessie. She lives around the corner. Jessie, these are my friends, Jeremy and Jayd." She looks up at us through an alcohol haze and starts to speak, but is stopped by her urge to vomit.

"I think I'm going to be sick," Jessie says, running from the porch onto the front yard. Chance runs after her and holds her hair, putting her cigarette in his mouth, next to his own. What he sees in this girl, I just don't get. He's so sweet and generous. I know he could have any girl he set his mind on. Well, except for Nellie, who just ain't feeling him at all.

When we walk into the dimly lit house, it looks as if squatters live here. There's no furniture except for a card table and four chairs, where Leslie, Alia, Alec, and Carly are seated. People are passed out on the living room floor, in the hallway, and sitting in the entryway to what must be the kitchen. And, everyone's smoking something. I can barely breathe.

"Jayd, what are you doing here?" Alia asks. She's as surprised to see me as I am to be here.

"We came to check Chance out," I answer, grabbing Jeremy's hand before walking over to give her a hug. I'll be damned if I'm going up in here by myself. When I reach the table and bend down to give her a hug, I notice some sort of board on the table. It looks like a game, but I've never seen it before.

"Hey, guys," Jeremy says, nonchalantly greeting everyone at the table and ignoring the passed-out folks all around us.

"Hey, Jeremy," Carly says, a little too friendly for my taste. "So, are you two dating now?" she asks, turning her attention away from him and back to the game on the table. Alec hasn't looked up from the board since we walked over, and Leslie seems just as entranced.

"Yes, we are," Jeremy answers before turning around to look through the still open front door for Chance's return. If Chance weren't here, I doubt Jeremy would've come. This ain't his crowd at all. Lighting another cigarette, Carly continues her cross-examination.

"So, Jayd, how does it feel to date South Bay High's most popular dude?" she says, slurring her speech a bit. "Let's see, first there was Dalia, the Indian girl, then there was Trisha, the Black-and-White mixed one. Then there was—" Before she can continue her embarrassing tirade, Jeremy shuts her up.

"All right, Carly, that's enough. Everyone here knows just how ugly you can get. No need to remind us."

"Oh, come on, J. You know I'm just messing with you," she says, offering Alec a hit from her Marlboro Red before turning to Jeremy and offering him a cigarette from her pack.

"No, thank you. I stopped smoking a while back." I didn't know he smoked. I despise cigarettes. My dad and his entire family smoke, and it drives me crazy, especially the way the smoke sticks to my hair.

"Oh, what a shame. It was so sexy on you," she says, flirting with Jeremy right in front of her man and me. I should say something to this broad, but it doesn't seem like I need to. Jeremy's got this heffa on red alert.

"What's wrong with you, Carly? You used to care a little about yourself. Now you just seem like you gave up."

"You never cared about the way I look," Carly says, taking yet another cigarette out of her pack and lighting it. "I'm not dark enough for your taste." Oh, hell no, this broad didn't just say what I think she said. Does everyone know Jeremy has a taste for a darker shade of brown?

"What the hell is that supposed to mean?" I ask Carly, loud enough to wake some of the people passed out on the floor.

"Don't let her get to you, Jayd. She's just a bitter bitch. And jealous too. Did I mention that?" Jeremy says, reverting to his smart-ass mode, lightening the mood a little. But I'm not done. These White folks around here think they can say whatever they want and get away with it. Well, not in front of me. I can practice for my confrontation with Mrs. Bennett on this girl.

"No, Jeremy. I really want to hear what she meant by that little twisted comment. Because personally, I don't think you not liking her has a damned thing to do with her complexion," I say, looking Carly up and down. Alec, Alia, and Leslie look from me to Carly, ready for the blows to come. Carly and I are both known for our feisty tempers. Carly had her share of fights as a senior last year.

"Seems like you picked a lively one this time," Carly says to Jeremy, conveniently dodging an altercation with me.

"Do you want to play?" Alia asks me, ignoring the tension. "We just started."

I really don't want to fight with Carly, so I take Alia's out. "What are you playing?" I ask. I'm actually interested in this game. It doesn't look like anything I've ever played before.

"It's a Ouija board. My mom bought it for me. I've wanted one forever," Leslie says without looking up from the board. The only thing I know about these boards is that they're more than a game. Mama told me to beware of dark magic, especially where White folks are concerned. Jeremy looks at me and, noticing my obvious discomfort, answers for me.

"Jayd, we should go and make sure Chance and his date are cool."

"Okay. I guess I'll have to catch you next time, Alia. Thanks anyway," I say, allowing Jeremy to pull me away from the table. "What the hell was that?" I ask when we get outside.

"That's the way they get down. See why I stick to my beach crew? They may be a little out of it, but I don't have to worry about this kind of shit with them. I wish Chance would stop hanging out with these losers."

"Now, this is new. You being judgmental," I say, playfully caressing the back of his hand with my fingertips. His skin is smooth, and his hand feels good in mine.

"Not judgmental, just stating the facts."

"Hey, Jeremy. Got a cigarette, man? I'm all out," Chance says as he and Jessie share the last drag on hers.

"Nah, man. I quit," Jeremy says.

"I didn't know you smoked." I say. "But, according to Carly, there's a lot I don't know about you," I say with a little salt. I don't want to give Carly the satisfaction of seeing me upset with Jeremy, but I have to let him know I heard everything that broad said.

"Jayd, don't let her get to you. There's nothing good that comes out of her mouth, ever," he says, looking me in the eye. "Yes, I have dated a few girls in my past and yes, most of them weren't White. And yes, I used to smoke cigarettes," he says, pleading with his eyes for me to drop my attitude. His smoking doesn't surprise me. Most of the folks around here do. Even Mickey takes a hit every now and then. And, when Misty and I hung out she would steal her mother's cigarettes and smoke them.

"So, you used to smoke, huh?" I say, trying to lighten my own mood. I'll deal with his female fetish later.

"Yeah, had to quit, though. The smell stayed on me and in my car, and I don't like smelling like cigarette smoke." I knew he was my soul mate. "Besides, it doesn't taste good to kiss a smoker." He bends down to give me a kiss, eliciting taunts from Chance.

"You know, you can go upstairs with all that." Chance can't say nothing to us. Jessie's passed out on his lap, but it looks like something else completely.

"Dude, why don't you take her home? She's gone," Jeremy says.

"I wish I could, man. But she's too damn heavy. Her boots must weigh thirty pounds alone."

"So, are you really going to take Mrs. Bennett on for running off at the mouth?" Jeremy says, turning the conversation back to us.

"There's a difference between running your mouth and throwing racist slurs," I say, pulling away from him a little. How could he not be upset about her behavior?

"Yes, but you also have to know when to fight and when to take flight." That last statement really hit home. Maybe Jeremy's right about Mrs. Bennett. Maybe I should leave this battle for someone else to fight. But, I don't want to let Ms.

Toni down, and I especially don't want Mrs. Bennett to get away with her racist comments.

"You really think I shouldn't go up against Mrs. Bennett?" I ask.

"No, I don't. I think it's a suicide mission," he says, sitting down on the bottom porch step and pulling me down next to him. Chance and Jessie are sprawled out on the lawn in front of us, recuperating from the drinking.

"So, you think she should just get away with her comments? Is that how you want to go through life, not fighting?" I ask. I know Jeremy's hella mellow, but I can't respect passivity, especially not in a boyfriend. He's got to be willing to fight for something.

"I admire your tenacity, Jayd. And don't get me wrong. I know how much of a bitch Mrs. Bennett can be. I'm just saying you won't win because she is that much of a bitch and so are a lot of the teachers and administrators up there. And, she's got their ears. Why do you think it was so important for her to be my character witness? She's been teaching at South Bay for twenty years and ain't going anywhere anytime soon. It's not right, and it's not for me to judge. It just is what it is."

"And that's it? She wins by default, she's allowed to go around shooting off her racist opinion, and we all have to take it?" I say, feeling myself get hot. This is some bullshit. "How can you be so nonchalant about it? She basically said I was your flavor of the month, and you could care less."

"Jayd, let's be clear: Mrs. Bennett isn't my spokesperson, and neither is anyone else. You already know how I feel about you, and you shouldn't allow what anyone else says to influence your thoughts," he says, turning my chin toward his face. "You can't change the way people think, only the way you respond to them."

I hate to admit it, but he's right. I'll just have to wait and talk to Ms. Toni about this more on Monday. And, as for Carly, I have to shake her comments off, too. I really shouldn't trip off of her because I actually feel sorry for her. If this is her life out of high school, I can see why she's so damn bitter. Right now I have to get this boy to take me home and get ready for work tomorrow. I also have to go with my Dad tomorrow afternoon, which is another battle all its own.

After Jeremy dropped me off last night, I went right to sleep, not worrying about the smell of smoke in my hair. But it's been bothering me all day at work. And, after being with my dad's family this afternoon, I'm sure I'll need to do a rare hair washing at Mama's house tonight if I don't want to smell like smoke all week.

Don't slip up and get caught. Restricted caller. It must be my Dad.

"Hello," I say.

"Hey, girl, it's your daddy. What time you get off work again?" he asks.

"I get off at three today." I check the clock to see how long I have until the reunion. One hour.

"All right, I'll be there at three. And, did you bring your stuff with you? No need to go to your mother's house if you did." He's always trying to get out of seeing my mom. After all the shit he's put her through, I don't blame him. It must kill him with guilt to see her.

"No, I didn't, and I need to change out of my work clothes."

"Oh, okay then. Well, I guess I'll see you in a little while."

After cashing out the register with Shahid taking over my spot, I clock out and sit outside to wait for my daddy. He pulls up in his black Acura TL five minutes late. He always has to make an appearance.

"Hey there, Jayd," he says through the driver's side window. "Sorry I'm late. There's always so much traffic on the 405." No shit. That's why he should leave earlier. But, as usual, he needs a reason to start the complaining marathon about driving to this side of town, and the congested traffic is the perfect culprit.

"Hi, Daddy," I say, opening the passenger door and sitting down on the hot leather seat. Thank God I'm not wearing shorts.

"So, how was work?" he asks as he pulls out of the parking lot and toward my mom's house. "Did you get paid today?" Like I'd ever tell him when I get some money. This dude is the brokest property owner I know of and the most selfish too. You'd think he'd put my mom and me in one of his houses or apartment buildings, but no. She had to sue him for child support, and he's always late on the payments.

"No, Daddy, I didn't. Did you remember to give me an allowance?" I ask.

"You got a mouth just like your mama, you know that, Jayd?" he says, making a left onto LaBrea as we head to my mom's house. I hope she ain't home because if she is, she's liable to come downstairs and say hi to him just to piss him off. Because of the foul way my dad divorced my mom, Mama's had a gris-gris on him from the time I was born. He can't set foot on Mama's yard, and he doesn't try to, either. He's got enough sense to be afraid of her, and my mom too.

"We don't have to talk at all, if you like." He hates when I get passive aggressive on him. I love playing with my dad's head. He's just too easy to piss off.

"Fine, Jayd. Have it your way. All I know is you better hurry your little sassy ass up and come on. I've got the family waiting at the house, and it'll take us at least forty-five minutes to get back to Lynwood in traffic. You could at least say thank you."

"Thank you," I say as I slam the door and make my way up the walkway to my mother's apartment. I can't wait to get the rest of this afternoon over with. It's impossible for me to be in a good mood around my dad.

When we finally arrive at his house, the entire family's here waiting for us. I'm sure they want to grill me about my mom's love life, school, and their favorite subject, my loser uncles. They just love to rub it in how my oh-so-powerful grandmother has raised some trifling men. And how, in their opinion, my mom's on the same path.

"Hey, Jayd. How's Lynn doing these days?" asks my aunt Trish. My dad has seven sisters and five brothers. And they all have children and grandchildren. They're a tight-knit group, making those of us not raised in the family feel like outsiders. Unfortunately, I'm the only outsider here this afternoon.

"My mom's good, Aunt Trish. How about your family?" I ask.

"Oh, everyone's just fine. You see, Kim, just pledged AKA over the summer," she says, referring to my cousin wearing a pink and green sweater with the Black sorority's letters across her chest. "We're so proud, she being a legacy member and all. Tina and her husband, Mark, just had their third baby, and he's being relocated to Spain for his job at the engineering firm. And, Preston over there started Stanford this fall. As you can tell, we're doing just fine."

"Cool," I say. I'm ready to go. Mama's house is only a twenty-minute walk from here. If I didn't have my stuff in my dad's car, I would sneak out like I did last year at his Christmas party. After my little stunt, my dad didn't talk to me again until I called him for Father's Day.

"Jayd, I want you to say hi to your uncle Willard," my dad says, pulling me away from my post up against the wall and toward the Bid Wiz table. Everybody's drinking and smoking and having a good time, except me. All the kids are outside playing in the backyard. And, the cousins my age are somewhere talking about me and what I'm wearing, I'm sure.

"After this can you please take me home?" I ask. "I have a lot of homework to do."

"You know you could try to be social, Jayd. It wouldn't kill you."

"I was social. Didn't you see me over there talking to Aunt Trish?" I say.

"What about your cousin Nina and the other kids your age? What's wrong with you, girl?" he asks.

"Hey, Uncle Willard. Congrats on the marriage, the lung, everything," I say, giving him a big hug. I don't have anything against him. I really don't know him all that well, so I don't know where he fits in.

"Well, thank you, Miss Jayd. So, did your mama get married again? Oh, who am I kidding? It was hard enough marrying her off the first time, I'm sure, with that fiery temper of hers." Well, that seals it. Everyone in my dad's family has something to say about my mom. Why would I want to be around folk who really don't like me? I just want to go home and forget this part of my day ever happened.

~ 12 ~
The Sell-Out and the Sistah Lover

"Seems like you got a hold on me/
It must be voodoo, cause baby, I want you."

—YOYO

"Jayd, don't you hear that alarm clock, girl? Get up before you're late," Mama says, half asleep herself.

"I hear it, and you, Mama," I mumble, automatically checking to see if my pink do rag is still tied to my head. "I'm up."

Damn, the weekend went by fast. All I can think about is seeing Jeremy again. I love school now. I wish I could get there a little earlier on a regular basis to watch him and his crew surf. But I know Mama would know I wasn't going to school early for any productive reason and then, out of spite, make me get up early every morning and do my spirit work. I've learned to stay one step ahead of Mama at all times. She always knows when I'm up to something.

I crawl out of my bed and grab my clothes for the day off the back of the bedroom door. As I reach for the knob, I stub my toe on the side of the dresser drawer.

"Ouch," I say rather than my first thought, only because Mama can hear me.

"Be careful, Jayd. You act like you don't know your surroundings." Something about Mama's words or the way she says them brings on an intense feeling of déja vù, like I've done this before, which makes me remember last night's dream.

"You're out of your element, Jayd. You don't belong here."

"Who are you?" I ask, to a voice with seemingly no body. I'm stuck in a dark room with no visible doors or windows. It feels like a big, black box, and I'm in the center. The voice is coming from all directions. It's a woman's voice, and it sounds like Jeremy's mother.

"You don't belong here. You don't have the sight, child. You can't see."

"Jayd, what the hell is wrong with you?" Mama asks, grabbing my arm.

"Nothing, I'm fine. I just thought I forgot to do something last night, but I didn't," I say, lying through my teeth.

"Funny. By the look on your face, I thought you'd seen a ghost or something," Mama says, smiling slyly. I know she knows I'm not telling her the truth, but she'll wait for the shit to hit the fan before letting me know she knows.

"Nah, I'm fine. Let me hurry and get in the bathroom before Bryan wakes up."

"Have you done your homework for me, Jayd?" Mama asks, already knowing the answer.

"No, Mama. I haven't had time."

"Well, little Miss Jayd, you better make time. Meet me after school at the beauty shop. Netta and I will have a quiz ready for you."

"It's Monday, Mama. What are you going to Netta's for today?" I ask, confused that Mama's standing Tuesday appointment has been changed. Netta doesn't even take any other clients on Tuesdays so she and Mama can talk about whoever and whatever they want for as long as they can.

"Netta has a doctor's appointment tomorrow, so we'll be at Kaiser all afternoon and won't have time. Besides, Mondays are usually slow," she says.

"Mama, please not this week. I have a major English test and I need to study," I plead, hoping Mama will cut me some slack, although I doubt it. I've been seriously slacking in my spirit work.

"No, Jayd. There will always be something else. You need to learn how to balance both your worlds. That way you'll never be out of your element." And with that last hint at what she knows, Mama gets back in her bed and goes back to sleep.

"Damn," I mumble under my breath as I close the door.

"What did you say, young lady?" Mama asks with serious attitude in her voice. I swear she stole Lexi's canine hearing.

"Nothing, Mama," I say, stepping toward Daddy's room. As I enter to grab my stuff out the closet, Bryan turns over and looks at me from his bottom bunk bed.

"Wake me up when you come out the bathroom, Jayd."

"All right," I whisper, trying not to wake Daddy and Jay.

"And don't stank it up either," Bryan says.

"That's all y'all's nasty asses. I smell like roses, punk," I say, pushing my Hefty bags back into the closet and heading for the bathroom. As I rewrap my cornrows before my morning shower, I see Mama has left one of her usual notes for me on the mirror. She must've just put it there while I was in Daddy's room. As if I needed something else to do, now I have to run to the backhouse and make this bag. I hope I don't forget any ingredients in my haste.

As soon as I step foot on campus I head straight for my locker, only to find KJ already there waiting for me. When I reach my locker, he rushes me, knocking me off balance and into his arms.

"I know you miss this," he says, like he's really the pimp he's not.

"Fool, you need to get up off me. You're messing up my

clothes," I yell, pissed that he caught me by surprise, but loving the way his athletic body feels. "What the hell do you want?"

"I want a second chance," he says bluntly and almost sounding sincere. I'm not prepared for his madness this morning.

"KJ, what are you talking about? You've had more than two chances already. It's time to give someone else a chance," I say, not meaning to be cruel, but it's over, and he needs to accept that. I wish he hadn't hurt me like he did because I think we made a good couple. But, not anymore. I will not give in to my soft spot for him.

"Oh, and the drug-dealing, rich surfer boy is more worthy than me," he says, like a wounded puppy. I think this is really getting to him. Not because he cares about me, but because his ego can't take being replaced by Jeremy.

"KJ, please. You act like your homies and you don't get your hustle on," I retort, pushing him away from my locker and turning the lock. I can still smell his cologne on my clothes, just like when we were together. Damn, why does he have to smell so good?

"Hey, what's your new combination? You know how forgetful you can be," he says, making me remember how he used to go to my locker for me during summer school to get my books because, as usual, I had left them in my locker.

"Don't try and sweet talk me now, Negro. It's over, which means you are no longer privy to combinations, bear hugs, or anything else for that matter," I say, shaking off memories of good times. People otherwise absorbed in their own worlds are starting to look at us, including Misty, who's headed our way.

"Here comes your girl," I say, opening the locker door and retrieving my Spanish book.

"Unless you've got a double," KJ says, reclaiming his position in front of my locker as I close the door shut. "I don't know who you're talking about."

"KJ," Misty snaps at him like she really is his woman and he just got busted with the next-door neighbor's wife. "What's wrong with you?" she asks, not acknowledging me at all, which is just fine with me. I'm sick of the broads and drama this dude carries with him. If I could've been his only one, he wouldn't need a second chance.

"Misty, let go of me and mind your own business," KJ says, snatching his arm away from her tight grip.

"You are my business. And, you're humiliating yourself over her," she says, pointing at me but still not looking me in the eye. This broad's got her nerve, talking about somebody humiliating themselves. She could write a book on the subject, I'm sure.

"Misty, stay out of this, please," he pleads, stepping away from the locker and in between Misty and me. There's the warning bell, just in time. As I walk away from the soap opera still going on at my locker, KJ yells to me right over Misty's head, "We'll talk about our reunion song later, baby."

When I turn around to send him hate radars, Misty catches my eye instead. Out of all the looks I've ever seen Misty give me—hate, vengeance, envy—never have I seen her send me a jealous vibe so clearly. She does want KJ all to herself. If that's really the case, maybe she's been playing me and him from jump. And if that's true, we do deserve a second chance—at least at being friends.

"Hey, Jayd," Jeremy says, catching me by surprise and giving me a big kiss on my cheek. "I'm running late this morning—high surf and all."

"High surf?" I ask.

"Yeah. It means it's a good morning," he says, smiling

brightly. "See you at break?" he asks as he walks away from me toward his class. I remember Ms. Toni's warning last week and had planned on catching up with her.

"No, baby. I have to talk to Ms. Toni this morning. How's lunch?" I ask as the bell for first period rings over my head. I'm officially late. Luckily, Mr. Donald gives us an extra minute to get to class before he marks us tardy. After all, it is first period.

"Lunch, it is," he yells as he runs off to class. I don't know how I'm going to justify my blossoming love for Jeremy to Ms. Toni, but she'll just have to understand.

As I sneak into the ASB room, I can see Ms. Toni sitting at her desk, as usual, with a huge orange sweater on that looks radiant against her mahogany skin.

"Good morning, Ms. Toni," I say, wrapping my arms around her neck, surprising her.

"Well, well, well," she says, grasping my wrist and turning her neck up to look me in the face. "Look what the cat dragged in."

"Ha, ha, ha," I say, releasing myself from her grip and taking a seat in the chair opposite the small desk.

"So, have you thought any more about what I said regarding Mrs. Bennett," she asks, getting right to the point.

"Yes. But, truth be told, I don't know if going up against her will honestly do any good. She's been here for too long and shares the mindset of most of these folks up here," I say.

"Yes, Jayd, that is true. But that doesn't mean your voice shouldn't be heard. And how do you know what most of the folks up here think?" she says, twisting her face up as if to say I think I know it all. "Maybe most people are too afraid to voice their opinion and just go along to get along. Your voice may be the one to change that."

"My name is Jayd Jackson, not Sojourner Truth. And honestly, I'm tired of fighting with ignorant people. It just doesn't do any good," I say.

"Yes, it does. If nothing else it'll let Mrs. Bennett know you aren't afraid of her. And, instilling that fear in her is more powerful than your little young self can imagine right now. Take my word for it, Jayd. Confronting Mrs. Bennett is the right thing to do. And going through the proper channels is also the most effective way to do it." Damn, she's good.

"All right, Ms. Toni. I'll do it," I say, feeling the gravity of my decision.

"I knew you would. That's why I already scheduled a conference tomorrow morning during second period. Your English teacher has already been notified of your absence. So, be ready, girl."

"Well, thank you for leaving it up to me," I say. "Did I ever really have a choice?"

"Well, of course you did. I just knew you'd make the right one, unlike with that Jeremy boy. Speaking of which, how's life with the ex-con?" she asks, turning her chair toward me and letting me have what's been coming to me for almost a week now.

"He was found not guilty," I almost whine.

"This time, but what about the next?" she asks while bringing a hot coffee mug to her lips. "I've known these Weiner boys for a long time, Jayd, and they're all alike: typical rich, spoiled P.V. brats," she says.

"Well, I met his family this weekend, and they seemed pretty nice," I say, feeling like I'm Jeremy's attorney. "Besides, Jeremy's his own man."

"Yes, and as his own man, you should respect the fact that he will make his own mistakes. I just don't want you to be a part of his downfall." I know Ms. Toni's only looking out for my best interests, but right now she's getting on my nerves. I don't need anybody else telling me what to do with Jeremy.

Will we ever have a chance to just make our relationship work without all this outside drama?

"Whatever happened to just being with the one you want to be with?" I say, like I'm talking to someone who doesn't know about love and heartache.

"Jayd, I know it can be all exciting and everything, finding a new man, especially after what you went through with KJ," she says. "But remember, baby, trouble comes in all shades. Now, unless you've come to tell me something new, or help me with this stack of paperwork," she says, picking up a full manila folder, "I've got business to handle." Ms. Toni can be a cold sistah sometimes.

"All right, Ms. Toni," I say, realizing her patience with me has run out, "I'll talk to you in the morning." I pick up my backpack from the floor and get up to leave.

"I know you'll, again, make the right decision, Jayd," Ms. Toni says from her desk without looking up at me. I think she's way off base here. I also think she has a little bias when it comes to the Weiner brothers. Apparently there's more to their story than I know. I'll have to get Jeremy to tell me more about his brothers over lunch.

Before Jeremy and I have a chance to leave, KJ, Misty, and crew catch a glimpse of us heading off campus. I see them too, so I know Jeremy must see them as well, but he doesn't say anything. It never seems to faze Jeremy that people are watching him. I'm just glad to get off campus and talk to him. I don't need an audience when I tell him about tomorrow's conference with Mrs. Bennett.

"So, what do you feel like eating? Campos Burritos, Taco Bell, McDonald's," he says, reading off the names of several fast food joints in the area.

"McDonald's sounds good," I say, noticing the restaurant

on the left. He pulls into the drive-through and orders. We pull up to the payment window and wait for our food.

"So, how was your talk with Ms. Toni?" he asks.

"It was cool. She convinced me to file a formal complaint against Mrs. Bennett," I say, and wait for his reply. After our talk Saturday, I'm sure he thought I'd forgotten about it by now.

"I figured as much," he says. "You don't seem like the lie down-and-take-it type. Just be prepared for the backlash," he says, taking our bags from the cashier and handing them to me before getting our drinks.

"It won't be as bad as you think. Ms. Toni will be there to act as my ombudsman. So, it won't be me against her."

"That's what you think. You have to remember, Jayd, Mrs. Bennett's going to not only be your teacher next year, but she's also the A.P. sponsor, which means you'll have to see her at every study session before the A.P. exam. She's never going to forget this and will use every chance she gets to make your life a living hell."

"Damn, you're really afraid of her, aren't you?" I ask as we head back to campus.

"Not at all. I just know how she gets down. And, I know saying something won't do any good because I've already tried. Chance was in my English class the last semester of our sophomore year. She kicked him out for making a joke about her glasses. I said something to her then, and she called my mom and told her I was being disobedient and probably needed more sleep. So, as a result, my mom didn't let me surf in the morning or hang out late on school nights for the rest of the semester. Now that I know how Mrs. Bennett is, I just don't mess with her anymore. My freedom's too precious to me."

When we get back to campus with our food, we decide to park in the back parking lot and eat our lunch in peace.

"Jeremy, what else did you and your brothers get into that I don't know about?" I say, not wanting to be too nosy, but I have to know the truth.

"Oh, not too much," he says in between bites of his Double Quarter Pounder with Cheese. "It's just we always got caught at some point, you know," he mutters, covering his mouth with his hands, trying to be polite. As I snack on my large fries and chicken nuggets, I think of the best way to ask my next question.

"Be honest. Are you and your brothers some typical rich, spoiled P.V. brats? Or do you guys actually have a purpose in life?" I ask, trying to be both funny and serious at the same time. "Inquiring minds want to know."

"I can't speak for my brothers, but I can say I do have a purpose in life, even though we are P.V. brats." He smiles. "A lot of people have always tried to judge me according to what my brothers have done, like the time Michael stole a car or when Justin got caught having sex in the teacher's lounge," he says, taking another bite of his food and looking me straight in the eye. "I try and surf to my own wave, you know what I'm saying?"

"Yeah, I do know what you mean." Now I have a big lump in my throat from feeling guilty. How could I judge him? I knew who this boy was the first time I laid eyes on him: a rebel with a soul. And, like rebels before him, he's loved when he's popular and hated when the ride's over. "So, what's your purpose in life?"

"Oh, right now my purpose is to get to know you better, Miss Jayd Jackson," Jeremy says, leaning in to give me a kiss. "Why so many questions?" he asks.

"Well, ever since your hearing, a lot of people have been questioning your character," I begin. "Not that I care what people say, but it does make it easier when the people I love,

love each other back," I say, realizing I just said I love him. How do I take that one back? And, do I really want to?

"So, you love me?" Jeremy asks with the biggest smile on his face I've ever seen. Oh, shit. How do I explain this one without seeming crazy? I mean, I could fall in love with him very easily. But, to say I love him right now is a bit premature, and I don't want him to think I'm moving too fast or in the wrong direction.

"You know what I mean," I respond, trying to make it seem insignificant, like a slip of the tongue.

"No, Jayd, I don't know what you mean. We haven't discussed it, but I'm getting impatient. Will you or won't you be my girl?"

"Jeremy, you've already got me," I say, initiating a kiss for the first time. In my heart, I really feel for Jeremy. So why not make it official? As I pull away, not wanting to let go of his lips, I look at Jeremy and I look at the school. What's the worst that can happen if I do become his girlfriend?

"So, does that mean I can start calling you my girlfriend?" he asks as he kisses my nose and then my forehead. "Inquiring minds want to know," he says, mocking me.

"I just think it's a little soon after my last relationship to commit right now." I hope he understands it's not that I don't want to be his woman, because God knows I do. It's just I'm not ready to be on lockdown again.

"I understand, baby. And like I said before, there's no pressure. It's just I want to make sure we're on the same page."

"And what page is that, Jeremy?" I ask. I love teasing him. I get such a kick out of it.

"On whatever page it is that says we're more than just friends, more than just kickin' it. I want to get to know you for a long, long, long time to come."

There's the bell, damn it. Just when things are getting good, we have to return to reality.

"There'll be plenty of time to get to know each other and to be boyfriend and girlfriend," I say, kissing him on the lips as we both reach for our door handles to get out of the car. It's quite a hike from this parking lot to the main campus, but it's worth it for a little peace and quiet. "See you after school?" I ask, hoping he's still willing to take me home, even though he has no claim to the cookies quite yet.

"Of course. I look forward to our daily ride to Compton," he says, taking the lunch trash out of the car and throwing it in the bin on our way to class. I hope I don't miss the opportunity to be with Jeremy. It's a dream come true; it really is. I still have my reservations and not so much because I miss KJ or anything like that. His aloof attitude and my wanting him to be a little more like KJ in some ways is keeping me from being my full self around him. And, until these issues are resolved, I can't fully say I'm his woman yet. But damn, I want to be.

After Jeremy drops me off after school, I realize I didn't kiss him goodbye. He still makes me so nervous. I get all unsettled inside when he's around. KJ never made me feel like this—ever. I enjoy my afternoon walks home from the bus stop. It gives me a chance to clear my head of all the day's drama at school. At least Jeremy and I are finally on the same page. It's just so lovely, the way he makes me a priority in his life. We spend our time talking and just overall chilling and getting to know each other; it isn't always about making out.

Even though it's chill between me and Jeremy, I miss the passion KJ and I shared. He gets me all hot and bothered just by the way he looks at me or when I catch a whiff of his cologne as he passes by me in the hall. It's just something about a good-smelling brotha that makes me weak in the knees.

As I walk up Alondra toward Wilmington to Netta's beauty shop, I see my neighborhood haters and crew. Damn, I don't feel like dealing with Monica and them today. It's already bad enough having a quiz I'm not prepared for.

Instead of going straight, I make a right by the Miracle Market and cut through the back way up Kemp, just to avoid confrontation.

"That's just like a sell-out, running from Black folks," Felicia yells, loud enough so the whole block can hear. She's such a broad. And, did she just call me a sell-out? What the hell? I'm sure Misty had something to do with that coined phrase. Otherwise, how would they know I was dating a White dude, because that's exactly what that comment means. She's the only other link between the haters at South Bay High and the haters around the way.

Ignoring Felicia's comment, I make a left on Greenleaf, crossing over Wilmington to where Netta's shop is located. Her sign's so bright I'm sure astronauts in space can see it. As I approach Netta's Never Nappy Beauty Shop, I see Mama and Netta through the front window chatting up a storm. I hope they're not talking about my quiz.

I reach into my little wannabe Coach purse and pull out the charm bag I made this morning. Usually Mama has me write something on the bag in a particular color. But this morning when I made the bag, she just listed the ingredients and measurements on her note. Nothing more.

"Princess Jayd, why you standing outside? Are you waiting on a handout, like Pam?" Netta says through the intercom as she stops scratching Mama's scalp to buzz me through the door.

"God don't like ugly, Netta," Mama says, defending Pam.

She's got a real soft spot for the needy, especially crack heads.

"Oh, Lynn Mae. I was just teasing. Come on in here, girl," Netta says.

"Hi, Ms. Netta. Hi, Mama," I say, walking over to give them each a hug and kiss on the cheek.

"How was your day at school, baby?" Mama asks.

"It was all right," I say, trying to avoid the impending inquisition.

"All right? Sounds like diversion to me," Netta says, applying a hot oil treatment to Mama's scalp. It helps control the dandruff while Mama's hair is locked in her twist all week.

"That's all right, Netta. We'll get to that in a minute. Right now we've got other business to handle."

"Oh, that's right, Lynn Mae. We have a quiz to give," Netta says, smiling at me. Netta has the most intense brown eyes I've ever seen. They're so dark they almost look black, especially up against her light skin. Netta's high-yellow, like my daddy's folk.

"Jayd, hand me my purse, please," Mama says, pointing to the sofa in the lounge area. I love coming to Netta's shop. It's so inviting, bright, and tranquil, even amid the sounds of running water, blow-dryers, and sizzling hot combs.

The comfort Netta's shop brings me is odd because ever since I was a little girl, I've hated getting my hair done. I can remember when I was about five years old, my mom came to pick me up from my old elementary school, Caldwell, and told me I was going to Netta's to get my hair done, which I thought would be like getting strapped down to a table and having someone saw my head open. I screamed bloody murder. I don't know what I was afraid of, but I've always been a little on the dramatic side. All the same, I don't let anyone touch my head, except Mama.

"Here you go, Mama," I say, handing Mama her oversized

Liz Claiborne bag and sitting down in an empty salon chair, opposite Netta's station. She reaches in and grabs her notebook and reading glasses.

"Stop moving your head, Lynn Mae, or this oil won't settle into your scalp," Netta says, cocking Mama's head to her right.

"I need to put on my glasses so I can see, Netta. Damn, you're so bossy."

"You know, we can do this another time, y'all," I say, trying to get out of this pop quiz any way I can. I could be on the phone with Jeremy or Nellie or studying for my English test.

"Here, Jayd. This is a list of the ingredients in your charm bag from this morning. You need to write next to each one what they're used for. Then, you need to write the word for their combined purpose on the other side of your bag, in the proper color, of course."

She digs through all the junk in her purse: Doublemint gum packs and wrappers, a sunglass case, a huge billfold wallet, tiny bags of herbs, extra earrings, rings and other jewelry, pictures of everybody's kids but her own, and finally, her personal pouch. Inside Mama's pouch are all the important things: ID and credit cards, an extra bottle of Paris perfume, her portable prayer book, a Rosary, and her pens. Mama hands me seven multicolored pens and shoos me away with her right hand as Netta talks about her purse.

"Lynn Mae, I don't know why there's always so much crap in your bag. Now, you know what they say: You can tell how much junk a person's got in their life by how much junk they got in their trunk, or in your case, purse," Netta says.

"You know what, Netta?" Mama says, stuffing everything back inside her purse. "Mind your own business, which is my hair at the moment. And you, lil' Miss Jayd, get to work. I have a feeling you're going to need as much time as you can get."

Mama's right about that because I have no idea what to do about anything, especially not Jeremy. Can I trust him with my heart? Or will he just break it like KJ? And that's another reason I'm not ready to commit to a relationship, because I can't separate one man from the other. Yes, at the beginning it's all great and grand, and yes, at the beginning they're each very different from each other. But, I think that's because I'm seeing what I want to see, which is a second chance at love.

"Girl, what's on your mind?" Netta says, seeing what Mama doesn't because she's got her head under water. I haven't started yet.

"I'll tell you what's on her mind. It's those damn little boys she's running after," Mama says. "She ain't got time for her spirit work, schoolwork, or nothing else for that matter. You better be careful about them boys, Jayd. They'll get your head all twisted up, especially the White ones," Mama says as Netta takes the long water hose connected to the sink and rinses Mama's hair.

"Oh, Lynn Mae, you act like you ain't never been in love before. Ignore your mama, Jayd. She's just hatin'," Netta says, laughing at her use of my language.

"Oh, I know you didn't just call somebody a hater, Miss Netta," Mama says, ready to jump out the chair. I guess it doesn't matter what age you are. Nobody likes being called a hater.

"She's just jealous because it's been a long time since she had two men fighting over her. And Jayd, your Mama told me about the new White boy you're dating. Back home, White men used to salivate over Lynn Mae," Netta adds, on the verge of a good story, I assume.

"Netta, don't make me get out this chair," Mama says, sounding more relaxed than she means to. She can't help but be relaxed when Netta's scrubbing her head with home-made shampoo—the scents of lavender and eucalyptus rise with the steam from the hot water in the sink.

"As I was saying, White men used to salivate over your mama. Thank God we didn't have octoroon balls in those days."

"Funny you mention White men's fascination with Black women. A teacher mentioned something similar to me the other day, and it really pissed me off," I say, remembering my disturbing conversation with Mrs. Bennett. She really got under my skin, and so did Carly's punk-ass comments on Saturday night.

"What teacher?" Mama asks, trying to look up at me through her shampoo-soaked head.

"Oh, Mama, you know who," I say.

"Not that heffa Mrs. Bennett, I hope." Mama hates Mrs. Bennett from every story I've ever told her. I didn't really want to get into this today, but it's still bothering me, and it has a little bit to do with why I haven't fully committed to Jeremy. What if I'm just a fading curiosity for Jeremy, like the broad said?

"Yes, of course it was her. And she basically told me that White boys, especially the White boy I'm dating right now, all have uncontrollable curiosities about us little colored girls," I say, waiting for Mama to go off about Mrs. Bennett's stupid ideas, but she never does.

"Not that I want to agree with Mrs. Bennett, but she does have a good point, Jayd. From my experience, White boys do like Black girls, and some even fall in love with them. But, more often than not, it's just a simple curiosity which usually ends up hurting the girls more than the boys." I'm shocked that Mama thinks this way—more shocked that she agrees with Mrs. Bennett.

"Yeah, Jayd, you better listen to your mama on this one.

She knows what she's talking about when it comes to those White men. They courted Lynn Mae from the time she was a little girl. Every White woman in New Orleans had it out for your mama."

"Netta, please don't start filling that girl's head with all those damn stories," Mama says as Netta rinses her head clean, making a squeaking sound as her hands tightly pull the water from Mama's shiny hair. Taking the towel tucked into Mama's cape, Netta covers Mama's head with it and leads her back to the station to blow-dry Mama's hair straight before setting it.

"I wouldn't need to if you would just tell the girl yourself. Her path is obviously very similar to yours, even if she doesn't have your green eyes and it's a different time and place. The bottom line is to be careful; you never know what's in a man's head." And with that last comment Netta turns the blow-dryer on full blast, leaving me to concentrate on my quiz.

"You need to have that done before you leave the shop," Mama yells over the loud noise, pointing to my paper and many colored pens. "If your path is similar to mine, you'll need to become an expert in your spirit work to help you walk it." Even though I'm still confused about Jeremy, I'm more confident about my abilities to master my spirit work ever since whipping up that batch of cupcakes for him. Although I'm still not sure if I put enough him-never-leave-me potion in them, since it wasn't technically part of the recipe. I guess I'll just have to trust that Jeremy wants to be with me for me, and not because I'm his mocha for the month.

~ 13 ~
I Said, She Said

"Uppity, who me?
'Cause now I'm speaking my thoughts, no longer secrets."

—KINA

When I get to school this morning, the vibe is chill. I'm a little nervous about confronting Mrs. Bennett. But, I'm more nervous about the impending backlash from her, no matter how this thing turns out. I'm going to repeat everything she said to me verbatim, and I'm going to tell her what she can do with her words.

Walking into the main hall, I notice my girls already at my locker, waiting for the dish of the day. I've been debating whether or not to tell them about this morning's hearing. I'm not sure they'll really care. They already see me as never being able to shut my mouth about the injustice of our school. But going up against Mrs. Bennett's enough for them to think I've gone completely mad.

"Hey, girl. What's up?" Mickey asks.

"What's up is the latest on your boy toy," Nellie says, not waiting for a good morning, hello, or anything before getting to the point. "Misty told KJ she saw Jeremy in the mall with this girl named Tania a few weeks ago. Apparently, they had a thing over the summer."

"Oh, I know that girl. She has gym with me," Mickey says. "I think she's Persian or something."

"Yeah, I've seen her around. She's barely here, though. You know her, Jayd. She's tall, brown eyes and hair, big horse-tooth smile. Hangs out with the other absentee girls," Nellie says, referring to a small group of hella rich girls who ditch every day to go shopping, get their nails done, play tennis, or whatever other activity they think supersedes school.

"As vivid as your description is Nellie, I still can't picture who you're referring to. And besides, what difference does it make? We just started dating. A few weeks ago Jeremy could have seen me walking through the mall with KJ." For a minute, I remember splitting a Cinnabon with KJ. We did have our good times.

"Yeah, but aren't you the least bit concerned that she could want him back?" Nellie has too much time on her hands.

"Nellie, I've got bigger fish to fry," I say as I slam my locker door shut and head for first period. "And, if she wants him, he doesn't seem to want her because I've never heard anything about this girl."

"Even more reason to be suspicious," Mickey says in between sucks of her Blow Pop.

"Nobody's got to be suspicious. Have you two ever heard of a little thing called trust?" I ask.

"Yeah, it's right after 'trifling' in the dictionary. And, your man's just that if he ain't told you about Tania by now. At least you knew about KJ's other broads. It's worse when you don't know what's coming at you," Mickey says.

"KJ didn't exactly tell me about Trecee, now, did he?" I shout as they walk toward their class, and I toward mine.

"That was an exception. She was crazy. This is just Jeremy keeping secrets from you, and you need to front his ass on it, ASAP," Mickey says with Nellie nodding in agreement.

"Yeah, Jayd. Not that I believe everything Misty reports, but I do kinda remember them being together last year. Not really my crowd. But, maybe you should ask Chance about it. See you at break," she shouts before the bell for first period rings. As if I don't have enough drama to deal with.

I barely paid attention to Spanish class today thinking about Mrs. Bennett and now Jeremy's ex. I wish I could picture this girl Tania. And not that I'm really worried about it, but why didn't he tell me he recently dated someone up here? Walking toward Ms. Toni's office, I see Misty lingering in the hall, as usual. I hope she doesn't know about the hearing. All I need is for her to report back to everyone I'm in trouble with Mrs. Bennett. By the time she finishes telling her version, I'm sure she'll have me crying, cussed out, and near expulsion.

"Hey, Jayd. How's your new man doing?"

"Shut up, Misty," I say, passing her by and going straight into the ASB office. I don't have time to deal with her bullshit right now.

"Touchy, touchy. I guess you heard about his flavor over the summer, huh," she says to my back. She's such a broad.

"Good morning, Jayd. Are you ready to face Mrs. Bennett?" Ms. Toni asks, meeting me outside her office door.

"I guess so. How about you?" I say, realizing she's taking quite a risk herself, going up against an influential teacher like Mrs. Bennett.

"Oh, girl, please. Mrs. Bennett doesn't scare me. And besides, I live for justice." She leans in the door and makes an announcement to the crowded ASB room. "I'll be back by break. Get to work on those Homecoming signs and don't make too much noise," she says to Reid and the rest of the ASB clique.

"Have you considered running for Homecoming Princess," Ms. Toni asks me as we walk down the hall toward the main office.

"Are you trying to distract me from our meeting? Because I know you can't be serious."

"Why not? I think you'd make a great princess. You're smart, beautiful, and you've got courage. Those are all the qualities you need to win."

"You forgot the most important quality of them all—popularity," I say, opening the door for her to walk through. The air is thick with tension, and all eyes are on us. Every secretary, counselor, and administrator is in the main office this morning. I'm sure the other teachers wanted to be here, but they do have to teach. Luckily, Misty's mother isn't here yet. Otherwise, I'm sure she'd have a front seat too.

"Good morning, everyone," Ms. Toni says, taking some of the heat off me. I follow her as she walks straight into the principal's office, not waiting for a return greeting from anyone.

"Good morning, Mrs. Crowe," Mrs. Bennett says as Ms. Toni walks in ahead of me. "Jayd." After Ms. Toni takes her seat next to the Special Needs counselor, Mr. Schaeffer, there's only one seat left, and it's directly across from Mrs. Bennett, and that's just fine with me.

"Good morning," I say, not wanting to seem rude to the other adults in the room.

"Well, let's get started, shall we? The principal had urgent school business to tend to. So, it'll just be the four of us present," Mr. Schaeffer says, starting the meeting. "Miss Jayd Jackson has filed a formal complaint against Mrs. Bennett. Can you please tell us the nature of your complaint, Miss Jackson? And, speak clearly so the recorder can hear."

"Last week, while I was outside her classroom waiting for a friend, Mrs. Bennett called me into her room," I begin, only to be rudely interrupted by Mrs. Bennett.

"Uhmm, actually, Mr. Schaeffer, Jayd came in of her own free will. I asked her what she was doing near my room, since she's not a student of mine this year and it was well after the last bell rang. That's when she rudely stepped into my room." Oh, no this bitch ain't about to lie right up in the office.

"That's not true," I say. My heart's beating so fast I want to jump across the table and choke her. "I was waiting for my friend, and she called me in. Why would I willingly go into her room?"

"Well, that's why we're here, Jayd," Mr. Schaeffer says, but I'm not quite sure what he means. I look at Ms. Toni, and she quickly intervenes.

"What are you talking about, Mr. Schaeffer?" Ms. Toni asks.

"Well, it seems Mrs. Bennett is concerned about Jayd's aggressive behavior toward her and doesn't want her anywhere near her class for the remainder of the semester. And, we'll have to see about next year, since you are on the A.P. track," Mr. Schaeffer says as Mrs. Bennett smiles like she's just won the battle.

"What?" I exclaim. "She called me into her room and then proceeded to talk to me in her usual racist tone, and she's filing a complaint against me? Are you serious?" I ask Mrs. Bennett, who's sitting calmly in her seat, like we're wasting her time.

"Jayd, it's your word against hers. And, right now, you're displaying the exact demeanor she's complaining about. As for the racist exchange that supposedly took place, we have no proof." Mr. Schaeffer has already made up his mind. Jeremy was right about Mrs. Bennett's power, and Ms. Toni looks completely defeated.

"Proof?" I ask. "You need proof when she has a reputation for not liking any people but her own and for belittling students in class? What kind of school allows teachers like her to get off scot-free?" I know my speech is falling on deaf ears at this point, but I refuse to let her feel like she's won a thing.

"Miss Jackson, please calm down and lower your voice. Now, I think you owe Mrs. Bennett an apology for speaking to her disrespectfully. Insubordination is cause for detention under the student bylaws and constitution. But, we'll let it slide this time." This fool must be tripping if he thinks I'm going to apologize to this broad.

"In all fairness, Mr. Schaeffer," Ms. Toni says, "why would Jayd waste her time filing a complaint if she didn't have grounds to do so? As you pointed out, Jayd's an A.P. student and doesn't have time to waste. She could be in English class right now. But instead she's here standing up to a teacher whom she has to face in class next year. Doesn't that deserve some credit?" It seems Mrs. Bennett's not the only teacher with Mr. Schaeffer's ear because he appears to be listening.

"Yes, it does. But, unfortunately it's a case of she said, she said. My hands are tied. For the record, Jayd, unless you have official school business, don't go near Mrs. Bennett's room," he says as he rises from his seat and begins to head out the door. "Off the record, I think you should both apologize and put this ugly episode behind you. Most issues like this one are better resolved between the two parties. Not in an official meeting." Well, I agree with him there. I stare hard across the table at Mrs. Bennett, letting her know this ain't over. I'm nowhere near finished with her.

"Well, Jayd, Mrs. Crowe," Mrs. Bennett says, rising from her seat and walking toward the door. "You are both way out of your element."

"We'll see about that," Ms. Toni says. That last comment from Mrs. Bennett gives me an instant hot flash, like I'm about to have another déjà vu experience, but it never comes.

"Jayd, I'm so sorry about this," Ms. Toni says as we walk back to her office before the bell for break rings. "I had no idea she'd do something like this."

"It's all right," I say, feeling sorry for her. She really put herself on the line for me, and we both got burned. "She'll get hers sooner or later." As I walk away from Ms. Toni I feel the power of my statement. Mrs. Bennett will get what's coming to her, and I'll make sure of that. Maybe not today, but someday.

After the hearing with Mrs. Bennett, I decide to get to government class early to see if I can catch Jeremy, but to no avail. I guess today's another high-surf day. I sit in my usual seat, waiting for Jeremy to walk in.

"Good morning, sexy lady," Jeremy says, hugging me from behind and kissing me on my neck. As he sits down next to me, all I can think about is my conversation with Mama and Netta yesterday and the hearing with Mrs. Bennett this morning. I want to talk to him about it, but I'm still so hot I don't think I can without crying. Besides, the class is hella noisy, even though everyone's seated at their desk. Before I can say a word, the bell rings, and Mrs. Peterson begins class.

"Okay, class, today you need to read chapter three and answer the study questions at the end of the chapter. Please choose a study partner and turn in one combined paper by the end of the period. I have tests to grade, so don't bother me, and whisper quietly amongst yourselves," Mrs. Peterson says, settling in behind her desk. Jeremy and I look at each other and smile. We don't even have to ask anymore.

"Are you the writer or am I?" Jeremy asks, reaching for his backpack.

"Your handwriting is much neater than mine. Why don't you be the writer this time," I say, telling the truth. My handwriting is so bad, most of the time I can't even read it. He pulls out his textbook and a pen. I hand him a piece of notebook paper, and he puts both our names at the top.

"Jayd Jackson and Jeremy Weiner. Sounds good together, doesn't it?" he says with a sly smile.

"Yes, it does," I say, smiling right back at him.

"So, Jayd, what are we waiting for? When can I start calling you my girlfriend?" Jeremy asks, looking so sincere.

"How did we get to this from class work?" I ask. Jeremy's been trying to get me to commit, but I'm just not sure. KJ's still jocking, and I don't want to write him off completely, at least not as my friend. Not yet, anyway, per everyone's advice. And this flavor-of-the-month thing is still bothering me.

"Jayd, you and I both know what we want, don't we? Or, maybe I'm just being presumptuous." Damn, he's beautiful, and he's also hella intelligent. I don't know anybody who ever used the word "presumptuous" voluntarily except for me. Nor could anyone I know be so bossy in such a sweet way. KJ would just tell me that we should be together. See, there I go again comparing and contrasting, like KJ and Jeremy are paragraphs on my English test. That's so unfair, for KJ especially, 'cause at the moment, the brotha's coming up short.

"No, you're not being presumptuous at all. But, you know I'm not ready for all that yet, baby," I say, taking the pen from his right hand.

"What is it?" Jeremy asks, clenching his jaw.

"It's me," I say. He ain't buying it at all. "Look, Jeremy, I want to be with you, but not with all this drama still so fresh. Let's just continue as we are, taking it slow, and building our relationship so that it's right."

"I've waited this long, Jayd. I'm not going anywhere," he says, smiling at me with his perfect teeth on full display. He can certainly change up quickly, but I'm glad he doesn't seem angry anymore. "But, I'm also not going to ask again. The ball's in your court now," he says, handing me our history textbook. "Now get to reading," he orders playfully. I turn to chapter three and start reading.

"You know, the last guy I was with liked to play games, and I'm just no good at it," I say, playing with my braids.

"I'm not playing any games here, Jayd. That's your thing." Oh, no he didn't just go there. Who does he think he is, sassing me like that?

"Jeremy, may I borrow a pencil," interrupts this wannabe White girl who pretends not to be whatever ethnicity she is. I usually don't get jealous about girls talking to Jeremy, but this broad's energy is hella loud and all over my man.

"Sure, Tania. How've you been?" How've you been? Is he reminiscing with an ex-lover right in my face? Damn, I know he has a past, but this chick? And she's in class with us too. What the hell?

"I've been good, Jeremy. How about you?" she asks, flipping her heavy-ass, blow-dried straight, honey golden brown #3 hair over her shoulder, just like a White girl.

"Ah, you know how it is. Everything's chill as usual," he says, sitting up in his chair, fully engaged in this broad's conversation.

"Chill? Well, how are you handling, you know, that whole ugly drug bust thing," she says, whispering like the whole class doesn't already know Jeremy was busted and acquitted, I might add.

"Everything's cool. Thanks for your concern," he says.

"Thanks for the pencil. And let me know if there's anything I can do for you in return," she says, while biting the tip of the pencil. When she turns to walk back to her desk on the other side of the room, the switch in her hips is obviously for Jeremy's benefit.

"What the hell was that?" I ask. I'm trying not to sound too jealous, but, damn, why didn't she just lay the cookies in his lap? That would have been more subtle.

"What was what?" Jeremy asks, laying back in his chair.

"That. Tania, the pencil, all of that. How come you didn't tell me your ex was in class with us?"

Jeremy puts his head down on the desk and starts laughing. "Just a second ago you weren't sure you wanted to be my girl, and now you're jealous. You can't have it both ways, Jayd."

"Something funny, Mr. Weiner?" Mrs. Peterson asks from her desk. The otherwise uninterested class looks up from their work and at us, hoping for drama.

"Yeah, actually, there is. Did you know that Jayd's an excellent chess player?" Jeremy answers, being a smart-ass, amusing the rest of the class. They may think he's funny, but I don't.

"Very funny, Jeremy. Now, get back to work, everyone," Mrs. Peterson says, returning to her stack of papers.

"Jayd, I'm no good at this kind of shit. All I know is I like you. And, if you like me, then we should be together. But, like I said before, there's no pressure from my end. Take your time."

Yeah, but how long will he wait? I don't want to lose him to Tania or anyone else. If he's a good guy, he'll wait. But even the best guys won't wait forever, especially not when there's a flock of females waiting to take my place. Just look at what happened with KJ. I've got to make up my mind, and fast. But, I'm just not sure which way to go. We'll just have to talk about this more at lunch.

~ 14 ~
Men's Stuff

"If you wanna do right, all day woman/
You gotta be a do right, all night man."

—ARETHA FRANKLIN

Before meeting up with Jeremy and his crew for a rare on-campus lunch, I decide to stop by South Central to say what's up to my girls. When I arrive, Nellie and Mickey are already sitting on a bench, chatting it up. I sit down next to Nellie and join the conversation.

"Hey, girls," I say. "What's up with y'all?"

"Well, good morning, Miss Jayd," Nellie says snidely. "How's your morning going so far?"

"I think what Nellie means to say is: Where the hell you been, girl?" Mickey asks. "It seems like we haven't seen you in days," Mickey says in between sips of Diet Coke.

"That's because we haven't. She's been spending all her time with her new man." It's not like Nellie to be jealous, but I swear that's what I'm feeling from her now.

"Okay, Nellie. What now? I thought we'd already discussed your problems with Jeremy. But, because you're such a good friend," I say as I place my arm around her shoulders, trying to lighten the mood, "we can do it again, if it'll make you feel better."

"My problem is not with Jeremy; it's with you. How dare you not chill with your girls at lunch sometimes," Nellie says, putting her arm around my waist, letting me know she's not jealous and only missing me. I sure am glad, because the last thing I need is one of my girls turning on me right now.

"Well, you know you two are always welcome to join us off campus for lunch. You just can't take the whole damn crew with you," I say, gesturing with my free arm around the quad. Just as I do this, KJ comes over to finish where we left off yesterday, I assume. I hope he doesn't touch me again. It weakens my defenses against his player games.

"Well, well, well. If it isn't Miss Jayd Jackson," KJ says, grabbing my free hand.

"Hey, KJ," my girls chime in.

"Hey, y'all. Did your girl Jayd here tell you that we're picking out a reunion song?"

"KJ, don't tell lies to my girls; they know the real deal," I say, pushing him away, guilty about letting him hold my hand a minute too long. "Look, y'all can always come and hang with us. I'm about to go over there now. Are you two coming or not?" I say to my girls, ignoring KJ.

"Well, I'm not too comfortable being around all those White boys. It's bad for a sistah's reputation, you know what I'm saying, Jayd?" Mickey says, telling the truth. If word gets around Compton that Mickey's hanging out with surfer boys, other girls on the block might think she's getting soft. And that's not good for her reputation as a hard-core gangster's girl, indeed.

"Yeah, Jayd, and my reputation is solid as not hanging around dudes who sell drugs," Nellie says, unrelenting in her judgment of Jeremy as the biggest drug cartel leader she's ever known. I guess she's never really met Mickey's man. Or, if she has, it's different to her because he's Black and from the hood.

"I won't be ignored, Jayd," KJ says, stepping in front of me, blocking my escape route.

"I'm not ignoring you, KJ," I say, mapping out a new path

through the quad. "I just don't have anything to say to you. When will you give up on us? I have moved on, KJ, and you need to do the same." My patience is wearing thin. "Well, since no one's interested in going to hang out on the other side of the quad, I'm out," I say, eyeing my girls, moving KJ out of my way and walking toward Jeremy and his friends, who are on the other side, completely oblivious to what's going on over here. The only time the White side pays any attention to us is if they think a riot's about to go down.

"Not so fast, Jayd," KJ says, grabbing my left hand and turning me around to face him. "We're not finished. Now, I've played this little game with you long enough because you've played so many with me," he says, sounding like he's about to say something really profound, which would be new for KJ. "But, enough's enough. I deserve another chance, Jayd. And if I'm going to be replaced by somebody," he says, pulling me in close to him, forcing me to smell the Lucky cologne, "it's not going to be some drug-dealing, surfer boy." KJ's really upset, and I'm angry too, but still I can't help but notice how nice he looks today. He's wearing a Steelers jersey with some baggy jeans—Levi's, I assume. I love the way his clothes hang off his muscular frame. I must admit, there's just something about a Black man with a nice body who smells good that really gets a girl going.

"You've got to stop this, right now, Jayd. People are really talking about y'all, and not in a good way," KJ says, releasing me from his tight embrace. Nellie, Mickey, and everyone else within earshot are now staring at us, waiting to see what'll happen next.

"If you haven't noticed by now, KJ, I don't really give a damn what you or anyone else at this school think of me and who I date," I say, not wanting to make more of a scene than we already have. But, I agree. Enough is enough.

"You need to care, Jayd, because you don't know what

you're getting yourself into," he says, hinting at I don't know what.

"Is there something you want to say to me, KJ?" I say, offering him a chance to fess up if there's anything to tell.

"I just did. You need to pick your company a little more wisely, Jayd. Anyone who cares about you will tell you the same thing: this dude's bad news. And, you're only going to get hurt in the end." This is the most sincere I've ever heard KJ talk to me. Well, except whenever he was trying to get in my pants or under my skirt. And I do have to admit he's right. Everybody's telling me pretty much the same thing, except for Mickey, that is. But she's really not all that excited about the two of us getting together, either.

"You mean, like I did at the end of our relationship, KJ? Or, did you conveniently forget you just broke my heart a few weeks ago?" I say.

"Good point," Nellie says. She, Mickey, Shae, and Tony across the way are watching us go back and forth like they're watching Venus and Serena on the tennis court. Everyone else has moved on to getting their lunch.

"You're right, Jayd. I did hurt you, and I'm sorry. If I could do it all over again, I would never let you go," he says, taking my left hand into his right, casting the player's web. Luckily, I know a spider when I see one. And, no matter how cute he may be, I know his bite is lethal.

"Your player bullshit doesn't work on me anymore, KJ," I say. I must admit, though, the thought of hugging KJ is very appealing. I would love it if we could just be friends, but I think that's the farthest thing from his mind. The way he's looking at me now makes me think if I were to drop the cookies in his lap at this very moment, he would take it and run. Well, too bad second chances only happen in the movies. The pain from our breakup is still too fresh on my mind.

"It's not bullshit, Jayd," KJ says. "What can I do or say to make you believe me?"

"You can give me some space and let me go, KJ." Before KJ releases my hand, Misty sees us from the lunch line and heads our way. Shit, just what I need—more drama.

"I don't need this right now, KJ. If you're really and truly sincere about changing your ways, then maybe we can be friends. I'm willing to talk about that. But not right now. I'm late for a lunch date, and your girl's headed this way," I say as he finally releases me and looks in Misty's direction. I give my girls the peace sign and grab my backpack from the ground.

"I wish you'd stop calling her that. She's not my girl. And, for the record, the only girl I'm interested in right now is you," he says. But I'm already running off to meet Jeremy and his friends. Talking to my girls will do me no good. I guess I'm going to have to wait until I get home to deal with these issues.

When I get home, Mama's out back, working. There's a small patch of grass in between her spirit room and the fence separating our yard from the neighbor's behind us on Dwight Street. This is where Mama does all the gritty work: making and molding black soap and shea butter, planting her herbs and other essential ingredients, and other mysteries I'm not yet privy to.

"Hey, baby. I didn't hear you come through the gate. How was school?" Mama asks, looking up from her big, cast-iron pot filled with shea butter. Mama makes the best shea butter ever. I don't know exactly what she puts in it, but it works wonders on my scars and dry feet. It also smells really good, like lavender and cedar.

"Mama, KJ's such a little punk. He makes my skin crawl," I say, taking my backpack off and sitting down next to her on the grass, cleaning my hands in the bowl of cold water next to the iron pot. I take a small portion of the shea butter and begin to mold and shape it into a bar.

"Oh, Lord. What's the boy done now?" Mama asks, pouring more lavender oil into the pot. As Mama kneads the shea butter with her hands, I notice her skin is glistening from her work. No wonder she's ageless; it's a natural by-product of her work environment.

"During lunch, he came over to me and started talking a bunch of crap. He acts like he didn't just dump me last month for some other broad, never mind the fact she was crazy," I say, pounding the butter harder than necessary.

"It's not the butter's fault KJ's a jackass, Jayd," Mama says, gently stopping my hands with hers. "You know me and your daddy don't always have the best relationship," Mama says.

"Yes, Mama, I'm well aware," I say, returning to the gentle motions of molding the butter bar.

"Well, smart-ass, you should also be well aware of the fact that I'm the one in control of our relationship. If I wanted to, I could get your daddy back in my good favor. I just don't want him anymore," she says as bluntly as if she were talking to Ms. Netta.

"Mama, that's my grandfather you're talking about. And, that's just way too much information," I say, turning my head like I just saw something I wasn't supposed to. If I could cover my ears, I would. But the shea butter is all over my hands.

"He may be a grandfather to you, but he's a man to me. And only one of many, I might add."

"Mama, I don't know if I want to hear about all of this . . ."

"Jayd, what do you think? All of these children and grandchildren just appeared? No. We have to have relationships with men to get families here. But, men don't necessarily have relationships back with women. I know this may be a

little over your head right now, since you don't want to see
me as a woman," Mama says while placing small bars of shea
butter on wax paper, ready to individually wrap and label.
"But you as the female have all the power in relationships.
Think about this household, Jayd. You have lived in a house
full of men all your life and you haven't learned that yet?"
Mama sounds just like Bryan. What am I not seeing about
this whole male/female power trip?

"So, what you're saying is to be more forceful in the way I
deal with KJ?" I ask, assuming she means to act more like she
does with Daddy, Jay, and my uncles.

"No, Jayd. I mean you need to be as sweet as honey to get
what you want, and to get them to see that what you want is
what they want too," Mama says, retrieving a small, yellow
pouch from her pocket. "This should help you be a little
sweeter," she says, sprinkling the yellow powder from the
pouch onto my butter bar. Whatever it is gives off a sweet
aroma.

"What is that?" I ask. "It smells like night-blooming jas-
mine, honeysuckle, and Egyptian musk, and something else I
can't quite make out."

"Honey," she says. "Put this on your body every morning
after your shower until it's gone. You and the object of your
desire will be far more pliable. Now, I'm sure you have plenty
of homework or something to do. I need to finish my work,
chile." I knew Mama would help me figure out what to do
about KJ and Jeremy both pressuring me, each in his own
way, to be their woman. I just need to be sweet, and the
problem will solve itself. No more fighting with KJ or arguing
with my girls or Jeremy. I'm taking the sweet road from now
on. We'll see if this sweet shea butter works on my attitude.
And, after today's little flirt fest with Tania, Jeremy needs to
watch himself too. Both these dudes are working my nerves,
and so are the haters, as usual.

~ 15 ~
That Green-Eyed Devil

*"Trying to crush my world with jealousy/
And I'm about to catch a fit."*

—MARY J. BLIGE

Bryan actually beat me to the shower this morning, so I had to eat breakfast first, which is just not right. I need my morning shower to get me ready for the new day's drama as I watch the night's layers of dreams and sweat go down the drain. How's a sistah supposed to start her new day of sweetness off right if I don't get in the bathroom before the Negroes in this house funk it up?

"Bryan," I say, tapping on the door. The water's not that loud, so I know he can hear me.

"I'm almost done, Queen Jayd," he says. Why is he testing me? When he opens the door, I'm ready with hella attitude. Oh, no, I'm supposed to be sweet today. Got to be cool.

"Well, if it isn't little miss 'I always go first in the mornings,'" he says in a singsong voice, walking out the bathroom like a diva, wearing nothing but a raggedy blue towel around his waist. These men up in here can work a nerve.

"What the hell, Bryan? Are you PMSing or whatever the male equivalent is? You know I have to catch the bus. I don't have time for your childish games," I say, pushing him aside and stepping into the steamy bathroom.

"You don't own this house, Jayd. I'm saying that's why you can't keep a man. You have this attitude like you're not only better than us, but you don't need or respect us. And that isn't attractive in a girl at all. Think about it," he says, taking off his towel and smacking me with it hard before running into the boys' room.

"I hope you catch pneumonia, you little punk," I yell, but not so loud that I'll wake up everyone else. What the hell kind of day am I going to have if it starts out like this? Bryan reminds me of the gnome in *The Lord of the Rings, Part Three*. I never know which side he's on, and he makes my skin crawl. But, I still have to love him. And there may be some truth to Bryan's words. Am I too hard on these dudes? I'm taking my time dealing with both of them, and I can't leave Jeremy hanging indefinitely if I'm going to be his girl all the way. I also have to make up my mind whether or not I'm going to be KJ's friend; the sooner the better. Maybe today will be peaceful enough for me to think things through clearly.

The bus ride was uneventful and unusually quiet this morning. Not too many extra stops and there weren't too many people, just enough to make it interesting, but not annoying. And, for the first time this school year, the bus driver smiled at me and said good morning. Usually, he doesn't even look my direction.

With all of this newfound peace on my morning ride, I had some time to think about my options. I'm wrong every time I judge a guy, and I always end up getting hurt. What if Jeremy's an undercover player and KJ can change? I know. It's a twisted thought given KJ's patterns of behavior, but anything's possible. I mean, I don't really know Jeremy that well, and if my friends are tripping off me being with him, maybe they know more than I do. I'll try to talk to Nellie at break and get her honest and unbiased opinion, which may be impossible. But, she's my girl, and I'm willing to listen to her.

* * *

Unfortunately, South Bay High isn't as peaceful as the Metro line. As soon as I step foot on campus, I hear the rumors Misty has started, based off nothing but made-up bullshit in her twisted little world. Apparently, I wouldn't give it up to KJ because I'm too uptight, but Jeremy's just the one to loosen me up, or that's what Mickey told me when I got to my locker this morning. Now it's break, and my girls and I need to have a meeting. How am I supposed to be sweet with all this going on? As I walk toward the quad, I stop at the vending machines to get some Fritos where Misty and Shae are also hangin' this morning.

"So Jayd and that White boy done it, huh, Misty?" Shae says, passing her a water bottle from the vending machine. They act like I'm not standing right here. Shae's never liked me, but she's usually smart enough to stay out of Misty's mix. But, this is her chance to prove I'm the sell-out she thought I was when I first got to South Bay High.

"I don't know. She's kinda uptight about giving up the cookies. Like she's the damn Queen of Sheba or somebody," Misty says, looking to make sure I'm within earshot. What a broad.

"Well, everybody ain't gone wait on her ass, especially not no White boy," Shae says, walking toward South Central.

"Yeah, and not even the Black one's still on her jock. He's slowly fading from her wait list too," Misty says, following Shae. I should go over there and set them both straight. But for what? Them heffas ain't got nothing on me.

"Hey, Jayd. Did you get me some chips?" Nellie asks, looking around the quad to see if Byron's outside yet. She's been jocking him on the low ever since his party. It's only break and it's already ninety degrees by the beach. By lunch, it'll be hot as hell out here.

"Not yet. Where's Mickey? She's usually not late for the morning news," I say, looking for her around the quad. All I see is KJ in the distance, walking this way.

"She had to stay after class and finish last night's homework. That girl needs to get her priorities straight or she'll find herself back in the eleventh grade next year."

"Why she didn't finish it last night? It ain't like she got to go to work or nothing."

"No, but she does have to go to her man's and check in, which could take all night, knowing them."

"W. T. M. I., Nellie. Way too much info."

"Hey, Jayd, Nellie," KJ says as he walks up to us, blocking my clear view of the ocean.

"Hey, KJ. Where's your entourage?" Nellie asks while waiting for the vending machine to release her chips.

"Very funny, Nellie. Jayd, can I talk to you for a minute?" KJ asks with that charming smile of his.

"No," I say flatly. The last time this brotha talked to me, I wound up falling for his bullshit again and that ain't happening. But, I will try and maintain my sweetness.

"Jayd, we really need to talk. Misty's out to get you because she thinks you're playing me, and you know how she is." Is he actually defending her? Has he lost his mind? "And, I don't want you to think I'll be the same if we get back together, 'cause I won't," KJ says, taking my hand and looking into my eyes. "I love you, Jayd. I meant it when I first said it, and I mean it now. I won't put any pressure on you for sex, and you'll be my only girl, for as long as you want to be." Damn, this brotha's good.

"KJ, you think Jayd's just sitting around waiting for you to apologize?" Nellie says, snapping me back into reality.

"Yeah," I say, trying to ignore the fact he's got me remembering how good his arms feel. "It's not that easy, KJ. Remember, we've already been down this road."

"Don't lie, Jayd. You know you miss us," he says, as full of himself as ever before. "And I miss us too. I miss picking you up from work. I miss seeing Mama and talking to your uncle without it being uncomfortable, like I'm not supposed to be there when we both know I am." As KJ leans in to kiss me, I step back, letting him fall forward, almost losing his footing.

"Damn, KJ. You got played," Nellie says loud enough for anyone within earshot to hear. Luckily his boys haven't arrived yet. KJ doesn't look amused.

"What the hell, KJ? I know you know I'm dating Jeremy. So why would you try to kiss me, especially in front of everyone, like we're still together," I yell at him, pissed that I'm secretly flattered by his gesture.

"I just got caught up, that's all. You could've let me sneak one in, though. No girl's ever complained about my kisses," he says, licking his lips like he's L.L. Cool J.

"Well, find yourself someone else to get caught up with. Nellie, let's go find Mickey," I say, grabbing her arm and pulling her away from the vending machines and KJ. That's when I notice Misty, Shae, and the rest of the folks hangin' in South Central watching the whole scene. Poor KJ. I know his rep is taking a blow, but he needs to give it up. I'm just not interested in getting hurt by him again.

"This ain't over, Jayd. We deserve another shot at us. I'm calling you after school, so you better answer," he says, flipping open his cell and pressing send. "There's Luda, right on time," he says, referring to my ring tone. "So, don't act like you don't hear the phone when I call you later. We'll work on resetting my personal ring tone later. I'm insulted to ring with the masses." He must be the cockiest dude I've ever met.

"Whatever, KJ," I say, leading Nellie away from KJ and the spectators. "I'm so sick of this. When's he going to give up?" I ask, not really expecting an answer.

"When you give it up," Nellie says, smacking on her Nacho Cheese Doritos. "Men love that shit," she says in between bites.

"What shit are you referring to," I ask, wondering where Jeremy is. I haven't seen him all morning. I wonder if word travels as fast on the White side of campus as it does over here.

"The hard-to-get shit. Like Beyonce says: 'I know you want to taste it, but I'm gone make you chase it,'" Nellie says, popping her booty like Beyonce does in her video.

"You're so silly." I giggle, pushing her in the arm. "And, I'm not playing. KJ's a little too much for me," I say, telling Nellie the truth.

"He wasn't a few weeks ago," she says, stopping in front of Mickey's class and turning to look me in the eye. "Look, Jayd. Now, you know I'm not rooting for either one of these dudes. But, KJ's definitely the better of the two, in my opinion. I think you should definitely make him sweat for the way he treated you," she says, pausing her lecture to peek her head through the classroom door, looking for Mickey. She nods her head at Mickey, I assume, and continues.

"You have to give it to KJ. He's really humbled himself for you," Nellie says, smacking on her Doritos.

"What?" I say, a little louder than I meant to. But that's a shocking statement coming from her. "Humbled himself how, Nellie?" I ask with my hand on my hip, in full Foxy Brown mode.

"When have you ever seen KJ, or any brotha, chase after a girl as hard as KJ's chasing after you? Doesn't that warrant some sort of forgiveness, Jayd?" I hate to admit it, but she has a good point. But still, I'm not backing down.

"Forgiveness, yes. Forgetting and making up, no. I'm not looking backwards," I say, trying to fool myself.

"I'm not saying you should look backwards. I'm just saying you should look at KJ with fresh eyes and be a little nicer to him. He's not such a bad person or you would've never dated him in the first place, right?" Damn, why does she always have to make such good points?

"You just don't want me dating Jeremy," I say, knowing that's only half true.

"It's true, I don't like Jeremy or his little crew. They're not good enough for us, girl," she says just as the bell signaling the end of break rings. At least I know I'll see Jeremy in third period. "When KJ calls this afternoon, pick up the phone," she says, poking her head back through the door to see if Mickey's done yet.

"I'll think about it," I say, remembering my oath to be sweeter. I just pray my being nicer to KJ doesn't mess up my chance with Jeremy. Truth be told, I would consider giving KJ a second chance if I didn't like Jeremy so much from the start. Yeah, KJ's cool and all. But, Jeremy's where it's at for me now, even if I do miss the passion KJ and I shared. Maybe if I talk to KJ and let him see for himself why we can't be together, he'll back off on his own and leave me and Jeremy to ourselves, without his ego being crushed in front of everyone. Okay, I'll talk to him after school. But after Jeremy takes me home. Any time we get to spend alone is precious.

When I get out of class, everyone's rushing as usual to catch a ride or a wave, depending on their priorities. I'm heading to my locker to meet Jeremy when I run into Misty leaving the main office.

"Hey, Jayd. Waiting for the White boy, as usual, huh, girl?" she says, switching her wide hips as she walks by.

"Watch it with those things, girl. They should be registered as lethal weapons," I retort. Actually, her curves are quite flattering. When we were girls, we used to tease each other all the time. But now, I'm sure she took that little joke personally, as I did hers.

"We'll see if KJ thinks so," she says, putting her hands on her hips and turning toward me, ready for a confrontation.

"Is there something you want to say to me, Misty?" I say, returning the pose, less dramatically because my hips aren't as powerful as hers. But, my stare is just as penetrating and gets my point across exactly.

"Are you really that naïve, Jayd?" she says, like she's been dying to ask me this for a while now. "KJ's obviously sprung over your stupid ass, but you could care less," she says, shifting her weight from one side to the other. "And, that trifling-ass little White boy you chose to date instead of him is just insulting to us all."

"I'm sorry, but what business is this of yours?" I ask with much attitude.

"When you hurt someone in my crew, you hurt me. And right now, you're humiliating the sweetest brotha at South Bay High for some White guy who smokes weed and surfs all damn day. I knew you weren't down, but I never pegged you as a sell-out, Jayd," she says, sounding sincere.

"Misty, the last person I'd ever take advice from on anything is you. And, as far as KJ's concerned, I know you're just jealous because you want him for yourself and he still wants me," I say, elevating my already loud voice. "I'm sick of everyone having an opinion on my love life."

"Oh, so you do have a love life now. I knew you'd give it up to him. What, Jayd, afraid you can't handle a brotha?" she says.

"Unlike you, Misty, for me to get what I want from a dude, I don't have to give up anything in return." Just as I shut her up and give all the nosy-ass people listening something to chew on, my cell rings. It's KJ of course.

"Well, aren't you going to answer it," Misty asks, waiting for me to pick up the phone. I wonder if she and KJ planned this little scene. I'm not going to get hyped. I'm staying cool and chilling with my baby. Nothing's going to distract me from our plans today. Not Misty and not KJ. He'll just have to wait until I call him back. And Misty can do whatever she wants. I'm through with her for today. I see my man coming now.

"As pleasant as this little exchange has been, I've got better things to do," I say, leaving Misty standing in the middle of the hall with her hands still on her hips, while I walk to meet my man. He's just what I need right now—some peace.

~ 16 ~
Salt In My Game

"Explorer like Dora these swipers can't swipe me/
My whole aura's so mean in my white tee."

—LUDACRIS

Ever since Jeremy and I started hanging out, my whole vibe has become chill. I used to be so concerned with being stylish like my girls. Now I want to be stylish, yet more laid back, like my new man.

I like my new style. After school, Jeremy and I decide to hang at the Galleria. While walking hand in hand through the mall, I spot this cute white tank top with yellow rhinestones with the Bebe logo across the front. I love Bebe, but I can't afford it, and from what I know they don't have too many sales.

For whatever reason, Jeremy wants to go to Bebe, because if it were up to me, I would've just kept walking by on our way to the escalator, up to the food court.

"Do you like these shoes," Jeremy asks, stopping in front of the store window.

"Those little yellow flip-flops?" I ask, pointing to the cutest sandals I've ever seen.

"Yeah, I think those would look good on your feet," he says, guiding me into the store, past the long sales counter and toward the back, where the lush couches and dressing rooms are. It's so big in here, I could get lost inside.

"Jeremy, I work too hard for my money to spend it all in this store."

"I didn't ask you all that, Lady Jayd," he says, taking the pretty slipper off the display and leading me to the seating area, where a saleslady is waiting and ready to please.

"Size eight, right?" she says, retrieving the shoe from Jeremy's hand before we have a chance to ask. Damn, she's good. When she returns, Jeremy takes off my out-of-season Jordans and slips the very pretty and dainty sandals onto my ashy feet. Damn, these shoes feel like butter.

"Jeremy, why are you teasing me?" I say, posing in the mirror.

"Oh, those look really nice on your feet," the saleslady says. "Have you seen the tee to match?" she asks, taking a white tank off the rack and putting it against my chest so I can see my reflection.

"Oh, that's cute. And I love how the yellow rhinestones shine on both the shoes and the tank," I say, feeling as pretty as a princess.

"You've got to get them both. They go so well with your complexion," she says, smiling at my reflection in the mirror.

"Oh, I wish I could. But the shoes alone are one paycheck for me," I respond, feeling a little less pretty already. Jeremy momentarily disappears into the vast store and leaves me to dream about being able to afford a $60 tank top and $120 pair of sandals.

"Would you like to wear them out or should I put them in a bag for you?" another saleslady asks as I reach down to slip the sandals off my feet. Jeremy walks up behind me, puts his arms around my waist, and kisses my neck.

"Happy three-week anniversary, baby." He then pulls out a tiny blue box from Tiffany's, and my mouth drops open. No one has ever bought me something so expensive before. And Jeremy's not even my boyfriend yet.

"I've never heard of a three-week anniversary before," I say, still shocked.

"It's been three weeks since you got kicked out of government class and I started to fall for your sassy ass."

"Here's your receipt, Mr. Weiner," my original saleslady says to Jeremy. She then takes my new tank and old shoes to the counter to wrap up. It's obvious the sandals aren't coming off my feet.

"Jeremy, I don't know what to say."

"You don't have to say anything. Just get used to it. Now, please open your gift."

I carefully unwrap the pretty blue box to find a perfect gold bangle inside, with the letter "J" engraved in the center. It's the most beautiful piece of jewelry anyone has ever given me.

"Damn, baby," I say for lack of a better response.

"Do you like it?" he asks nervously. His arms are still around my waist. I turn around and give him the biggest kiss ever.

"I love it. It's gorgeous. Thank you," I say, kissing him again. The salespeople clap as we walk to the counter to get my shopping bag, before heading up to the food court. "But, Jeremy, it's too soon for all of this," I say.

"Why would you say that?" he asks, looking puzzled. "I bought it to show you how much I appreciate you and your feet," he says, smiling and making me laugh.

"These sandals are cute," I say, eyeing them as we glide up the escalator.

"And so are you. So, why shouldn't you have something to compliment your beautiful features? Why aren't you worth it?" he asks, really hitting home. Why don't I think I'm worth a rich guy buying me some shoes at a price that would make even my mom say I've hit the jackpot?

"It's not right. We're not even officially a couple yet," I say, still feeling guilty. Slowly, though, these sandals are molding to my feet, making me a little more accepting of the idea.

"Jayd, I don't only buy things for my girlfriends. Friends are worthy of shiny things too, don't you think?" As we approach Mrs. Fields' for some oatmeal raisin cookies, he takes me by the hand and pulls me in close to him, forcing me to look up into his blue eyes. "But, if you were my girlfriend, there'd be no holds barred on me spoiling you." He bends down and kisses my mouth, allowing me to return his kiss at my own pace.

"Oh, he can bust the same move and it's all right. But when I tried it earlier, you left me hangin'," KJ says from out of nowhere. Where the hell did he come from?

"Earlier? When did he try and kiss you?" Jeremy asks, waiting for my reply.

"It was nothing, Jeremy," I say, trying to diffuse the situation. But Jeremy doesn't look satisfied with my answer, and KJ looks like he's ready for a fight.

"If it was nothing, then why didn't you tell me about it?" Jeremy asks.

"Because it was something," KJ says with a smile on his face like he's just caught me in a lie. "What Jayd and I have is special, and ain't no White boy gone come between us. Ain't that right, Jayd?"

"Hell no, that ain't right," I say, pissed KJ's ruining our afternoon. "Like I told you earlier, I've got a new man now, KJ. Your kisses and anything else you have to offer are no longer welcomed by me."

"You need to shut up with all that bullshit, Jayd. We both know the real deal," KJ says, stepping toward me.

"Hey, man. You don't need to talk to her like that," Jeremy says, coming to my defense.

"Hey, dude," KJ says, mimicking Jeremy's surfer accent, "like, stay out of this. It doesn't concern you, dude."

"What's this guy's problem?" Jeremy asks me.

"His ego's too big for his own good," I answer, ready to leave without the cookies. We need to find another mall to hang at.

"You need to lose the zero and get back with the Negro, Jayd," Del chimes in from the background. He's so silly. If the situation weren't serious, I'd have to laugh. Ignoring Del's comment, but not my obvious discomfort, Jeremy takes my hand and leads me away from the food court and back toward the escalator.

"That's it, run like a little—" Before he can say what I know is about to come out his mouth, I turn around and silence KJ with the most intense look I've ever given him.

"Now you see why I didn't answer the phone? All you do is bring drama into my life, and all I really want is peace. Can you please chill out?" I ask, surprising myself with my calm words. I was ready to cuss him out a minute ago. But then, just as I felt myself getting hot, I also caught a whiff of Mama's shea butter still lingering from this morning.

"How can he chill when you keep throwing rejection in his face?" Misty says, following Shae and the rest of the crew up to the scene we've just created. Did everyone in South Central decide to come to the mall today? And where are my girls when I need them? Jeremy's not enough backup for all this heat.

"It wouldn't be thrown in his face if he'd stop following me around," I say, unsure if I should be talking to KJ or his attorney, Misty. Just as we get into it for the second time today, Chance and Matt walk though the door from the rooftop parking lot and head our way. Thank God. Finally, some relief.

"What's up, dude," Matt says to Jeremy, unaware of the drama taking place. Chance, a little more keen than Matt, senses the awkwardness and takes my other hand, ready to lead me toward the door.

"Hey, Jayd. What are you two still doing here? I thought we were meeting at Matt's after school," he says, providing a diversion to the chaos.

"No, I guess Jeremy decided to take her on a shopping spree instead," KJ says, walking up to us and grabbing my left hand away from Jeremy's, revealing my new bracelet for everyone to see.

"Hey, man, you need to watch yourself," Jeremy says, reclaiming my hand from KJ's grip and slightly knocking KJ off balance. KJ catches himself and stares Jeremy down like he's doing a drive-by on him with his eyes. Then he steps up to Jeremy like he's going to sock him, but turns his attention to me instead, making me feel a rush deep inside. I've never had two dudes literally fighting over me. I have to admit, this is kind of cool.

"Sock the shit out of his White ass," Misty yells suddenly. Jeremy doesn't move a muscle and neither does KJ, who's still looking right at me.

"You need to step back," Jeremy says, stepping in between KJ and me. KJ slowly looks from me to Jeremy before doing something I never expected.

"And, if I don't?" KJ says, pushing Jeremy's shoulders and knocking him off balance. What the hell? When Jeremy regains his footing, he returns KJ's push, and the fight is on.

"Fight, fight," Misty yells through the crowded food court. I'd better stop this before we all end up in jail. These police officers in Redondo Beach don't play.

"KJ, let him go," I say, knowing he's not listening to me. "Jeremy, stop it!" Jeremy does hear me and untangles himself from KJ's grasp before they both fall to the floor. Wiping a trickle of blood from his lower lip, Jeremy grabs my hand and catches his breath.

"Let's get out of here," Jeremy says, looking at Matt, Chance, and me. I feel so bad for getting him into this mess.

"So, that's what it takes to get the cookies from Jayd Jackson: the bling-bling," Misty calls, adding salt to KJ's already open wound.

"Shut the hell up, you little instigator," I say, trying to get Misty to realize her part in all this. I then step from in between KJ and Jeremy, feeling both of their bodies extremely close to mine. There's that rush again. "Jeremy, let's just go. They're not worth our time," I say, allowing Chance to lead us out the door following Matt, who's already in the parking lot.

"This ain't over, dude," KJ calls to our backs as the rest of the spectators laugh at his imitation of Jeremy.

"No, dude, it isn't," Jeremy says in a tone so calm it's almost frightening. I guess he can get down and dirty with the rest of us when he needs to. But, he can also maintain his cool, which makes any doubts I may have had about his character fly out of my head.

I know there will be some sort of backlash from this scene tomorrow. I wonder if we can just hide out until the weekend comes. I don't want to deal with KJ, Misty, or even my girls anymore. Jeremy and I were having a great afternoon until they messed it up. And I don't care what Nellie says. KJ hasn't changed a bit. I know he's hurting, but he doesn't have to act like this. Only Mama can help me with this. She's with clients tonight, so I'll just have to wait until tomorrow afternoon to get some advice.

It's been a long week, and I'm glad to go to my mom's tonight. I started packing my bag last night, so all I need is to finish and wait for my mom to swoop me up when she gets off work.

"Jayd, come back here and help me find my shoes, please,"

Mama yells from her closet. I'm barely through the door and already working.

"Which shoes are you looking for?" I ask, immediately looking under my bed, then hers.

"Any pair of black ones that match," she says, frantically searching through the pile of shoes on the closet floor.

"What y'all doin' in here?" Jay asks from the hallway.

"Looking for Mama's shoes. You can help if you want," I say, glaring at him from my crouched position.

"Naw, that's okay. I'm going down to Ms. Prichard's house. I'll see y'all later," Jay says, turning around to leave.

"Jay, take some of this cream to her. Tell her this will help with her arthritis," Mama says, grabbing a jar from her bookcase and handing it to Jay, who steps over me to reach Mama's hand.

"Dang, Jay. Watch out before you crush me with your boat feet."

"And don't be down there all night, either, boy. You hang out with them girls too much," Mama says. She don't want no premature babies from no one to raise.

"Yes, Mama. Bye, Jayd. Tell Auntie Lynn I said hi." And Jay was gone to chase after some broads while I'm still here looking for Mama's shoes, doggy style.

"Jayd, where'd you get that bracelet from?" Mama asks, noticing my new bling.

"Oh, Jeremy gave it to me yesterday. You like it?" I ask, waving my arm around like a star.

"Yes, very much. It matches your shirt and shoes quite nicely," she says sarcastically, referring to my new tank and sandals.

"How's it going with KJ and Misty? Are they still causing you problems," Mama asks, still digging through the closet.

"Oh, yes. KJ's jealous and so is Misty," I say, pulling out several black shoes, none of them matching.

"Jayd, just be careful with both of them. Men can get real petty when egos are involved," Mama says, tossing several almost identical shoes out of the closet and into my pile. "One of those has got to match one of your shoes," Mama says, giving up and taking a seat on her bed.

"KJ's ego is just too much for me, Mama," I say, finally finding a match to one of her shoes. "And, I feel bad for him, especially because I found another dude so quickly. But I don't know what else to do," I say, handing the matching pair to Mama and getting up from the floor to sit across from her on my bed.

"Have you tried listening to KJ? Maybe he just wants to be heard," she says, slipping on her shoes before grabbing her purse and heading out the door. She and Netta are hosting a candle party at the beauty shop, and Mama's running late, as usual.

"All I do is hear KJ because he won't leave me alone."

"Okay. Then maybe it's time you changed your approach. Instead of fighting his advances, allow them in and see where they lead. If there's nothing there anymore, then you have nothing to be afraid of." And, with that last bit of advice, she's off, and I'm left waiting for my mom, who's also running late. Just then, my phone vibrates, letting me know there's a text message in my mailbox.

"Peace, Jayd. Didn't c u at school 2day. Just want 2 say sorry 4 yesterday and I want 2 c u this weekend so we can talk face-to-face. Please call me when u get this message. KJ."

This fool must be tripping if he thinks I'm calling him after the scene he caused at the mall yesterday. Jeremy and I did an excellent job today of avoiding everyone we didn't want to see at school. That's one good thing about going to the second largest high school in Southern California. It's easy to avoid people if you know all the hiding places, like Jeremy does.

Speaking of my honey, we have a date tomorrow night, and I think it's time we made this thing official. I'm tired of waiting for everything to be just right, and it'll obviously never be a cool time for us to get together. So, the only thing really stopping us is me. Well, no more. I'm ready to give Jeremy and me a chance at love. I can't wait until our usual Saturday night date. I'm getting used to him being a part of my weekend routine.

~ 17 ~

Second Chance, First Choice

"If I'm seen with a girl then she gotta be just (like u)."

—LIL BOW WOW WITH CIARA

As usual, our date ends up at the beach, which is just fine by me. I love coming to the beach at night, especially with Jeremy. I always wear my hair pulled back in a ponytail, making sure the fog doesn't affect my do. He usually lets the top down, allowing the water's cool air into the car.

"Are you cold?" Jeremy asks, reaching into the backseat and retrieving the overstuffed down blanket.

"No, I'm good. I'm getting used to the weather out here," I say, allowing him to pull me close into his arms as he gets comfortable in the driver's seat.

"What do you want to listen to?" he asks, grabbing his CD case from under the front seat.

"How about the radio," I offer, tuning the dial to 93.5 KDAY, my favorite station.

"How do you know about KDAY?" Jeremy asks, looking impressed with my choice in music.

"My uncle used to listen to the original station back in the day when it was on AM." Bryan told me all about how the powers that be took it off the air because it was getting too politically conscious. I'm just glad it's back on because I really enjoy the music. "Let's see what they're playing," I say, readjusting my position in his arms. As we both get comfortable, waiting for the music to start, the DJ announces a dedication from KJ in Compton. No, it can't be . . .

"KJ says for his sweet, lovely Lady Jayd to call him when she hears this song. He knows you're listening. Here's to you, Jayd, wherever you are. The brotha's got it bad if he's dedicating Al Green to you, baby," the DJ says as "How Do You Mend a Broken Heart?" begins to play. It's KJ's and my second favorite song after Aaliyah's "Let Me Know."

"I'm so sorry about this, Jeremy," I say, instantly feeling embarrassed for him. When will this brotha quit?

"It's cool, Jayd. I'm not sweating it," he says, lying back in his seat like nothing just happened. I'm so shocked by his nonchalant attitude I don't know what to say, so I say nothing. Maybe he feels like he shouldn't have to. Whatever the case, I must admit, no one's ever dedicated a song to me over the radio before. And, it's making me feel special, just as special as buying me gifts does. Why didn't KJ do stuff like this when we were together?

"Are you cool with it?" Jeremy asks, not moving from his relaxed position. He's a little too damn relaxed sometimes. "It's your song," he says, in a tone I don't recognize.

"I'm well aware of whose song it is, Jeremy. I thought you just might, you know, be a little upset, another guy sneaking up on your territory and all," I say, rubbing his stomach.

"It's not my territory to sneak up on, is it?" he asks with a little venom on his tongue. I decide not to push the issue any further. We can talk about this tomorrow, when it's not so fresh. He may act like he doesn't care, but I know this bothers him a little bit. It has to, right? And, if it doesn't, what does that say about his feelings for me? Men are so confusing. And I'm going to have to deal with KJ sooner or later. I just don't know what to do now. Jeremy's aloof behavior has turned me off a little, and KJ's persistence is starting to turn me on. Maybe I'll give my girls another chance to help me out on this one tomorrow, because I'm stuck in neutral and don't know which way to go.

When I get to work this morning, Jeremy and KJ are all I can think about. And, because it's been so slow, as Sunday mornings usually are, I don't have much work to distract me. At least Shahid let me take an early lunch, giving me a chance to sort out my confusion over some comfort food and sunshine.

Don't slip up and get caught, 'cause I'm coming for that number one spot.

"Hello," I say in between bites of my spinach pattie.

"Hey, Jayd. It's Nellie and Mickey," Nellie says.

"Hey, y'all, what's cracking?" I say.

"So, how was your date last night?" Mickey asks, beside herself with excitement. I know they heard KJ's little dedication.

"It was fine," I say, suddenly losing my appetite.

"Are you sure, girl? I know my man would've whipped KJ's ass for some shit like that."

"That's because your man's a thug, Mickey," Nellie says. "Jayd, is everything all right with you and Jeremy?" Nellie asks, sounding genuinely concerned.

"Yes, we're fine. Actually, a little too fine for me," I say, playing with my food. I was hungry a minute ago.

"What do you mean?" Nellie asks.

"He didn't react at all, y'all," I say, still in disbelief myself.

"What?" they scream simultaneously.

"Oh, that's just plain weird, Jayd. See why I couldn't date no White boy. Where's the passion?" Mickey says.

"There's a difference between passion and rage, Mickey," Nellie says, putting her in check. "But, I do agree with Mickey. That's a little bit strange."

"Well, I agree with both of y'all," I say, though I don't want to admit it. "But what do I do now?" I ask.

"Girl, if I were you," Mickey says, like she's about to offer me the Holy Grail of advice, "I'd hang up the phone with us right now, call KJ, and pray Misty hasn't laid that booty on him yet."

"Not that I agree with everything she just said," Nellie says, "but Mickey's right. You do need to call KJ and see where you two stand." I don't know if she's right about me and KJ, but I do know I really don't feel like dealing with him right now.

"I'll see," I say, wanting to get off the phone and just spend the rest of my lunch break relaxing, looking at the cars ride down Overhill Drive. "Right now I just need to chill."

"All right then, girl. We'll talk to you later," Mickey says.

"Call us when you get back home," Nellie says.

"I'll call after I finish my homework. I've avoided doing it all weekend."

"Homework? Sometimes I think we go to different schools. Later, Jayd," Mickey says, before hanging up.

"Talk to you later," Nellie says, leaving me to my own thoughts, or so I think. I've only got about fifteen minutes left on my break to relax before the after-church lunch crowd hits, but wouldn't you know who I see walking up?

"Hey, Jayd. What does it take to get you to call a brotha back?" KJ asks when he gets close enough for me to hear him.

"What are you doing here?" I ask, a little glad to see him. He's just not going to give up that easy, is he?

"I'm here to see you, obviously. And, you can't run from me here," he says, and he's right, unless I want to get fired.

"Look, KJ. As flattered as I am by this newfound love you have for me, I'm still not moved to completely forgive you," I say, readjusting my position on the metal bench.

"Okay. But can we at least start as friends again?" he says in that charming way of his with that golden smile. "I can't let this go, Jayd."

"And maybe that's the problem, KJ. I think you can't let it go because I'm a challenge. And, it's not going to always be this way," I say, pulling out my reserve of buried wisdom. After Jeremy dropped me off last night, I decided not to react with emotions, which is exactly how Jeremy tries to live. It seems to work for him, so I thought I'd give it a try.

"I know it's not always going to be like this. And, I'm not worried about sex anymore; it'll happen when you're ready. I'm just worried about you coming back to me, where you belong."

"KJ, do you hear yourself when you speak, or does the bullshit just flow continuously?" I ask, rapidly losing my patience with him. "What if I'm never ready?" I say, challenging his newfound patience.

"Don't be ridiculous," he says, shrugging his shoulders as if I've just made a joke. "Everybody has sex at some point, Jayd."

"You see, that's my problem with you, boy. You expect sex as a part of our relationship. What if it never gets that far? What if I decide not to have sex until I'm married?" I say, knowing that's not true. I'd never marry a guy before knowing everything he has to offer.

"You're so difficult," he says, pacing back and forth in front of my table. "You know what, Jayd?" he says, slamming his hands on the table and looking me square in the face. "When you're ready to get with a real man, let me know. If you're lucky, I'll still be here. Just be careful with that White boy. I hear he picks a new flavor every year." And, just as quickly as he came, he goes. He practically sprints back to his car and drives off in a huff.

When KJ leaves and I finish up the last of my lunch,

Jeremy calls to remind me he's coming to pick me up after work. It's becoming our routine. And then he takes me back to Compton, inadvertently saving my mom some well-needed gas money. He's so sweet.

"Hey, baby. How's work?" he asks, sounding as cool as ever.

"Work's work," I answer, not feeling the need to bring up KJ's surprise visit.

"I'll see you at three o'clock. And, Jayd," he says.

"Yes, Jeremy?"

"It did bother me. I just try not to act on first emotions. It's not Zen like," he says, dropping some knowledge on a sistah.

"Well, I'm glad you're different from the norm. It's refreshing," I say, working up the nerve to ask my next question. "Jeremy, do you think you could give me another chance?" I ask, leaving him hanging.

"Another chance for what?" he says, making me ask him outright, even though I know he knows the rest of my question.

"A second chance to be your woman," I say, feeling like I'm finally making the right choice.

"It's your world, Lady Jayd. I'll see you after work," he says.

"So, just to be clear. We're now officially a couple, right?" I ask, just to be sure we're both on the same page.

"Yes, you are definitely my girl now. You can tell everyone you know," he says, hanging up the phone and leaving me to day dream about later. It feels so nice to be in love again. And, this time, I'm sure he loves me back.

Epilogue

Although Jeremy and I are still new, I feel closer to him than anyone I've ever dated. I'm so glad we got through our first little crisis successfully because school would be no fun without my man.

Speaking of which, I wonder if he's going to ask me to Homecoming in a couple of weeks. It's the first official dance of the year, and it's always fun to see which couples end up going together. Usually I'm not into hangin' at a dance full of folks who can't dance and girls hating on me and my crew for being dressed the best. But now that I have Jeremy's arm to escort me, I want to show off a little.

Don't slip up and get caught.

"Hello," I say, already knowing it's Nellie again. I'm actually glad she called back. I want to share my good news with her, even if she thinks it's a mistake.

"Jayd, guess what?" she asks, unusually excited.

"Well, hi to you too."

"Oh, Jayd, don't get salty. Just guess," she says, torturing me into playing her game.

"Chicken butt," I say.

"You're no fun. Chance just called me and told me the Drama Club wants to seriously give the cheerleaders and athletes a run for their egos by sponsoring a Homecoming Princess candidate for our class," she practically shouts through my cell.

"Jayd, Shahid said break's over," my coworker, Alonzo, calls out to me.

"Okay, Nellie. I have to get back to work. Can you speed up this guessing game?" I say, getting up from my table and brushing the golden patty flakes from my green apron.

"I'm running for Junior Class Homecoming Princess!" Chance and the Drama Club want to sponsor Nellie? Why not me?

"What? You're not even a member of the club, and I thought you didn't like my pot-smoking, White friends," I say, momentarily envious and reminding her of the salt she's been throwing at me lately.

"Jayd, I was tripping. They're actually really cool, just a little misguided. Maybe I can bring some salvation to the crew, and that doesn't mean I've changed my mind about Jeremy," she says, now sounding like the Nellie I know and love. "But still, can you believe it? They're sponsoring me to run as the first Black Homecoming Princess. I'm so exited I want to go shopping right now for my dress. What are you doing after work?" she asks, obviously forgetting I have homework every day of the week.

"I'm going back to Mama's and finishing my homework for both school and Mama. Like I said before, I'm already back inside the store heading to the bathroom to wash up and finish my workday." I can't wait to see Jeremy after work. I love riding in his Mustang with the top down. I feel so free every time I'm with him. "And, Jeremy and I are officially a couple," I add, not so subtly changing the subject.

"Whatever, Jayd. I already told you what I think you should do. If you don't want to heed my advice, that's on you," Nellie says. "Mickey and I are going to Fox Hill's mall later on if you want to roll. Have fun at work," she continues. "And, Jayd, they wanted to pick you but thought you'd bring too much controversy to the campaign," she says, even though she doesn't have to. That's a real friend.

"Nellie, anyone who's the first to do something is going to bring controversy with them," I say. "Besides, I know they're right. Controversy's in my blood."

Drama High, Volume 2:
SECOND CHANCE

L. Divine

ABOUT THIS GUIDE

The following questions are intended to enhance
your group's reading of
DRAMA HIGH: SECOND CHANCE
by L. Divine.

DISCUSSION QUESTIONS

1. In *Second Chance*, Jayd crosses the line to date a White boy. What would you have done in Jayd's situation? Would you have tried to make it work with KJ just because he's a Black boy or would you have done what Jayd did—date Jeremy?

2. Have you or someone you know ever dated a White boy? Under what circumstances would you or would you not date a White boy?

3. Does race really make a difference in relationships? Can you be just as happy with a White significant other as a Black one?

4. Who treats Jayd better: Jeremy or KJ? Is the difference in how each boy treats Jayd due to his race?

5. Is there interracial dating at your school? Is it the problem that it seems to be at South Bay High School *aka* Drama High?

6. Is it brave to date someone of the opposite race?

7. Are Jayd's friends supportive of her decision to date Jeremy? Would your friends support you if you decided to date someone of another race? Would you be supportive of a friend who decided to date someone of another race?

8. What do you think about the preference the boys in Jeremy's family seem to have for Black girls? Is their wanting to date Black girls unusual? Should Jayd be careful in dating Jeremy given the apparent history?

9. Do you think Tania is any competition for Jayd when it comes to Jeremy's feelings?

10. In *Second Chance*, Jayd goes up against Mrs. Bennett. Jayd says Mrs. Bennett is a racist. Do you agree or was Mrs. Bennett, in her own way, trying to help Jayd?

11. Do you think Jeremy truly likes Jayd for Jayd or is Mrs.

Bennett right? Does Jeremy just have a thing for Black girls?

12. Do you know teachers like Mrs. Bennett at your school?
13. If you were confronted in the way Jayd was by someone like Mrs. Bennett, would you have filed a grievance or let it go? Was Jayd right to file a grievance or did she make too much of the situation?
14. Jeremy is substantially more well off than Jayd. As a result he buys her expensive gifts. Should Jayd have accepted the bracelet and items from Bebe before they were an official couple? Do you think Jeremy was being sincere or was he trying to buy Jayd's affection so she would agree to become his girlfriend?
15. Should a boyfriend a girl has in high school buy her very expensive things?
16. Was it fair that Jeremy was suspended only for a day after being caught selling marijuana? Was his punishment fair? Was Jeremy treated differently than KJ would have been treated if he had been caught selling marijuana?
17. What do you think of Jeremy's reaction to KJ's song request for Jayd at the beginning of chapter 17?
18. Why does KJ want to fight Jeremy? Is it just because Jeremy is seeing Jayd?
19. Misty seems to be very protective of KJ and KJ's hurt feelings over the breakup with Jayd. Do you think KJ will end up with Misty? Do you think Misty may be better for KJ than Jayd? Why or why not?
20. Who's better for Jayd: Jeremy or KJ?

Stay tuned for the next book in this series
JAYD'S LEGACY,
available in February 2007
wherever books are sold.
Until then, satisfy your DRAMA HIGH
craving with the following excerpt
from the next installment.

ENJOY!

Prologue

*T*he smell of freshly cut grass permeates the crisp night air. The crowd is cheering loudly and my heart's beating fast. I don't know why, but I feel like something's about to go down.

As I get up from the bleachers and start walking toward the football field, the halftime show has already begun. The parade of fancy cars starts to cross the football field, each carrying a club sponsor's candidate for Homecoming King, Queen, Prince and Princess. Nellie's sitting in the passenger side of Chance's classic Chevy Nova, looking like a queen with the drama club's other candidates seated in the back. As the cars stop in the center of the field, Nellie's car is second in line and very close to the people in the bleachers.

I come down the bleachers as quickly as I can, trying to reach Nellie and Chance. But it seems with every step I take I'm farther and farther away from the scene.

As Chance gets out of his car to let the ladies out, three people in hooded jackets rush the football field, causing a stir. As Nellie steps out of the car, three people step out from under the bleachers and take out what appear to be big water guns from underneath their jackets and attack Nellie at full force. It turns out that they're not water guns but *paintball guns. Chance, trying to protect Nellie, leaps in front of her but gets taken out by the gunman instead.*

"Jayd," Bryan says, peeking his head through the bedroom door. "Get up or you're going to miss your bus, sleeping ugly," he says, before slinking back to the bathroom, leaving me to worry about my dream. I hope I'm way off on this one because Nellie's too excited about being the first Black Homecoming Princess for South Bay High.

"Did you hear your uncle? Get up, girl," Mama says. I jump at the sound of her voice.

"Alright Mama, I'm up," I say, stumbling out of my bed toward the door. I hate when Bryan beats me to the bathroom. It's never a good start to my morning.

"Don't forget about your homework for me due tonight Jayd. I'll be waiting for you when you get home," Mama says from beneath the covers.

"Okay, Mama. I'll see you when I get home," I say. As I head into Daddy's room to retrieve my morning necessities, Bryan opens the bathroom door and cuts in front of me.

"Excuse me," he says practically pushing me out of his way.

"It's a little late for that now," I say, referring to the stench he's left for me in the bathroom.

"Just thought I'd freshen it up for you before your morning shower, Queen Jayd," he says reaching up to the top bunk where he sleeps and grabbing his deodorant from under the pillow.

"Next time please don't do me any favors," I say as I locate my toiletries in one of my oversize Hefty garbage bags in the cramped closet, before leaving Bryan to his morning routine. I don't have time to deal with his bull today. After Jeremy dropped me off at the bus stop last night, he made a point to tell me that from now on he would be picking me up from the bus stop in the mornings when I reach South Bay. I want to look extra cute this morning, being that it's our first official day as a couple at Drama High. I'll worry about Nellie later. As with all my dreams, it'll come to pass one way or another. I just hope I can learn to control them sooner than later with Mama's guidance. Until then, I'm just going to go with the flow and enjoy my man and my friend's turn at catching a little drama of her own.

~ 1 ~
New Territory

*"In the middle of the madness/
Hold on."*

—SADE

I love Jeremy's new habit of picking me up at the bus stop by school every morning. Last night while driving me back to Mama's, he insisted on starting this morning and I don't mind at all. It'll give my feet a well-deserved rest and keeps me from dealing with the uncomfortable stares of the neighbors. It also gives me a few private moments with my baby before the impending drama of the days begins. After last night's dream, I can only imagine what's coming our way.

"Nellie doesn't know what she's getting herself into," Jeremy says, practically shouting over the loud music as we slowly cruise toward campus.

"I know. I told her to be careful. These folks around here will smile in your face and be all happy for her publicly. But, when the shit hits the fan, they'll scatter like roaches," I say, recalling my personal moment of betrayal from the Associated Student Body when I first joined.

"Ooh. Sounds like a sore spot. I'm intrigued," Jeremy says. The bass from Jeremy's car is so smooth the people walking around outside with their spoiled dogs can't even complain about the loud reggae bumping from his speakers. He turns down the volume slightly, ready for my story. I readjust myself, straightening out my red Apple Bottom cuffed Capri jeans and matching red shirt as I turn to face him.

"It's not funny," I say, playfully socking him on the arm. "It was a very painful experience, having the entire Associated Student Body turn against me for speaking up against the favoritism the cheerleaders, athletes, and ASB members receive during the monthly student senate meeting." Almost veering off the road, Jeremy looks at me shocked.

"When did this happen," he exclaims, almost laughing.

"Last spring. And, it's not funny," I say, again socking him in the arm, this time a little harder. "I was really hurt when they all turned on me."

"I'm sorry I laughed. It's just I don't understand why you would join an organization and then speak out about the perks, especially during a meeting where the principal and teacher sponsor are present. But, I've got to give it to you baby. You've got guts. So, then what happened?" Jeremy asks as he slows down in front of the main parking lot, really interested in my story.

"I resigned and joined the Drama Club," I say. "I was already enrolled in the class and played Lady Macbeth in the Drama Festival. So, I already knew everyone."

"It just goes to show you how ridiculous these people are up here. Nellie doesn't even know what she's getting herself into, especially running against ASB."

"I'm with you one hundred percent, baby. I know how these cliques up here work and I'd never run for anything just because I know how vicious they can get," Jeremy says as we join the long line of cars waiting to get into the parking lot. The first bell hasn't rung yet and students are hanging out all over the place.

"Has she ever run for anything before?"

"Not that I know of," I say, not really sure. She went to another high school for freshman year, just like me and Mickey. So, I don't know much about her life before South Bay High.

"Well, the competition ain't pretty. During Homecoming Week, the opposition can be very dirty," Jeremy says, finally pulling into a parking spot and barely missing a squirrel.

"Jeremy, did you see that poor squirrel?" I ask, reaching into the backseat for my backpack.

"Poor squirrel? You mean that oversized, rabies infected rat," he says, grinning at my sensitivity toward small animals. I can't even stand to kill a roach, let alone a small animal. It gives me the creeps.

"Well I'm just a damn riot to you this morning, ain't I," I ask, stepping out of his ride. As if I hadn't said a word, Jeremy takes my hand and backpack in one quick motion.

"Did I mention how good you look in those jeans?" he asks, eyeing my goodies like he wants to take a bite right now.

"No you didn't. But, I can tell by the look on your face you meant to." And, he's right. These are my favorite pair of jeans. They fit perfectly and feel good, just like the two of us.

"Not that I need to remind you, but you always look good, girl. I'm glad you stopped being so stubborn and decided to take me up on my offer," Jeremy says, slipping his arms around my waist and pinning me up against his Mustang. He kisses me softly and makes me forget all about the squirrel. I could stay here all day, but the school day calls.

"Come on Jeremy," I mutter in between pecks. "I have to catch up with my girls before the bell rings."

"Okay, just one more kiss," he says, pulling me in closer. I wish we could ditch. His kisses are so worth the unexcused absence in Spanish class.

"Okay you two, break it up," Chance shouts from the top of the stairs leading from the parking lot to campus, com-

pletely ruining our flow. "There are young, impressionable
minds here. Keep it moving," he says, gesturing his arms like
a traffic control officer, drawing even more attention from
the nosy onlookers all around.

"Don't you have other happy couples to harass," Jeremy
asks, wrapping his right arm around my shoulders and leading me toward campus.

"Yeah, Chance. Can't you see we're busy," I ask.

"Jayd, you're never too busy for your boy," Chance says,
kissing me on the cheek and falling into step with me and
Jeremy while the other students rush past. "And, did I hear
you say couple?" he asks.

"Yes, which means no more free kisses," Jeremy says,
pulling me slightly away from Chance.

"Hey, just because you're my man don't mean my cheeks,
or any other part of my body for that matter, belong to you,"
I retort, as sassy as ever. I do like Jeremy's newfound posses-
siveness. It's kind of sexy, as long as he doesn't get too car-
ried away.

"Hey dude," Matt says as he and Seth walk up to us.
"Chance, Jayd."

"What's up dude," Chance says, giving Matt and Seth dap.

"Well, don't you two make a picture perfect couple," Seth
says as Jeremy and I stop and lean up against the bicycle
racks next to the Science building.

"How's Nellie handling the nomination," Matt asks.

"I think she'll be fine," Chance says looking around the
buzzing campus. "Do you know if she's here yet?" he asks,
taking his cell phone out of his pocket and flipping it open to
check the time.

"No, but I'm about to find out," I say. "I have to get to my
locker before the bell rings. I'm sure I'll catch up with her
then," I say, reluctantly rising from my comfortable position
next to Jeremy.

"Could you please tell her we need to talk," Chance says. "She needs to know how to handle the nomination, know what I mean."

"Yeah. Tell her we've got her back if any shit goes down," Matt says.

"Yeah, I can't wait until the Reid gets wind of our nomination. He's going to be so pissed," Seth says, looking like he's been waiting for this moment all his life.

"Why did y'all nominate Nellie?" I ask. I hope it doesn't sound like I'm hating because I'm not. Why they're now her personal cheerleaders is what I don't get.

"Honestly Jayd, we think she can win. She has that princess quality about her that gives her the competitive edge necessary for full domination," Matt says. It sounds like he gave this a lot of thought.

"And also, she's just enough of a bitch to instill fear in all the other candidates, which is exactly what we need to win," Seth adds.

"Don't be calling my woman a bitch," Chance says, punching Seth in the chest. I knew he had a thing for Nellie.

"Your woman? Did I miss something?" Matt says.

"Nah, you didn't miss nothing. My boy's just got it bad for Nellie and she could care less," Jeremy says, rising from his spot on the bike rack to walk me to my locker.

"I'll relay all the messages," I say, instinctively taking Jeremy's hand and leading him up the walkway toward the main hall.

"I'll catch up with y'all later," Jeremy says, leaving his crew behind.

"Later, you two," Chance says. "And, tell Nellie if she needs anything at all, hit me up." Poor Chance. He's picked the wrong Black girl to have a crush on. Although, I think it would be cute if he and Nellie became a couple. Then, we could all hang out together and start our own crew. But, I'm sure Mickey would have a serious problem with that. She's already not feeling hanging out with the White side of campus. If Nellie crossed over, she'd be liable to leave us both behind.

When we reach my locker, Nellie and Mickey are already there waiting for me to arrive.

"Hey girl. What took y'all so long? The bell's about to ring and we haven't even had a chance to catch up," Nellie says, reaching out to give me a hug.

"Sorry. It was my fault. We ran into my friends, a.k.a. your fan club," Jeremy says.

"Her fan club? What are you talking about," Mickey asks. She's already on the phone with her man, I assume, and I'm sure they just saw each other. He comes to her house every morning before he goes to work, bringing her fresh donuts from Randy's donut shop. They are too cute.

"Chance, Matt and Seth are looking for you. They want to give you some pointers on being the Drama Club's nominee for Homecoming Princess, with the first round of voting taking place at lunch and all."

"Oh, that's so sweet," Nellie says, twirling strands of her hair around her index finger; she must have gotten a fresh perm this weekend. "I'll have to catch up with them at lunch."

"Voting? What the hell we got to vote for," Mickey says, completely out of the loop. When it comes to school business, Mickey couldn't care less. She might as well not even come to school sometimes, as oblivious as she is to the ins and outs of Drama High. All she cares about is what she's wearing, who's hating, and getting her diploma on time so she can go to beauty college. Everything else is secondary.

"Girl, where you been?" Nellie asks. "You have to vote for

the top three candidates for each grade level," she says, filling Mickey in while I retrieve my books from my locker. The bell has just rung and the race is on, with students bustling around the spacious hall, rushing off to first period.

"I don't get it. If you're nominated, doesn't that mean you've already been voted in," Mickey asks, putting her man on hold to get a better understanding of the voting process. I guess she cares now that her girl's on the ballot. Jeremy shakes his head, amused by my girls' conversation.

"No silly. I have to win a place on the actual ballot for next week's election. This is just the beginning," Nellie says all dreamy as if she's running for Miss America.

"Shit, that means I have to vote twice," Mickey says, resuming her phone conversation. "Baby, I got to go. The bell's about to ring," she says before hanging up her cell.

"That goes for me too," Jeremy says, giving me a kiss before sprinting down the hall. "Check y'all later," he says to my girls.

"Bye Jeremy," they say at once.

"So, when is the voting supposed to take place?" Mickey asks, truly annoyed. Anything that takes away from her chill time aggravates her.

"At lunch. And the finalists will be announced Wednesday at break. Make sure you tell everybody in your classes, Jayd. I have to make it onto the ballot," Nellie says as we all head toward our classes.

"Will do, Princess," I say, teasing her. I'm sure she's popular enough to make the ballot on her own accord. I really don't want to get involved with all the election business. It's too volatile here. These folks take their politics very seriously, as Nellie will soon find out.

When I get to Spanish class I notice our teacher/football coach, Mr. Donald, is dressed in a dress shirt and tie like he does on game day every Friday during the regular football season. I wonder what's going on.

"Good morning class," Mr. Donald says, waiting for the bell to finish ringing before continuing. "I have a new student coming in this morning and I'll need to talk to him outside for a few minutes. You'll need to complete page eight in your workbooks. And, if you finish before we're done outside, you can start your homework on page 25 of your textbooks," he says, picking up his teacher's edition and writing the homework assignment on the board under today's notes.

When I reach into my backpack on the floor next to my seat, I notice my workbook's not in there. Damn it. I can't go more than two days without leaving one of my Spanish books in my locker. Reluctantly, I have to ask for yet another hall pass.

"Mr. Donald?" I ask while raising my hand. He's turned toward the board and doesn't turn around to look at me. He already knows what I'm going to say.

"Let me guess, Miss Jackson," he says. "You left your books in your locker."

"Yes, I did," I say. "I'm usually not this forgetful." Mr. Donald turns toward the class and looks straight at me with no emotion.

"Here, Miss Jackson," he says, handing me the hall pass. "And, please make this the last time."

"Thank you and I will," I say, feeling a little embarrassed. I like to remain somewhat anonymous in my elective courses. I just want to pass, not make friends or enemies.

As I rise from my desk to open the door, someone's already on the other side pulling it open. I step outside, almost losing my footing, to see a familiar face from the past.

"There she is," Nigel, my old friend from back in the day says as he releases the door to give me a tight hug. "How's my girl been?" he asks. He looks too good to be visiting, dressed in a dark blue pinstriped suit and dress shoes.

"Nigel, what's up?" I say as he lets me go just enough to look up at him. Damn, he gives good hugs. "And more importantly, what are you doing here?"

"Girl, it's been a while and we miss you around the way," he says, allowing the door to completely close and leaving us outside to quickly catch up.

By his "we" I know he means Raheem. Whenever we'd get in a fight, which was often, Nigel would always play the middle man. But, this is the longest we've gone without talking, mostly due to us all leaving our old school, Family Christian, at the same time. Both of them now live in Windsor Hills, which isn't far from Inglewood, but still a completely different hood from my mom's.

"A while? Try two years," I say, releasing myself from his embrace to look him in the eye.

"So, you're balling like that now, huh," he says, grabbing my wrist and eyeing my gold bracelet. "Must be nice chilling with the White folks," he says. "But I'll know soon enough."

"What do you mean by that," I ask. "Is Westingle turning all White or something?" I say, referring to their school. It's basically the Black South Bay High. My mom tried to get me to go there, but no such luck. Her address wasn't in the right area and she missed the deadline for submitting a transfer request.

"No, but the coaches from South Bay said they could promise me a starting position, basically guaranteeing me recruiters from the top schools in the nation looking at me for scholarships. Now, a brotha can't pass that up, can I?" he says, throwing me off a little.

"So, you mean to tell me you're going to my school?" I ask, almost shouting. Oh, hell no. This can't be good. And, knowing Raheem, he'll be at every game, if not trying to transfer himself. They are each other's clique, no other members allowed or needed.

"Yeah, you got a problem with that?" Nigel asks, smiling. "Don't worry; I won't blow your cover, as long as you don't blow mine."

"No, not at all," I say as Mr. Donald opens the door. But, hell yeah I got a problem with it. First Nellie's nomination and now this. What the hell?

"Jayd, you know our new student Nigel?" Yeah, a little too well. But, Mr. Donald doesn't need to know all that.

"Yeah, me and my girl here go way back," he says, putting his arm around me and giving me one last hug before I head to the main hall.

"I was just going to get my book," I say, leaving the two of them to talk.

"I'll catch up with you later, Jayd. Raheem gave me a letter for you, but I left it in my locker." A letter saying what, I wonder? All I need is more drama to deal with.

After voting, Nellie, Mickey and I decide to hang in South Central for the remainder of lunch. Although I miss my man, I need to chill with my friends, too. Most of the usual suspects are still voting in the cafeteria. So, it's unusually peaceful in the quad area.

"Do you think I made it?" Nellie asks.

"I think so. The other names on the ballot weren't nearly as recognizable as yours. Well, except for Laura," I say. Laura's the first lady of ASB and that unofficial position always has its perks.

"What's the big deal," Mickey says, picking at her hamburger. We each settled for cafeteria food today, which isn't so bad. But, the voting line was long and our food has gotten cold. "So what if you don't win. Does it really matter?" The look on Nellie's face surely makes Mickey regret her statement.

"How can you say that?" Nellie asks, beginning what I predict to be the tantrum of all tantrums. Whenever her voice raises ten octaves, I know she's about to throw a fit. "This is very important to me. And, it's good for our social status," she says, giving Mickey the evil eye.

"Okay, whatever. Slow your role and bring it down a notch," Mickey says, taking a bite out of her lukewarm burger. "All I meant was you shouldn't be disappointed if you don't win."

"That's just the type of negative thinking I don't need. And besides, I wouldn't be worried about our social status if Jayd had come to Byron's party with us as planned," Nellie says, bringing up old news.

"Why are you dragging me into this," I say as I get up from the bench where we're seated to throw away my chili fires. If there's one thing I can't stand, it's cold potatoes.

"Because Jayd, not showing up to Byron's party wasn't a good move. It seems like you just don't care about your popularity anymore," Nellie says, sounding truly concerned. "Yes, it helps you're dating Jeremy. But, he's not concerned with popularity at all and that's okay for him. He's a rich White boy. You, on the other hand, need to think more seriously about your reputation." Both Mickey and I look at Nellie like she's lost her damned mind.

"What the hell are you talking about?" Mickey says, finishing off the last of her fries. To be as skinny as she is, the girl can out eat all of us combined.

"I'm talking about me winning. It doesn't help my campaign if I hang out with someone whose reputation is taking a turn for the worst."

"What the hell?" I exclaim, almost choking on my Coke.

"My reputation is just fine, contrary to popular belief. And besides, if it weren't for your affiliation with me you wouldn't have been nominated in the first place," I say, checking my uppity friend. Just then, Misty, KJ, and Shae return from the cafeteria to their usual post at the table across from our bench.

"Hey y'all," KJ says, smiling at me like he's just won something special.

"Hey KJ," Nellie says. Mickey and I are still in a state of shock over Nellie's growing head.

"I don't even need to ask who y'all voted for, do I?" Nellie says, hot on her campaign trail. She's taking this princess thing a little too seriously. But, I guess Seth had it right this morning. Nellie does have just enough bitch in her to make it to the top.

"Of course we voted for you, Nellie. I made sure everyone in South Central did," KJ says, unwrapping his sub sandwich while Misty sits next to him, holding his Snapple in her hand. This girl's so sprung on him I'm almost embarrassed for her.

"Yeah. We Black folks stick together, ain't that right Mickey," Shae says, obviously trying to say something to me without directly saying it.

"Don't ask me. I couldn't care less about all this homecoming shit. Although I am going to the dance." Now, that's a shocker. Last year her man was on lockdown in county jail and Mickey didn't attend any school functions. But, this year is different I guess.

"And, was that supposed to mean something to me Shae?" I ask. I don't really want to confront her, but I can't let her get away with that little comment of hers. How come she thinks I'm such a sell-out? Black folks get on my nerves with that mess.

"Not at all," Shae says, smiling. "I'm just saying if there's a Black name on the ballot, you know we're going to pick it because that's how we get down over here." Yeah broad, clean it up why don't you. Frankly, I've had enough of her and Nellie. Besides, I can't stand to watch Misty practically feed KJ for another second. I wonder what my man is up to. Maybe I can catch up with him on my way to drama class.

"Well, as lovely as this little chat has been, I've got to roll," I say, grabbing my backpack from the ground before getting up to leave.

"Can't keep the White boy waiting, huh," Misty says.

"Better than being someone's maidservant," I snap back at her before saying bye to my girls and heading away from the quad and down the hill. "I'll catch up with y'all after school," I say to Nellie and Mickey, ignoring Misty's evil glare and KJ's intense eyes.

"Jayd, I'll walk with you," Nellie says, hurriedly picking up her bag and tossing the rest of her chicken strips into the trash can before following me. It's not like her to leave Mickey, so this must be good. "I'll see y'all in class," she says to Mickey and everyone else, since they all have fifth period together.

"Jayd, I'm sorry if I hurt your feelings about the whole reputation thing," she says. "I just never imagined I could get nominated at this school for anything," she says, looping her arm into mine, forcing me to listen. Honestly, I don't want her to win if this is what's going to happen to her. She's already enough to deal with. Becoming princess will just make her ass even more uptight and stuck up.

"I know. And, for the record, I couldn't care less about what people up here think of me," I say, not letting her completely off the hook while letting her know we're still cool.

"I know. And you're right. If it weren't for you, I wouldn't have been nominated. So, thank you, girl. This means so much to me," she says, returning to her princess dream. "I can't wait until the nominees are announced tomorrow. I just know I'm going to win." For Nellie's sake, I hope if she does, Matt, Seth and Chance are going to be right there for her. Because, folk won't be happy with her nomination and when the shit hits the fan, I don't know what she's going to do. She's never had to face any drama of her own up here. And, if my dream predicted correctly, they'll be plenty to go around.

Start Your Own Book Club

Courtesy of the DRAMA HIGH series

ABOUT THIS GUIDE

The following is intended to help you get
the Book Club you've always wanted
up and running!
Enjoy!

Start Your Own Book Club

A Book Club is not only a great way to make friends, but it is also a fun and safe environment for you to express your views and opinions on everything from fashion to teen pregnancy. A Teen Book Club can also become a forum or venue to air grievances and plan remedies for problems.

The People

To start, all you need is yourself and at least one other person. There's no criteria for who this person or persons should be other than having a desire to read and a commitment to discuss things during a certain time frame.

The Rules

Just as in Jayd's life, sometimes even Book Club discussions can be filled with much drama. People tend to disagree with each other, cut each other off when speaking, and take criticism personally. So, there should be some ground rules:

1. Do not attack people for their ideas or opinions.
2. When you disagree with a book club member on a point, disagree respectfully. This means that you do not denigrate other people for their ideas or even their ideas, themselves, i.e., no name calling or saying, "That's stupid!" Instead, say, "I can respect your position, however, I feel differently."
3. Back up your opinions with concrete evidence, either from the book in question or life in general.
4. Allow everyone a turn to comment.
5. Do not cut a member off when the person is speaking. Respectfully wait your turn.
6. Critique only the idea (and do so responsibly; saying, "That's stupid!" is not allowed). Do not criticize the person.

7. Every member must agree to and abide by the ground rules.

Feel free to add any other ground rules you think might be necessary.

The Meeting Place

Once you've decided on members, and agreed to the ground rules, you should decide on a place to meet. This could be the local library, the school library, your favorite restaurant, a bookstore, or a member's home. Remember, though, if you decide to hold your sessions at a member's home, the location should rotate to another member's home for the next session. It's also polite for guests to bring treats when attending a Book Club meeting at a member's home. If you choose to hold your meetings in a public place, always remember to ask the permission of the librarian or store manager. If you decide to hold your meetings in a local bookstore, ask the manager to post a flyer in the window announcing the Book Club to attract more members if you so desire.

Timing Is Everything

Teenagers of today are all much busier than teenagers of the past. You're probably thinking, "Between chorus rehearsals, the Drama Club, and oh yeah, my job, when will I ever have time to read another book that doesn't feature Romeo and Juliet!" Well, there's always time, if it's time well-planned and time planned ahead. You and your Book Club can decide to meet as often or as little as is appropriate for your bustling schedules. *Once a month* is a favorite option. *Sleepover Book Club* meetings—if you're open to excluding one gender—is also a favorite option. And in this day of high-tech, savvy teens, *Internet Discussion Groups* are also an appealing option. Just choose what's right for you!

Well, you've got the people, the ground rules, the place, and the time. All you need now is a book!

The Book

Choosing a book is the most fun. THE FIGHT is of course an excellent choice, and since it's a series, you won't soon run out of books to read and discuss. Your Book Club can also have comparative discussions as you compare the first book, THE FIGHT, to the second, SECOND CHANCE, and so on.

But depending upon your reading appetite, you may want to veer outside of the Drama High series. That's okay. There are plenty of options, many of which you will be able to find under the Dafina Books for Young Readers Program in the coming months.

But don't be afraid to mix it up. Nonfiction is just as good as fiction and a fun way to learn about from where we came without just using a history textbook. Science fiction and fantasy can be fun, too!

And always, always research the author. You might find the author has a website where you can post your Book Club's questions or comments. The author may even have an e-mail address available so you can correspond directly. Authors will also sit in on your Book Club meetings, either in person, or on the phone, and this can be a fun way to discuss the book as well!

The Discussion

Every good Book Club discussion starts with questions. SECOND CHANCE, as will every book in the Drama High series, comes along with a Reading Group Guide for your convenience, though of course, it's fine to make up your own. Here are some sample questions to get started:

1. What's this book all about anyway?
2. Who are the characters? Do we like them? Do they remind us of real people?
3. Was the story interesting? Were real issues of concern to you examined?
4. Were there details that didn't quite work for you or ring true?
5. Did the author create a believable environment—one that you could visualize?
6. Was the ending satisfying?
7. Would you read another book from this author?

Record Keeper

It's generally a good idea to have someone keep track of the books you read. Often libraries and schools will hold reading drives where you're rewarded for having read a certain number of books in a certain time period. Perhaps, a pizza party awaits!

Get Your Teachers and Parents Involved

Teachers and parents love it when kids get together and read. So involve your teachers and parents. Your Book Club may read a particular book where it would help to have an adult's perspective as part of the discussion. Teachers may also be able to include what you're doing as a Book Club in the classroom curriculum. That way books you love to read such as the Drama High ones can find a place in your classroom alongside the books you don't love to read so much.

Resources

To find some new favorite writers, check out the following resources. Happy reading!

Young Adult Library Services Association
http://www.ala.org/ala/yalsa/yalsa.htm

Carnegie Library of Pittsburgh
Hip-Hop!
Teen Rap Titles
http://www.carnegielibrary.org/teens/read/booklists/teen-rap.html

TeensPoint.org
What Teens Are Reading?
http://www.teenspoint.org/reading_matters/book_list.asp?s ort=5&list=274

Teenreads.com
http://www.teenreads.com/

Sacramento Public Library
Fantasy Reading for Kids
http://www.saclibrary.org/teens/fantasy.html

Book Divas
http://www.bookdivas.com/

Meg Cabot Book Club
http://www.megcabotbookclub.com/